Diamond

Kyla Breene

A Note on Species and Politics

There are a lot of alien species in this series. This will help you keep track of which ones you have come across so far.

Manticorid: once empire-seeking, now mostly living peacefully. The origin of manticore mythology on Earth. Thivoll is of this species

- **Abstainers**: A sub-sect of manticorids with a strong political presence in Session. They believe venom is dangerous and cut off the tip of male manticorid tails at birth.

Genali: The slimes we all love to hate. Opportunistic, with a specialty in exotic goods, including people of all species.

Braceaaer: The origin of Little Green Men mythology on Earth. Violent, small, and much stronger than they look.

Drakonid: a dragon/dinosaur-like species that was once a servitor race to the manticorid empire. Drasuk is a drak.

Qendi: Kuret's species. They are from a primitive desert world, with green bioluminescent marks on dark gray skin.

We still don't know what species Wroahk is from.

Farsi Translations

Bābā – father
Māmān – mother
Allah – God
Ya 'llah – Oh God
Astaghfirullah – I seek forgiveness from Allah
al-Sheytân – Satan
Jannah – paradise
Jahannam – hell
Alhamdulil'ah – praise be to God
Keke – shit
Khar – donkey/ass
Iblis – devil
Haroomzade – bastard

Rin

"What do we want?"
  "FOOD, WORK, FREEDOM!"
  "When do we want it?"
  "NOW!"
  "What do we want?"
The crowd marches together, as if they are being controlled by one thing. In a way, they are.

Our need for rights.

"Food, work, freedom!" I continue to chant with the group of women and very few men, my arms hurting from holding a cardboard placard for well over an hour.

We shout out our demands. I feel myself getting swayed by the crowd as a disturbance happens somewhere far away from me. I don't relent, yelling even louder as sweat rolls down my face.

The disturbance pushes through a few of us, and I spot a hand holding something silver being raised in the air. I call out again when a gunshot crackles through the air and we all scream and cower, using our signs as shields.

"Shut up and go home!" the man causing the disturbance yells—his gun still raised in the air.

I swallow the lump in my throat, looking around me to find everyone cowering in place, too scared to run. Why? He is only one man, and we are over two hundred women. He is outnumbered.

I suck in a deep breath and stand up straight from my crouching position as he continues speaking, insulting us. I raise my sign up as high as my aching hands can go, and I chant again at the top of my voice.

"Food, work, freedom!" I scream, my eyes not leaving his, even as I watch them transform from anger to something more sinister.

My chanting does not stop, and his face falls, convincing me that maybe it is working. I look down at my sisters in arms and convince them with my eyes to get up and join me, but they don't respond. Their eyes are staring straight ahead in frozen fear.

I turn around to see what is scaring them, but he is right there in front of me, the next moment with his hand wrapped around my neck, squeezing.

I can't breathe and my eyes water. My hands drop my sign and try to pry at his fingers, but it is all futile. He raises his gun to the air and shoots before forcing the hot gun between my lips, bruising them until I relent, the barrel burning my tongue.

"If you don't stop yelling and get off the streets, I will kill you first and every single one of them will be locked behind bars for the rest of their miserable lives," he yells in my face, spit flecking my cheeks.

I groan, hoping that it sounds like I'm saying yes, like I'm trying to.

He holds me there in place for a few seconds longer before pushing me to the ground as he lets me go. "You are a woman. Act like one," he spits before turning to the crowd and beginning to scream profanities at them, too.

Not long after, we scatter, me headed back to my brother's, internally seething that it's my only option. All the while hoping he and his wife haven't heard about today, though already knowing word has spread faster than I could ever walk.

They will be even more vigilant not to let me leave again and my chest aches, breath coming in gasps as I imagine decades of being locked in those suffocating walls.

✳ ✳ ✳

This isn't much better than prison here in my brother's house, I grumble internally.

Then I chide myself sharply, remembering how women are treated there and thanking *Allah* for the safe confines of this small room.

Still, I am stifled here. Unable to do what must be done to put an end to all the ceaseless terror. I can't forget any of the violence. Every memory drives me harder.

As always, it makes me think of Laila and that night when I accidentally forgot my bag in our classroom and when I came out to where she was waiting and heard her screams.

Saw the men in dark clothing holding her limp body as they hit her, punch after punch.

The look on their faces when they caught sight of me. Rushing me. Grabbing my top and pulling it hard against my neck, me biting them, screaming.

Of help arriving, but not before Laila's body had gone far too still.

The violence on the man's face yesterday was the same. An assurance that what he did, anything he did, would have no repercussions.

Men and their violence are the reason Laila's family won't let me see her again. Why they keep her locked up, blaming me instead of the men who did it. It's why my own family decided to do the same, and why there is going to be an even closer watch on me after I slipped out yesterday.

I sigh and sit down, letting my palms rub over my sheets, seeking comfort, though finding none.

A lone tear threatens to fall as I stare at the framed picture of twelve-year-old me and my *bābā*, but I wipe it away, grab the picture, and run a finger over his smiling face.

He was always so quick to offer a smile, a witty joke, or his rich, bellowing laugh when anyone needed it. The crow's feet at the corner of his eyes and always-visible dimples were my favorite features on his face. Always pleasant, and he hoped I would be the same. It was no wonder he named me Nasrin... charming and pleasant. He expected me to live up to it, but here I am, being the exact opposite of agreeable.

But what else could I be? I can't be blamed for being as incessantly curious or willful as I am because I got all those qualities from him. He let me hide out in his study with him and use his computer, and he made sure I was educated.

If I only knew then just how cruel providing an education could be. The recipe for creating an imprisoned, angry woman.

I don't realize I'm clutching the frame too hard until the cracking of the glass brings me back to reality. "I'm sorry, *bābā*," I mutter, kissing the frame and placing it back on the stool.

No. I can't bring myself to regret it, or truly blame him. He simply wanted the best for his daughter. It's not his fault other people don't see the world the way he made me see it. I allow myself to stare at the photo for a little longer until I hear my brother's wife Bibi calling me to eat.

My brow furrows, since it isn't evening and the children aren't even here. Then I shiver. Anything to do with food becomes a fight, leading to a discussion of how I'll never get a husband looking like "a pregnant cow." Or how I must be stealing food from her children's plates since I never lose much weight, no matter how much she restricts my diet. As if I would ever steal from children. Not that she listens, she just keeps screaming about how disgusting I am.

Allah knows I could do without that for another week—or for the rest of my life, really.

As my *māmān* always said, this is the weight my body wants to be. I never really believed her before coming here, so I guess I have Bibi to thank for something.

It wasn't always like this with Bibi and me, but now the distance between us feels like a chasm. The very ideologies I am fighting against, she endorses and agrees with. But I push that thought aside and focus on thinking of my *māmān*.

I willfully ignore another call from Bibi, seeking solace from heavy thoughts as my *māmān* would, with movement. Bibi will scream no matter what I do now.

I'm mid-spin on a rather sloppy *Attan* dance, my *kamiz* flaring out, when a sharp knocking at the door of my room interrupts me. I throw a scarf over my head and scurry to the door. When I open it, Bibi's knuckle collides with my nose, and she lets out a chortle while I rub my face.

It seems unlikely it was an accident, though I suppose she does seem out of sorts.

"Forgive me, Rin. I was just excited. The children are with my mother and it's just us girls in the house," she chirps, and it takes me a moment to understand what exactly is going on.

Last time we talked, she was spitting on my face as she screamed at me for destroying her husband's reputation. Why is she suddenly being nice?

I look at her face, her freshly henna-colored hair peeking out from under her hijab and the sparkly look in her green eyes. She's excited about something, and I don't think I want to know what it is.

She's staring at me excitedly, waiting for an answer, so I wipe the surprised look off my face and replace it with a tight smile. "I'll be down in a few minutes," I say, and she nods her head, the look of pure joy still plastered on her face as I shut the door.

When I hear her footsteps retreating, I breathe out a long sigh and fall back on my bed. My ceiling fan is turning in lazy circles and I stare at it, wishing that it would break me out of the trance that is my stupid life.

The joy of dancing is rapidly retreating, the sense of freedom long ahead of it. Forever out of reach.

I know exactly what "us girls in the house" means and that there are a bucket load of chores for us—well me—to do while she leans against the kitchen door frame, throwing snacks in her mouth and spouting gossip I don't care for.

A groan leaves my lips again, and I look at the picture of *bābā* and me. I can hear him telling me to seize the day in a mirth-filled voice, with a loud chuckle following.

"I'm trying, *bābā*, I really am," I mutter in the direction of the picture before looking away.

The thought of having to live the same day over and over, stuck inside this place, sends frustration crawling through me, and I feel it about to jump out of my mouth in a scream. I swallow it down and press my warm hands to my face.

I can't let myself mess up again. My brother and his wife are barely tolerating me as it is, and none of my outbursts or angry rants will help. Especially not after I snuck out and did exactly what I was told never to do again.

I can't get married as a way to escape, though that would just be another cage. I will need to keep my head low until I can get out of here, somehow. The pounding of my heart and that persistent voice mocking me for thinking I have any choices aren't helping. I must ignore reality, or I will break.

I will leave this place. I will.

Until then, having "us girls" the only ones at home will have to do.

I wash up and pin my hair under my *al-amira* before making my way to the kitchen, my eyebrows raised at the small feast in one corner of the wooden table. I spot a lamb *kebab* with onions and colorful peppers between the chunks of meat, a bowl full of *qurut* balls, and an even larger bowl of *kabuli pulao* with extra raisins, just the way I like it.

"Oh good, you're here."

Bibi's voice stops my mouth from salivating, but does nothing for the tightness in my stomach. I've barely eaten in weeks. I turn to find her holding a plate with *naan*.

"What can I help you with?" I ask and she shrieks with laughter, as if I have just told the funniest joke in the world.

"You're not here to help me with anything, Rin Rin. You're just here to eat."

She places the plate alongside the other delicacies. It's her special plate that she only uses when we get important guests from my brother's work. My eyes widen in realization. She's about to tell me that my time here is up. As much as I want to leave, there is nowhere else to go.

"Go on, sit down," she chirps and watches me with that weird, plastic smile.

My skin crawls with it, but maybe it's just because I haven't gotten this warm reception from her since I was a child, and even then, I didn't get special plates or this much of a meal.

"Eat," she encourages me, and I pick a *qurut* ball and bite into it.

I can't help the moan that leaves my mouth, and she giggles like a girl. It makes me remember when all she did was giggle as the aunties showered her with praise, letting her know she was the most beautiful bride Afghanistan had ever seen.

I thought the same, and sometimes I still do, when she smiles or in the brief moments she remembers she is not just a wife and a mother.

"Is something wrong, Bibi? Did I do something?" I ask after I've finished the entire qurut ball.

I notice that she is not eating; instead, she's holding a cup of milky chai and sipping it slowly.

She looks surprised at my question and wipes a bead of sweat from her forehead. Then, she then pulls off her hijab, and her hair falls beautifully around her face, reminding me of how much I used to love it.

Mine has always been curly, and it used to be a nightmare until I grew up and learned how to manage it. But as a child, I used to idolize her wavy brown hair.

"Not at all, Rin Rin," she simply says, using the nickname my *bābā* gave me. It irks me the wrong way, but I swallow the feelings down.

She laughs. "Just eat!"

I follow her urging, picking up one of the kebabs and eating the tender meat and vegetables off it.

Since I got here, our relationship has gone from bad to worse, and maybe this is her own way of trying to mend it. I should also do the same on my side.

I clear my throat and swallow my pride. "This is thoughtful, Bibi. I know this has been a struggle, and I'm sorry for the shame I have brought you."

She grunts in reply, something flashing across her face before she returns to her too-wide grin.

If she tells me to leave, I'll figure something out, though I'm not sure what I will tell the authorities if I'm caught out after curfew.

I eat in silence, taking small bites from everything placed before me, while she watches like a hawk, probably to make sure I finish all the food and don't waste a bite. After so long eating so little, I'm not sure I can fit it all into my stomach.

Nothing about this sits right with me. She isn't eating and the Bibi I know loves to snack more than anything else. I pick up my second *qurut* ball and take a bite, but it doesn't go down my throat as my mouth starts to feel numb. I start to tell her that I've had enough, but the words are stuck in my throat along with the food.

Her face blurs, but I can recognize the smile on her face as one that is up to no good. She drugged me?

Vaguely, I hear the sounds of my brother coming in, and a surge of relief floods through me. He'll sort this out.

"Did you really have to waste that much food just to get the cow drugged?" he says in that terrible tone I hate.

The one meant to keep Bibi in check. Then my slow brain catches up with what he just said as I grasp that there will be no help coming. My heart drops to my stomach as I realize there truly is no one left I can trust.

I slump against the chair as the world spins around me.

Kuret

I don't realize that Samke is still speaking until he slaps a hand on my back and laughs at his own joke. I laugh with him, even though I have no idea what he just said.

I pretend I've been listening. "So, what happened next?" I ask, and he bellows once more before grabbing my shoulders and turning me to face him.

"What do you think happened? Her clothes fell right off, and she joined me," he exclaims, and suddenly I'm more interested in his words.

The blue-yellow sky is blazing hot from above us, and my ears twitch, tuning in to his words. "What was it like?" I urge, expecting him to throw my questions to the wind or laugh at me, but he leans in closer until our foreheads are nearly touching and begins to whisper.

"It was incredible. It felt like shedding my burden and just letting myself fall into something warm and welcoming," he explains, every word stressed as if to let me know exactly what he meant.

I can only imagine.

"Something you have to experience for yourself to understand," he emphasizes as I pull myself from his grasp.

"Well, we should take a moment of silence for the poor female you ensnared with empty words," I tease, and he throws his head back in laughter, scratching the strip of piercings on his ear, especially the fresh one at one of the points.

One I may never have.

"I did no such thing. She is forever my friend," he exclaims, and we fall into silence, our eyes pinned to the ground.

Regardless of his flippant tone, we both take that moment. Afterward, I go back to teasing him, setting the foundation for a barb with a compliment. "You are my closest friend, and I value you."

The glow of his marks undulate to show how much that means to him.

Then I call him out for being ridiculous. "No one is friends with a female, Samke Big Ears, and it would be wise to remember it. They are ours to protect, not to be friends with, no matter how good you are at talking."

His braids shift as he huffs out a breath, but he wipes a hand along the top of his other hand to acknowledge the truth of my words. The wind picks up sand and blows it away from us. My gaze follows and when it calms, Samke places his hand on my shoulder again.

"I will use my talking to find out which are mine when they release them," he jokes, and I shake my head.

"Your ears are the size of a whole child, Samke. The biggest of the qendi. I know that once she pushes out your sons, the entire world will figure it out," I joke and Samke waves me off.

He bumps his shoulder against mine, our marks flaring at the contact. "Forget that now. You should experience this too."

I tap a finger on my hand in disagreement, get up from my cross-legged sitting position, and dust the sand off. He joins me, and we stare out into the horizon, the fiercely partitioned sky looking back at us.

"I think about it sometimes, to be honest. You all describe it as some once-in-a lifetime experience, but I just think maybe it isn't for everyone." I glance at him. "Maybe it isn't for me."

"Nonsense, Kuret. If you want something, go out and get it. Do not think all these thoughts," Samke says, but I tilt back my head, the clinking of my braids soothing me.

"I have already decided it would probably be best if I don't take part in the selection," I inform him, and I can see his face fall from the corner of my eye.

Immediately, I look away.

His tone turns more serious. "You can't continue to keep yourself closed off, Kuret. Join the selec—"

I don't let him finish. "Samke, males and females are kept separate for a reason, and when they get together, the women only want one thing. I don't think I'm ready to give that," I explain, and Samke nods in understanding.

I give the horizon one last longing look before letting him know I'm off to patrol the cloister.

He stabs the air with his spear as he dips his body into an odd stance, eliciting a laugh out of me. "Me too. Predators have been a little too brave these days. They need to be taught a lesson."

We part ways, and I patrol along the walls, then inside the outer halls, listening for any signs of trouble. It's silent, except for the chittering of conversational voices. I walk out into the courtyard and look up at the sky for a few minutes before making my way back in to continue my patrol.

It's monotonous, but some things take priority, and right now, this is it. I walk along all the walls of the outer cloister, the brown stone reminding me of the rest of the desert. I make my way back to the courtyard and see a small crowd gathering.

They are mostly males, and they are not supposed to be here. I attempt to weave through the crowd, then spot Samke talking intensely with another guard.

I interrupt them. "What's happening? Why are there so many males here?"

He doesn't get a chance to answer before we hear cries of alarm, most of them talking about the sky.

We all look up, falling silent for a long moment as a silver and pink... object descends toward us before landing in the inner cloister. The place where no one but females may go, except when there is an immediate threat.

The screaming of women and younglings gives us a clear reason to intrude where we are normally not allowed. I know what I must do, as do my fellow protectors, and we roughly push open the forbidden gate, rushing toward the strange vessel.

It becomes a battlefield, with screams and loud crackles ripping through the air. I follow my brothers and Samke as we screech out our battle cries.

Horrific blasts of green lightning cut through buildings and people, leaving smoking ruins and bodies behind.

Still, I continue on, stepping on the dead bodies of my fellow protectors as I sprint through the inner cloister, unfamiliar with its halls and turns. Another lightning bolt goes through the air, and I hear a pained scream as another body adds to the pile on the ground.

I can taste sand on my tongue as I step on another singed body and almost lose my footing. I look down and recognize him instantly, watching with horror as his glowing cheeks come to a weak end.

I look up, glimpsing gray skin and bulging eyes through some sort of viewing area of the vessel. It sears into my mind, this strange sighting of our enemy.

My chest hardens with hatred for these beasts and the horrors they have brought upon my people. I turn around to search for Samke, hoping he will help me destroy them, but something hits me on the neck and I reach up with a hand to pull it out of me, the cold metal of it feeling smoother than seems natural.

My vision blurs and my legs give out. I fall on my side and try to use my hands to drag myself forward, but they fail me too and I lie limp in a pile of bodies, fighting against myself to just move, to do something.

Forcing all my strength into the only mobile part of my body, I struggle to turn and catch sight of the amorphous figure, bleeding pink as it makes its way toward me.

It makes a honking sound as black dots bleed into my vision.

Rin

The moment I regain consciousness, I know right away that something isn't right. What trouble have I gotten myself into this time? My brother will never let me back into his house again, not this time. I know it.

An odd, grating sound comes from above me, and I crack one eye open and see a blob... floating? No, there is glass between us. It's staring at me with beady obsidian eyes that radiate nothing but hunger.

Our eyes meet and its face contorts, making my breath hitch. I open my mouth to scream, but a sharp pain attacks my throat, and my hands instinctively press against it. It honks out a wet sound.

My brain is unsure of which horror to process first. Panic fully sets in. It isn't human or any animal I've ever heard of. I need to get away immediately.

"This one will give us a lot of credits," the blob above me says, making the short, honking sound again before sliding off the glass between us and walking away. My stomach heaves as I watch it through the pink-streaked glass, three short legs moving it as flesh jiggles.

I can understand it. Why?

There are more of them surrounding this odd cage I'm in, and I catch a better view of them, retching as I take in more details, my brain burning. The things are shorter than a human, though bigger, and they have no real shape—gray with something pink seeping out of them, leaving a trail as they slobber away from me.

I shut my eyes tight, willing it to be a dream, but when I open them again, the scene is the same, blurring slightly as a headache thumps right behind my eyes.

Where am I? There are odd trees above me, in colors and shapes I have never seen before, but the squelching sounds of the aliens brings my gaze back to them.

Is this a different... planet? My head spins at the thought, instantly rejecting it as ridiculous. Did he just say he planned to sell me? These are obviously bad people... things?

A sense of immediacy drives me. I need to get away, and my hands push against the glass, but nothing happens. It's some kind of glass and silver cage, seemingly made to fit my exact body proportions, and I realize that escaping is impossible.

Whatever these aliens have planned for me, I can't escape by fighting.

I lie there in a silent panic, ignoring my headache, wondering how I ended up here. If I could just retrace my steps, I might figure out how this happened—how I wandered so far from my brother's house and ended up in this strange place with these awful creatures.

My mind is blank, and all my former memories are fragmented, though something tells me Bibi is the cause of all this.

A wet squeal brings me back to reality. I look up to see one of the shapeless creatures in a pile on the ground, while another runs toward my chamber, its three limbs making an awkward gait and its body jiggling sickeningly.

A tall, silvery creature follows behind, walking with long, graceful strides as it catches up to the scurrying slime and stabs a long spear through it. Pink and gray splatter against the glass cover of the chamber, and I flinch, but remain as still as possible, hoping I'll be mistaken dead and left alone.

Unfortunately, I have no such luck. My savior approaches the chamber, looming over me with a strange expression. Its yellow eyes dart over me for a long moment before it turns and walks away.

He's beautiful, too angular to be human, with a shimmer to his silvery skin, and long, flowing green hair framing his features. Alluring, yet still very alien.

A chill runs through me, and I instinctively cradle myself, rubbing my palms vigorously over my goosebump-covered forearm. It's then I realize that my arms are bare. I look down at myself, and a startled yelp escapes my lips when I discover that I'm stark naked, save for a thin band around my waist that I almost didn't notice.

"Why am I naked? W-where are my clothes?"

I try to cover my breasts with one hand, accomplishing almost nothing given their size, and move the other to the juncture of my thighs. They do a terrible job of covering me up until something begins to creep up my stomach. I look down and watch the band expand into a black jumpsuit, stretching up my neck and covering my fingers and my feet.

Looking down, I see my nipples beaded and clearly outlined by the shiny latex material, and I cross my arms over myself again, thinking how this is barely better than being naked. Then I remind myself that modesty is the least of my worries right now. I'm still rattled, feeling like my brain isn't working correctly.

I hear steps approach—odd crunching sounds that don't align with anything human. My rescuer's face comes into view again, green hair falling forward as he bends over to press something on my cage.

He's opening it, I realize. As much as I want out, the idea of being unshielded from him makes my heart skip a beat. The glass slides away, and I finally get a clear look around me now that there's no pink blocking my vision.

His eyes pierce into mine, their yellow color too overwhelming to look at. I look away and wait for the cage to open, glancing around me.

It's a scene of carnage—gray blood and pools of dead aliens everywhere.

"We need to leave," the alien male urges.

Another pain shoots through my throat, and once again I can't seem to get any words out.

He grabs my arm, pulling me out of my dazed panic. "Don't touch me," I hiss.

His grip tightens instead of releasing, and he pulls me out of the cage, carrying me past the gore before placing me on the ground and dragging me along. I bite my tongue, suppressing the caustic words threatening to spill out until he finally lets go of me.

Then I remind myself that he just saved me, not to mention ensured I didn't touch any of the terrible ooze or alien blood.

A glimpse of green and purple sky through the dense tree canopy only disorients me further. Alien sky, plants... people.

None of it makes sense. None of it does. Fear is clouding my mind, and I work through all my usual mental exercises to push it back down so I can function. They work, just barely.

I glance back at one of the pink and gray blobs. It has completely melted into a puddle, dead and powerless, making me want to spit at it. Taking me to auction? A slaver deserves such an end.

I look up at the other strange alien who towers above me. I'm relieved when he lets go of me and returns to the silver container I was just in. It no longer looks like a cage, but more like something from a sci-fi movie.

My eyes go back to the gray puddle, my mind still spinning.

"Are you injured?" my savior asks from behind me. I whip around quickly and almost lose my footing. He grabs my arm to hold me upright, his eyes not leaving mine.

It discomforts me greatly. So, I look down to compose myself, only to find my nipples hardened and pressing through the jumpsuit, the ample flesh jiggling. My eyes widen, but I gather myself, standing up straight and pulling my arm away from his grasp.

I'm warm, especially between my legs, and a flush of embarrassment and shame rushes over me.

I straighten my shoulders and look at his face, my gaze getting caught by his long, elven-like ears. They're shaped like two long knives, sticking up and behind him.

Is he an elf? It seems like nothing is impossible here. I understood both him and the slime creature when they spoke to me, despite knowing they weren't speaking Farsi or even the same language as each other.

I realize I'm being rude and clear my throat. "Thank you for rescuing me. I don't know how I got here," I say, still dazed as the words leave my lips.

The burn in my throat has passed. My guess is that it has something to do with speaking and everything to do with those slimes.

"The genali are a nasty bunch. I am Tehlmar," he says, clacking his jaws at them.

I catch sight of a row of sharp green teeth and take a step back, swallowing hard.

It takes me a moment to process what he just said. "They are," I retort, glancing back at the puddle to confirm it. "You can call me Nasrin."

"I will check for supplies. Wait here."

I ignore his demanding tone and use the opportunity to get a better look at him. He is significantly taller than me by at least several feet, and his skin shines in the waning light of the forest, which I'm currently mostly ignoring so I don't panic.

He is thin, with his long green hair that almost reaches his waist. His legs move quickly, his foot spikes sink into the leaves and detritus in a way that my brain is struggling to process.

When he speaks to me again, I notice how soft-spoken he is. His language is melodic and soothing, almost like a lullaby being whispered.

"There isn't much this way," he says, pointing in the direction behind him as he walks past, his arm brushing against mine.

My nipples harden again, and the crotch of my jumpsuit grows moist.

I don't know what the genali have done to me, but this must be part of it—my body has never responded to a man this way before. Maybe it's the kind of men I've been exposed to, but I haven't found one attractive in a very long time. Even then, it was more out of curiosity than anything else.

He walks past me, and I catch a whiff of his scent, like some exotic spice. He may not be human, but I have to admit that he is good-looking.

I grumble to myself when another wave of wetness rushes out of me, pressing my legs tightly together. "Control yourself, Nasrin."

"Let's go," he calls to me and I nod, watching as his face twists into what I recognize as confusion.

He's an alien, and I might be the first human he's ever encountered.

A long, tired sigh escapes my lungs as my mind races, unsure of where to begin in figuring this all out. I'm on a different planet with a purple and green sky, I can understand two alien languages so far, and I'm dressed in a too-tight jumpsuit that either works with my thoughts or is some kind of magic.

Where does one even begin when everything is alien?

"You look dazed, but you are far calmer than I would expect," he comments, his voice sounding fake, though I'm not sure how I can know that in an alien language. I don't trust him.

I hear Bibi's voice in my head, scolding me for not trusting any men, reminding me how it only worsens my already terrible prospects. A memory surfaces with it... something about her. I shake my head, as if doing so will help rearrange all the confusion into something that makes sense.

"Fear is constant where I am from," I tell him through gritted teeth. "If you don't master it, you don't survive."

He huffs out a breath, but doesn't respond and it makes my hands twitch. Nothing feels right, but the basic foundation of my instincts seems useless now. Not trusting anyone is a default, but I'm certain I can't get out of this alone.

This is not the time to doubt the one person who literally saved my life from *Allah* knows what horrors they had planned for me. I'd better keep my head down and learn all I can. A towering, deadly-looking elf alien might just be the companion I need... wherever this is.

Kuret

It feels like I've been walking through the hallways of the outer cloister for ages.

I don't remember it being this long, but I keep moving forward, step after step, endlessly. In the distance, I hear a sound—like men screaming a battle cry-and it spurs me to quicken my pace, until I'm running, eager to reach them, to earn my honor on the battlefield.

When I reach the courtyard, I see the bloodied males marching toward me, their eyes vacant and dead, with Samke leading them. I raise my spear, trying to reason with them, but Samke lunges at me, open mouth, sharp teeth aiming at my throat.

* * *

"Samke!" I scream, pushing myself off the ground before I've even fully woken up.

I try to assume a fighting stance, but my legs are not steady, and I rock back and forth, tipping forward until a bush breaks my fall.

Pulling away from the surprisingly lush purple bush, I lay on the ground to collect my thoughts and make sense of where I am. The sky is an unnatural shade of purple-green, with a bright sun that warms instead of burning, and towering plants stretch far beyond my sight—unnaturally tall in a way that makes my marks itch.

This is not my home.

"Honorless animals," I grunt, hissing as a sharp pain shoots through my head.

How did I get here? Reality and dream blur in my mind, but one thing is clear; I failed.

I remember being captured, but my memory fractures after that. When I try to force myself to recall more, it feels like something's gnawing at my brain, all thanks to those disgusting creatures. I decide to stay down for a while, regaining my strength with deep breaths as I think of how to survive in this strange new place.

The sky is evidence enough that I cannot just walk home.

Am I the only one here? A sharp pang strikes each of my hearts, one after the other. I've never been alone before. There have always been males around me to speak with, to fight alongside.

I push down the rising panic.

A wet chatter pulls me from my thoughts, followed by a collective honking. My eyes shoot pen—I'd recognize that sound anywhere. The chattering continues, and I flip onto my stomach, rising slowly to avoid stumbling again.

I walk quietly, hiding behind a towering plant, and spot the source of the sound. Ahead, the forest leads to a ridgeline, where three of the aliens are ascending, moving away from the path that leads to me. A smile stretches across my face. They will never detect me coming.

They took my spear, but I remember the knife hidden inside my boot. I reach back with two fingers, pulling out the sharp dagger. Looking up again, I see that they've moved far enough ahead for me to follow them.

I trail behind them down the ridge, thankful for the odd plants that provided cover. I never imagined revenge would be so easily within reach, but as I follow the aliens, I can see all the entry points of attack.

There are plenty, since they seem to have no sense of survival.

When I close in, I note that they are holding weapons and realize that my initial plan to announce myself with a battle cry may not be the wisest. Their lighting puts smoking holes in warriors who have been in more battles than the years I've been alive. It is wise to be cautious.

As we near the top of the ridge, I hear a stream bubbling nearby, and the grotesque creatures make the honking sound again. I realize they have come up the ridge for the water, focused on it in a way that makes them ignore their surroundings.

I decide to wait where I am hiding so that I can find a second weapon while they get into position. A suitably thick branch lies a small distance away from me, so I pick it up and remove the leaves, carving the tip until it's sharp enough to be a point.

Such a valuable resource, just lying around in abundance. So strange.

I creep along the ridge, staying out of sight as I make my way toward them. They are sufficiently distracted, so I quicken my pace into a jog and drive the sharpened branch into the head of one of the aliens.

Pink slime and gray blood spurts from the hole as he deflates in front of his friends with a squelch. The second recovers from his shock quickly and reaches for his weapon, but my dagger is already through his eye, as he bleeds all over my hand.

The third one pulls out his weapon and aims it at me, but I dodge and fall to the ground behind one of the dying aliens. I spot a dagger in his holster and waste no time throwing it.

Peeking out from behind my temporary cover, which is rapidly deflating, I see that I have killed all three, and pride fills my body. I stand up straight and pull out my knife from one of their puddles, taking it with me as I wade into the stream to wash their filth off.

This is just the first of them I plan to kill.

For their invasion, for my abduction, and for the deaths of my friends—and probably the females at the cloister—I will not stop until I make every one of them pay. Until then, I must find weapons and gather supplies to protect myself.

I don't recognize some of their items and although it feels like a lost opportunity, I can still carry so much.

Although they are awkward in my hand, as a last resort, I decide to carry one of their daggers with me, attaching a cleaned holster around my waist. I make my way down the ridgeline, stepping into the thick, leafy plants that sway gently around me, noting how different it is from my home planet.

There, the air is harsh and dry, and the sun's brutal rays scorch your skin if you stay too long under it. Here, the breeze brushes softly against me, and the towering plants create a patchwork of shade. But I can't bring myself to appreciate my environment.

My hearts are pounding fast, drumming loudly against my chest, each feeding the rage building inside me. I want nothing more than to destroy these creatures, wipe them out completely, one by one.

Rin

The wind blows softly, and my hair flies into my face, brighter than I've ever seen it.

Grabbing onto a few locks, I pull them in front of me and see that it is a stark white, the curls longer and looser. With the shock comes anger, but I bite down on the comments that want to bubble up, my mind still reeling.

As Tehlmar and I move through the trees, my first thought is how the sky looks like a radioactive sunset, with a pale-yellow sun, like something out of a sci-fi movie.

A strained smile stretches across the side of my mouth as I remember that *bābā* used to really adore the genre. He wanted to be an astronaut as a child but inherited the family's butcher shop and threw away his dreams of traversing space, but he kept the faith alive with stories.

If he were still alive, I'd find a way to make it home just to tell him I left Earth. My smile fades as I think of how much of my life has centered around those few words.

If he were still alive.

My life shrunk to almost nothing because of his death, with people telling me I needed to simply move on. But move on to what? There was no room left to breathe, let alone live.

Now, here I am, with no restrictions on me, an open world and sky. It's terrifying.

I shake my head, frustrated that I'm letting my mind wander, even though it's hard to focus right now. My hand goes to my hair again, and I pull it to eye level. I'm still in shock at its whiteness after twenty-three years of having brown, extremely frizzy curls I never appreciated.

Why was it changed? The desire to cover it surges more than ever.

My mind drifts to my hijab collection, collecting dust on the wooden hangers in my room. What would be more helpful, though, is something to cover my body.

I lost a bit of weight after moving in with my brother, but my thighs are still thick, and my stomach is padded. Although I'm not ashamed of my body, it's not meant to be on display like this for anyone to see. This jumpsuit emphasizes every curve, and I know that if my parents had the displeasure of seeing me in this, they would be appalled.

Tehlmar strides forward, ignoring me. It's almost as if he forgets we're walking together, only remembering periodically when he turns to glance down at me, as if checking that I'm still alive.

I don't mind the silence because it gives me time to process my new reality and figure out how I got here. Not that I've made any progress in understanding that. Everything feels stretched out since eating at the table with Bibi, almost like I've been dreaming. But I know for a fact that I didn't dream those horrifying genali doing something to me.

With a start, I remember the look on her face. She did this to me. A shiver runs down my skin and my heart contracts painfully. Did she... sell me? Then I remember that my brother was there and it feels like a knife inserted through my ribs.

They did. They sold me so I wouldn't be a problem anymore. I didn't have any illusions that my life would be easy, but that is nothing I ever thought possible. And so here I am.

It's hard to breath for several long moments, but I force my mind away from it, concerned that if I let myself feel that betrayal that it'll make the fear harder to contain. That I'll be right back to that cowering child I vowed to never be again.

So, instead, I try to figure out what is going on.

It doesn't take a genius to see that this is some kind of interplanetary trafficking, and I'm not the first woman they have done this to. My head starts to throb again and I palm my temple, wishing I was back home with a bowl of eucalyptus oil.

Or maybe back home, period.

Eager to escape my thoughts, I turn to Tehlmar. "Are there more things like the genali out here?" I ask, stepping over a bramble.

"The genali are everywhere," he responds, "it is hard to avoid them. The braceaaer as well, devious little things."

I gasp. "There's more than one kind?"

A fresh fear settles itself in the pit of my belly and I almost lose my footing.

"Yes, they're the most dangerous species on this planet, aside from me. The genali are technologically advanced and their main targets are females. They abduct them and kill anything in their way unless it has some use to them. This is one of their hunting grounds. "

"They are horrible," I say, recalling the look in the genali's eyes as he leered at me through the glass cage.

"Not many people survive an encounter with them, so count yourself lucky I was there to rescue you."

His words have a gloating edge, and I catch myself judging him through a lens of distaste. It's not the first time he has made reference to his role as my "knight in shining armor," and it's starting to grate on me.

I was there; I saw it all and don't need the reminder.

Mid-thought, I shake my head, chastising myself. I shouldn't think this way about someone who saved my life. Besides, maybe I'm misjudging him because I don't understand his culture?

He continues to speak, and I listen eagerly. "The braceaaer are small, gray-green aliens that—"

I interrupt, "Let me guess, they hate women too?" He makes a chittering sound, then puffs, his shoulders shaking in amusement.

A laugh?

"Yes, they are worse. While the genali abduct females to make profit, the braceaaer capture them for personal use, sometimes to kill without reason. They are quite violent and brutal," he says, his tone making goosebumps rise on my arms.

I push my hair back and look straight ahead, aware of his gaze lingering on me. "I don't remember much from the abduction. I was home with my brother's wife; the next, I was here. It's all a blur." I sigh, reaching out to touch a feathery leaf.

The plants here look so similar, yet different from those on Earth. It's surreal, and I wish that I could truly enjoy it; I've dreamed of seeing more of the world since I was young. But this is far more exotic than I ever dreamed.

"Females can't protect themselves. It is a fact," he says simply.

My hands clench, and I bite back a retort just in time.

"Anyone who treats females that way should be exterminated. I have known males like that," I growl out.

The look on Tehlmar's face is strange—discomfort, maybe—but I can't quite tell.

I swallow my frustration and give him a tight smile. "Knowing their filthy hands tampered with my body makes me feel sick."

A heavy silence falls between us, one I hope lasts a while. Talking to Tehlmar sets off alarms in my head. I'm not sure if it's his choice of words or some deeper instinct, but it leaves me uneasy.

Not that I would trust him anyway, but it adds to the confusion and mental strain I'm already feeling.

As we walk across a clearing, his words echo in my mind. It seems there's absolutely nowhere in the galaxy where women are safe.

I wonder if he knows any women who were abducted, but the question feels too personal, so I keep it to myself. There might be other human women on this planet, and I hope we cross our paths, and find a way out of this together. No one should have to live this kind of nightmare alone.

It makes me curious about women's rights in his homeland. If women are such a prize for these aliens and other species know about it, are there any laws to help?

I turn to him. "At this point, I don't think there is any place where females are protected."

He huffs out an inarticulate response, his hair whipping around as he looks both ways, his long ears twitching.

"Are there any laws protecting them on your planet?" I ask in a low voice, but he is already moving faster, crossing over shrubs as I struggle to keep up.

I try to match his pace, but I'm panting and my legs are too short to close the gap.

"Tehlmar," I gasp, heaving. "Wait."

He glances at me, but doesn't slow down. "I recognize this area. There was a cart tied to a tree up ahead."

"Is it still there?"

"No, but there are tracks in the soil," he says, motioning for me to catch up. "If we hurry, I am sure we can find something useful."

I groan under my breath but follow, glancing over my shoulder to check for any hunters following us. Tehlmar looks back, his gaze briefly sweeping over me before he speeds up even more. I feel that strange sensation between my legs again, not arousal, just frustration at his pace that leaves me trailing behind. It's clear I'm in for a long journey with this alien, one I might not enjoy.

Thankfully, this time he pauses, waiting for me to catch up before heading into a small clearing with a long tree downed in the middle. There, the cart and an animal hitched to it come into view.

A long tug of excitement pulls at my heart; I want to run to the creature, but I hesitate, intimidated by its sheer size. I glance at Tehlmar to see if he shares my caution, but he's focused on inspecting the area, slipping behind trees and scanning to ensure we're alone.

I stay where I am, continuing to study the animal.

It is much larger than me and about the size of a draft horse, with beautiful deep-blue fur and wavy brown patterns scattered across it.

I take a few steps closer, relieved that it appears to be asleep.

Its legs remind me of a spider, with knees that jut out beneath as it lays down, three on each side. That's where the resemblance ends, though; its bulky body leads to a short neck tied to the tree with a thick rope halter.

The cart is secured to it with similar ropes, one thick buckle at the bottom, with the rest disappearing into the fur around its face.

Its face is endearing, with a short snout and wide nostrils that flare with every whistled breath it lets out. I'm tempted to reach out and touch it, even as a voice in my mind warns me to be cautious.

Its fuzzy tail, about half the length of a horse's, but shaped more like a dog's, flicks periodically, likely to swat any insects.

Tehlmar heads straight for the animal, and I raised an eyebrow in surprise. Is he really that bold or just arrogant? Approaching a sleeping animal this large could be dangerous, unless he's with it? I stay rooted to the spot, watching as he bends down to inspect it.

The animal stirs, glancing at him sleepily before shutting its eyes and opening its mouth in a wide yawn. The lack of sharp teeth helps me relax a bit.

My heart aches, wondering how long it's been trapped here. "Does it know you?" I ask.

"He's an argila, native to my home world. They're very docile creatures."

I hum a response, relieved that I'm not at risk of being attacked anytime soon. Tehlmar continues to speak as his thin fingers work to untie the knots of the ropes around the tree.

My gaze lowers to the animal's feet, which are gnarled pads of thick brown skin.

"Do you think there are genali nearby? I mean, it feels like a trap to leave a cart in the middle of a clearing like this," I say, a chill creeping up my spine.

I look around, feeling a spike of anxiety, as though we've walked right into an ambush.

"They are not here," he assured me. "Dust has gathered on the cart, there's no slime, and the animal seems smaller than it should be. It's a few cycles without proper food and water. Whoever left it probably doesn't even remember it exists."

Rage replaces my fear as I think of the poor creature, abandoned by its owners after they'd used it and moved on. The similarities between these hunters and some human sits very uncomfortably in my stomach. If it were a book or film, I'd assume they were just a metaphor for evil.

Despite its awkwardly bent knees, the argila is still taller than me and I have to stretch to reach its head. It lets out a soft whine as I touch it, revealing gentle, rubbery teeth that look more like the ribbed baleen of a whale than anything threatening.

Dust motes fly out from its fur and a musky, pleasant scent follows. Nothing like a horse, with a hint of pepper in it that makes my nose twitch.

Lowering my hands, I scratch at its neck, ready to speak, when I feel a sharp twinge in my own neck. Groaning quietly, I turned back to the argila. "Did they hurt you?" I murmur in Farsi. The animal's tail wags a little faster, and it lets out a long, braying sigh of contentment, its skin twitching with delight. It startles me for a moment, but when I look at its face, its eyes are tightly shut and its mouth is open, with the tip of its large black tongue peeking out.

I laugh as its eyes flutter open, skin still twitching, but much more gently now.

"You are so strange," I say to the argila and it bellows in a deep, tuba-like tone before bumping its head to me. I scratch its neck, feeling a surprising sense of comfort with this alien creature, who is sweet and guileless.

My musing ends as the argila nudges against me one last time for attention before crouching slowly in front of me.

Realizing that it wants to graze, I step back and watch it with horror as its knees jut out on either side until they are almost touching the ground as well. It must stay that way for its short, broad neck to reach the grass.

My initial revulsion quickly turns into amusement, and I wish I could communicate with it. I'd probably get clearer answers than from Tehlmar.

The argila, bending low like this, looks straight out of a horror movie, yet it's somehow the cutest thing I have seen. It says a lot about my mental state, but I don't care. My sense of nearly everything was warped the moment I woke up on an alien planet.

If I had come across something like this on Earth, I'd have screamed and run. Now all I want to do is pet it and make sure it's okay. I keep watching the animal as it eats, the rubbery stuff inside its mouth grabbing at the feathery grass. Big, dark lips pulling the blades into its hungry mouth.

It needs a name.

The argila lets out a small hissing bleat and I face it, smiling as a name flashes across my mind.

"Roshan," I murmur under my breath. The argila looks up at me, its warm, bright, beautiful eyes filled with what feels like recognition. I smile softly. "I will call you Roshan because you have brightened my day."

The argila brays joyfully, as if accepting the name, and I repeat it a few times, delighted by its reaction. Encouraged, I step closer, scratching at its neck while babbling nonsense to it, my words a mix of affection and relief. For a moment, it feels like a small, comforting reprieve from everything else.

I let out a soft, wistful sigh, gazing into Roshan's mustard-colored eyes. "It's not our day, is it?"

"Stop startling it. They don't handle surprises well," Tehlmar chides from behind me.

I open my mouth to protest; I hadn't startled Roshan, but before I can say anything, Tehlmar speaks again. His green hair falls forward as he leans down, picking something up from the base of the cart.

"Get into the cart," he says firmly, his voice brooking no argument. "We need to leave before someone else follows the tracks and finds us."

6

Kuret

Ahead, the dense foliage breaks into a small valley, splitting into three winding paths, each veiled by thick greenery. I pause, scanning the options, but my decision is made for me when I hear it, the rustling of leaves, followed by the sickeningly familiar wet sound of the aliens.

I don't hesitate.

Following the noise, I move silently, keeping low as the plants close in around me. My senses are still slightly dulled from whatever they used to drug me, the lingering effects tugging faintly at my focus. But nothing can deter me now.

I crouch behind a wide, leafy plant, my movements slow and deliberate as I peer through the underbrush. The edges of my lips stretch into a smile when I finally spot one of them, stumbling clumsily into my line of sight.

It circles in place, searching for something it won't find. Instead it will meet its end.

The alien drifts closer to the giant plant shielding me, and I hold my breath, counting down the moments until it comes close enough for me to grab. When it's just within reach, the snap of a twig nearby pulls its attention away. The distraction is all I need.

I lunge from behind the tree, my battle cry ripping through the air as my hands slam into its wet slimy head. We tumble to the ground, and I drive my fists into its face, relishing the wet crunch beneath my knuckles.

It reaches for a weapon at its side, but I knock it away, pinning it under my knee on the ground. A sharp pain radiates through my abdomen. I glanced down to find the alien has driven a knife into me.

Because of the hardened muscle, it doesn't go all the way in. Gritting my teeth, I press my knees tighter against its sides, watching its eyes bulge as it squeals. It tries to struggle against me, but my knees and one hand have pinned its limbs to the side of its body so that it cannot access any of the surrounding weapons.

My strikes grow wild, fueled by rage, until I reach for its eyes. My fingers dig deep into its eye sockets, and with one violent pull, I tear them free. It makes one last pained sound and goes limp, gray blood and pink slime spurting from its injured body. I fling its eyes onto the lifeless form, hissing in disgust.

Wiping my bloodied hands against the dirt, I notice the even bigger pack strapped to its back. Intrigued, I crouch and attempt to undo it, only to find no clasp or buckle. Frustration prickles at me.

With a sharp tug, I pull the knife from my torso, bitting down on my tongue as if to reduce the pain. The taste of my own blood fills my mouth, a distraction. Dark green seeps from the wound, but I ignore it. I will clot soon enough. I can't afford to leave a trail.

Blade in my hand, I begin sawing through the alien's pack.

"You are the fourth one I have killed, but you will not be the last," I murmur under my breath and immediately I hear a soft gasp in the distance.

I whip my head around to search for the source of the sound, then I hear a female's voice being carried by the wind from the same direction.

"Greetings. Can we come down to speak to you? We do not mean any harm," she says, and I am taken aback.

Why would a female want to talk to me?

The first thing I note is the distance her voice is coming from. Not too far but also not close enough that I can directly locate her. Her voice is strange, stilted in my language, her accent clumsy yet deliberate. She is not one of my kind, but neither is she like the gray slime I just killed. My ears twitch, catching every nuance of her tone, even as my grip tightens on my knife.

It could be a trap. It may be a trick of the disgusting gray aliens. I don't doubt their ability to use something like this to lure me into a trap, even with their previous attacks being as direct as they were.

My arm works harder at sawing through the strap when I hear her again, her voice even more amplified this time. "My name is Ree, and I was taken by the hunters. I managed to escape and find an ally and we are looking for other allies. Can we come and speak with you?"

Hunters? I pause, considering. She must be above me, high in one of these towering plants.

I don't know if I should respond, but I decide that there is no harm in trying. I've never been without allies and having a friendly face that I can ask about the workings of this place and maybe even the location of more of the slimes to kill wouldn't hurt.

"Where are you?" I ask, keeping my tone guarded.

"Not far from you, up high in a *tree*."

So that is what the giant plants are called.

"Are you alone?"

"No, I have a—" She hesitates briefly. "—a friend with me."

I run my tongue over my teeth, unsure. If they're larger or stronger than me, this could turn into a fight I'm not ready for. But if they're weaker, I could always deal with them later.

If they are friends, then they must both be female. Surely I can take on two females. The idea of it makes my marks pulse in horror, but I am injured and this is a new place, clearly full of dangers.

"Can you come down alone?" I ask.

"Sorry, no, but I promise we mean no harm," she assures me.

I make sure my weapons are placed correctly for easy access and that she understands just how serious I am. "I am Kuret. You can come down, but do not get too close. If you attempt to harm me, I will kill you and your friend."

She acknowledges my warning, her voice slipping into a hushed whisper as she speaks a different language I can't understand. I assume she is communicating with her friend and continue sawing through the bag, letting out a sigh of relief when it finally comes apart.

The silence of the forest is heavy, uninterrupted only by the distant hum of unseen creatures. Then faint, deliberate footsteps approach, soft yet precise. I want to step out from behind the large plant, but I am in too much pain from my wound. I can only keep my head low and watch a large, magnificent-looking beast walk toward me, its orange eyes glaring into mine.

Its eyes search me before it sits back, only a short distance away, orange and green fur waving in the wind when it spares a glance at the much smaller figure walking behind it. The female. I can't get a good look at her yet.

Its hands brush at its fur while serving as some kind of barrier between the female and where I am. I can barely make out more of her features than her oddly colored hair and eyes. Her skin is an odd pinkish color instead of gray, like our females.

A quick glance back confirms that she seems to breathe from the middle of her face instead of the sides of it. The sight of it unsettles me briefly, twisting my stomach. But I push the discomfort aside.

She speaks to me. "Hello Kuret, I am Ree, and this is Thivoll. Thank you for letting us come to you," she says, and I push myself up, standing tall despite the ache in my torso. I step into full view, watching her eyes widen slightly as they follow my movements.

"I will listen, but know I can defend myself if you try to harm me," I tell her, leaning my back against the *tree* bark for support. I make sure one of the weapons on my waist is visible, but she doesn't seem to catch it as she responds to me.

"I can see that. They hurt me too, me and my friends." I look over to the beast, eyes moving over its imposing frame and twitching tail.

The spike at the tip, poised and ready, leaves no doubt in my mind that it's venomous.

She must have seen the confusion on my face and lets out a small, pleased sound. "Not him. Thivoll actually saved me from them. They hurt him too, but he's healed now."

Her eyes soften as she looks at him, a glimmer of gratitude in her expression before she turns back to me.

"I killed three others a little distance from here," I inform her, a little confused at the ease of conversation between us but choosing not to question it just now. "They captured me from my home, and I don't know if I was the only one."

Her blue-green eyes dim with sadness. "Yes, they did the same to me, too. Changed me and a few others, gave us *nanite* translators, and treated us horribly. Luckily I found Thivoll, who they have been hunting. They are mostly hunters here, I think, not slavers. Thivoll is a manticorid, and I am human."

My jaw tightens when I imagine the females in the cloister going through the same torture.

"It is good we found each other," her tone lifting slightly. "Now I know there's someone else who hates the genali as much as we do." She lets out a trill of laughter, showing small, blunt teeth as her lips stretch.

I laugh too, appreciative of her humor. So that is what our enemy is called. I roll the name on my tongue, committing it to memory.

The laughter fades, and she turns to Thivoll, speaking in a language I can't understand. So this is what the *nanite* translators do? It seems like it is too useful to provide for someone and, once again, I feel suspicious.

I'd feel better with a knife in my hand, but something tells me I'd have that venomous tail flying at me faster than I could reach it.

She steps out from behind her manticorid protector, which means she must trust me more.

As she moves closer, my gaze takes in her full form for the first time. She is much smaller compared to the females of my species, her frame delicate but adult. Her features are striking yet strange, no marks, no ear spikes, no braids, blunt teeth, her coloring pale and her eyes a curious blue-green. Despite her differences, there's beauty to her, though she is closer in size to a youngling.

She wears a glossy black material, tightly covering her small frame. It outlines small breasts and pale skin where ours would be darker.

I look up at her "friend" and find that he is peering menacingly at me, orange eyes narrowing even as his lips move in response to Ree's words.

I do not believe they are friends, of course, that would be ridiculous. Just then, he says something that makes her laugh and slap a hand gently on his shoulder. Strange. She then turns over to look at me.

"I don't appreciate it when people look at me like that, Kuret. And Thivoll is thinking violent thoughts," she declares, the edge of her mouth twitching as if she is fighting back a laugh.

Realizing my mistake, I immediately bow my head in apology. However, I cannot help the question that shoots out of my mouth. "Is he your chosen donor? I assumed you were not compatible. Aren't you too young?"

She spoke about the genali, as she called them, abducting her and making changes to her. This manticorid looks older. His battle scars are visible across his body, and this purple-haired female does not look like she will be able to handle the sheer size of his children.

Still, I shouldn't have looked at her that way, regardless of how improper their relationship seems.

I shake my head as I continue to speak. "It is my error and a wound to my honor."

Despite my injury, my chest hurts, not just with pain but with regret. If I were at full strength, I'd challenge this manticorid for what I see as a grave violation, a young and fragile female being taken advantage of. Yet something in Ree's confidence tells me she is no victim, and it unsettles me further.

7

Kuret

Ree's brow furrows in confusion, the odd patch of fur above her eyes shifting as she scratches the top of her head. Her scaly arms caught my attention. "He is my, uh... donor? But no honor has been wounded," she assures me, her eyes shifting to my injury. "How about we take care of that one in your stomach? I will show you how to use the genali tools so you can heal any later wounds yourself."

I nod, lowering myself against the tree with care. Pain radiates through my body but I hold back a grunt.

Ree comes closer to me, dropping to her knees. Her attention is fixed on my hands as I start to undo the front part of my armor, revealing the shirt underneath. I bite my tongue to keep from making a sound.

"May I help?"

The question stops me; I glare at her, my brows drawing low in affront. Thivoll puffs out his chest and takes a step toward us, but he stands in place when I do not move.

"Is that a violent question?" she asks, her voice quiet, almost unsure.

"It is an insult."

A soft gasp escapes her, and she lowers her head. "My honor is diminished. I am a healer. I meant no offense."

"As you said, no honor is lost." I reply, softening. "You are different, but you are not offering violence. You may help."

A smile brightens her face at my words, and I offer a small one in return.

Her eyes lingers on me, traveling from my face to the point of injury, while her hands continue to help me undo my breastplate.

Once the armor is removed, I lift my shirt, exposing the bleeding wound. Ree leans in, assessing it closely. "I'll grab a tool," she announces, reaching for a pouch like the one I stole from the hunter and tears into it, pulling out a small, silver tool. I recognize it, but I don't know how it works.

Thankfully, Ree explains it to me. "This will tie your wound together. The ties will melt when your body no longer needs them. It will hurt when I use it," she warns, looking up at me through her dark lashes. "Did you get one from the other genali?"

"I did, but I left it under a bush," I admit.

"That is good." She nods her head. "Watch how I use it and ask questions as needed. May I touch you?"

"You may touch me."

"Okay. This will hurt," she says and I smile at her, watching as she returns a quick one before focusing on closing my injury. She assesses it. "Did it hit anything vital? Can I close it up?"

"It is only on the surface," I respond, amusement threading my voice as I observe the fuss she is putting up. Healers on my planet are vastly different, elderly males who are thorough to a fault. They ask no questions, yet their methods can bring even the strongest of protectors to whimper.

"Good," Ree says, digging into her pouch. "I am grabbing another thing."

I smile again, a stiff laugh following because I do not want to offend her, but she looks up and grins back at me before speaking again.

"This will clean your wounds," she announces as she sprays a liquid onto the wound. It burns slightly, but the pain fades quickly, turning into a prickling sensation as the clipping sound of the instrument echoes through the *trees*.

When she finishes closing the wound, she leans back on her knees, carefully inspecting her work. Her companion growls something in his gravelly language, and she turns to smile at him.

It discomforts me how little I know about her and her manticorid companion. My honor will not allow me to leave a vulnerable woman at the mercy of a creature she clearly can't defend herself against, especially not after her aid. At the very last, I must ask if she needs help.

"You look too young for a donor," I remark as I adjust my clothes. "Your teeth are worn. Are you actually old?"

"No. *Humans* just don't have that many natural defenses." She laughs and I cannot mask the shock.

She is a human; I remember her saying that before. How many other races are out among the stars?

"No natural defenses?" My eyes travel to the black scales on her arm, and I click my tongue in disbelief.

"But those black scales look thick."

They seem sturdy, capable of shielding her from many weapons. Ree touches the scales, rubbing them thoughtfully.

I don't know how or why it took me such a long time to realize, but she has four fingers instead of three. Odd, but they are small and nimble.

"Those are new. I got them from Thivoll," she says proudly and my eyes travel from her to the manticorid and then back to her.

Have I been wrong about her all along? Could she be the one dominating the manticorid, harvesting parts of him for herself? My hand moves slowly toward my weapon, but her wide-eyes reaction halts me.

"Wait!" she hisses out. "I didn't take them. I was captured by the same aliens you killed. It is because of them that I can look more like him."

Horror grips me as the implication sinks in. The genali's depravity seems to know no bounds, each revelation darker than the last.

"Why would they do that?" I ask, voice low.

"I was supposed to be a pleasure slave," she admits, her tone heavy with sorrow.

Rage floods my veins, both hearts poundings faster. Such a fate would be forced upon her without her consent, a death sentence for any male who dares to touch her.

"They truly have no honor, then," I conclude, and she lets out a disbelieving sound.

"No, I don't think they do."

"Then they will get no mercy."

She seems to like that, though something about her face lets me know she isn't used to violence.

"Would you join us? We can be stronger together."

She asks it quickly, nearly stumbling over her words, like she has been waiting to ask.

Her eagerness amuses me, though speaking so freely with a female still feels strange. "You seem like you have honor," I say, watching her face turn a deeper shade of pink. Her gaze darts everywhere but my face.

"Well, yes," she says and then hesitates, like she wants to take her statement back, "but maybe not like you think of it. I need to find other females like me and protect them."

Her response intrigues me. Protecting others has been my purpose since I was a youngling, It is one of the most honorable things to do as a male. Ree's tenderness, her resolve, draws me in. My ears twitch with interest as I lean closer.

"Where?"

Her eyes widen, surprise flickering across her face at my intensity. "We don't know. Well, except for one. Maybe two. We met another person—Szhe'ka... he looks like a very large *bird* man, except they cut off his wings—who is going to protect the one he saw. There are six more out there," she rambles, excited about my help.

"They would be found faster if I searched where you did not," I reply, lifting my face up to look around me.

Everything is a blur of green, purple, and brown but I am confident I can find my way back. Back home, the desert sand erases your tracks; you must know your way or risk being lost.

Many children and even some adults have vanished, unable to find their way back home. Some never return.

She lets out a sigh of relief and leans forward. "That's true, but we are safer together. This will be a risk for you."

Her concern nearly draws a laugh from me, but I suppress it.

I killed three genali with a single dagger and a hastily made wooden spear. I have nothing else to lose, and every moment of our being alive is a risk. "Danger is where the greatest honor lies"

Ree shoots me a joyful smile, and I cannot help but reply with one of my own.

There is something genuine in her gaze, like a brother's camaraderie. Her sincerity makes me want to stay and keep talking. It is no surprise a creature as mighty as Thivoll chose to be her donor.

She reaches behind her black clothing and pulls out something, revealing her hair. It is long, shining, and straight, even longer than my own, which I have never cut as a mark of my honor. Strands of orange streak through it, matching Thivoll.

I think it looks beautiful, so I tell her.

"Thank you."

Her face starts to turn pink again. "I hate it... but that doesn't matter. Each of us has different colored long hair like this. It isn't normal for us, so if you find them outside of a *cryogenic chamber,* they might have cut it off." She hesitates, glancing at me with a frustrated sigh, as if to articulate herself.

I wait for her in silence as she pushes out another laborious breath and continues speaking.

"I mean... they might be in a silver container, or maybe they are already out of it. It would be best if they stayed in it, and you carried them back to where we could protect them."

The red color on her face deepens and I almost laugh again. She is having a hard time saying the words and I do not want her to have more reasons to be... embarrassed?

Yes, I think that is what it means when her face changes color. Odd that it would be a redness, rather than the normal flickering of green.

"Does that make sense?" she asks.

"Yes," I answer. "I will start looking."

A grin spreads across my face, easing the lingering guilt over failing to protect my people. It also dulls the ache in my hearts urging me to stay with Ree and Thivoll instead of venturing alone. To not go out on my own and away from such allies.

But having a purpose, even a difficult one, is better than aimlessness. The thought of hunting genali fills me with renewed resolve. They will rue the day they attacked my home.

I fasten my breastplate, and gather all the supplies from the dead hunter's pack and stuffing them into mine. It's clear I'll need a bigger one soon.

Ree stands beside Thivoll as he combs through his bright orange fur and I watch as he is even more visibly relaxed now, muttering to her. It is odd to have a male here and to be talking to a female instead.

"What is he saying?" I ask Ree, breaking the silence.

Ree makes a trilling sound. "He appreciates your help."

Her face contorts into pain before she switches to Thivoll's language to ask him a question, and I squint. I saw her do that before and realize now that changing languages hurts her.

Of course, the genali would give something as precious as a *nanite* translator, but make it hurt. Ree and Thivoll continue in hushed tones, their exchange easy and genuine despite moments of disagreement. It fascinates me.

She turns back to me. "Thivoll says there is a ridgeline in that direction you could look for us at. Or we could meet back here."

She points toward the area where I killed the first three hunters. It seems like a stronghold for a rescue effort. I'm sure that I can keep it safe from the hunters once there is something to protect. "I know where he means. That is a better place than this."

Pushing myself off the ground, pain stabs through my body, but I mask it. "I hope to see you again soon, Ree."

She looks genuinely worried. "I hope so too. Please be careful."

"There is very little fun in that," I joke, and her lips press into a thin line, and her eyebrows furrow together.

These human expressions are surprisingly similar to my own. I let out a laugh and reassure her. "I will be careful with your females if I find them."

"Thank you."

I rub my arm to signal my departure, flick my head in silent acknowledgement to Thivoll, and turn to leave. I don't give my body time to adjust to the pain, breaking into a jog as I leave the area behind.

8

Rin

Tehlmar cracks the whip over Roshan's back, the sharp sound cutting through the air like a slap. I grimace, turning my face away as Roshan groans. The sight and the sound of his pain are unbearable.

Astaghfirullah. My thoughts churn uneasily. Tehlmar's actions paint him as someone unkind, but perhaps I'm overthinking again, as I often do. Roshan stumbles slightly while descending a short ridge, causing the cart to jolt and snapping me out of my thoughts.

Tehlmar jerks the reins roughly, and Roshan lets out an odd braying sound. Before I can protest, Tehlmar reaches for the whip again. This time, I place a hand over him, gently stopping him.

He grunts but lowers the whip, redirecting Roshan to the left at the fork below the ridge. "They are stubborn sometimes, and it doesn't hurt it."

I highly doubt it. "It doesn't mean you need to use violence all the time. He can be trained, you know," I counter and Tehlmar laughs. "What is so funny?"

He guides the reins tighter as we approach the slope. Roshan carefully picks his way down, slow and deliberate. "It seems that your people have strange views about animals. Back home, we use them for work, assisting us on the farms, and to be eaten. Not for treating like a lover."

His words hit like a slap. My jaw tightens, and I look away, swallowing the sting of his remark. I only care for Roshan's well-being, his accusation feels more like an insult than an observation. Like a lover? The nerve of him.

I grind my teeth together, and get distracted, but the biting cold seeps in, drawing my attention to my inadequate clothing. The genali, in their supposed generosity, gave me these thin garments that offer no insulation. I should be grateful to have anything at all, but it's hard not to resent them for this indignity. At least I'm not walking around naked.

Still, a scarf, or a thicker layer would go a long way.

Tehlmar seems to notice that I am chilly. "It is warmer where we are going," he assures, his voice neutral. Warmer than his attitude? He has gotten progressively less warm in his attitude toward me as the journey has gone on and I'm not sure if I can continue to ignore it. My instincts whisper that ignoring it may be unwise.

I thought we shared common ground, both of us captured and displaced on this weird planet. But now I am beginning to question my assumptions. "Where exactly are we going? Is it somewhere without the hunters?" I ask and he chuckles.

The laugh has no mirth in it at all, and it does not reach his eyes. Instead, it feels mocking, dismissive, a sound I know too well.

"You ask a lot of questions, Nasrin, and you are lucky I enjoy answering them."

Before I can respond, he continues. "We are heading toward a dock up north, You'll be safe from the hunters there. "

I cock a confused brow. "The hunters I'm so scared of? Do you not find them distasteful as well?"

He laughs at me, and it is definitely mocking, his face contorting into what I assume must be the equivalent of a sneer.

I cross my arms over my chest, keeping my expression composed. He needs to know I am serious.

He throws his head back in another cruel laugh and his hair blows back from the force of it. "Distasteful, yes. I find them absolutely abhorrent. However, I am not scared of them. They are easy for me to kill."

When he says that, his knuckles tighten menacingly on the reins in his hand, turning them nearly bone-white.

With a grunt, he wraps the reins around his fingers and pulls Roshan onto a path to the right instead of going straight ahead. It is easy, the way he just knows which way to go, almost like he frequents the path.

"You won't have to be scared of them anymore once we reach the dock." he says, his voice calm but firm.

"How do you know about it?" I ask, though I notice how the flex of his jaw betrays his irritation.

He leads us through a dense canopy of wide-leafed trees, the shadows swallowing the daylight once again. "I found out the same way many others find out, by asking the right people the right questions."

Roshan snorts, almost as if disagreeing with him, but the creature keeps walking, probably afraid of being hit again.

I'm struck by how much more human Roshan seems after giving him a name, perhaps, even more so than Tehlmar. But I focus my attention back to my companion and his clipped replies.

His response raises even more questions, ones I want to press. But what's the point? I don't know where north is or how to get back anywhere. I have no idea which place is safe or where to find other people. Most of all, I no longer trust Tehlmar.

If I ever did.

At this point, I'd rather be alone with Roshan than try to understand Tehlmar's sudden shift from savior to something far more unsettling.

Though I'm not sure what good my distrust does to me. I'm no match for him. He's huge.

When we emerge from the shadows, I watch him closely for any signs of strange intentions, but outwardly, everything seems normal.

The forest reflects our shifting moods—it started bright and familiar, but now it's dark and foreboding, the trees crowding together as if conspiring against us.

Tehlmar suddenly turns, his gaze burning into my face for an uncomfortably long time. "On my home planet, journeys like this are deeply interpersonal and are mostly shared by lovers and friends," he says, his tone almost casual.

He looks forward again, steering Roshan down a small but steep, grassy hill, ducking before a tree branch can hit him.

When his eyes flick back to me, I can feel the weight of his gaze shift to my chest. How can I not when he continues to leer at me, his yellow eyes shifting from my face to my cold-hardened nipples? I fold my hands over my chest and pretend to focus on something on the cart's wooden frame.

He just keeps speaking. "I think we would make good friends and even better lovers. Do you not agree?"

The answer jumps out of my mouth before I have the chance to think it through, probably because of years of practice. "I'm not the greatest at making friends."

He laughs, the tinkering melody of his voice floating around us. "Is it because you are afraid of something?"

I turn away, flustered, his words feeling like mockery. My face burns hotter as I stay silent.

"So, am I right?" he adds when I say nothing. "You know, you do not need to be so afraid when you are with me. Not of the genali, not of the braceaaer, not of pregnancy."

He whispers the last part and I whip my head around, unable to hide the shock on my face. "I am not scared of pregnancy. I just am not interested in having a lover," I explain slowly, leaving the sneer in my tone.

"Why would I fear pregnancy with you, though? We are different species." I look down at the dark skin of my hands and his silvery one, trying to imagine what a hybrid between us might look like. The thought disgusts me, and I close my eyes tightly, willing the cursed images away.

Tehlmar clicks his tongue. "It's possible between species, but that's not why I mentioned it."

Ya Allah, is he really going to make me beg for answers because I rejected his appeal? Even if I were going to decide to settle with him or anyone else, I would at least have to know them for longer than a few hours.

I don't know anything about him besides the fact that he rescued me from my doom, and he doesn't know anything about me either. How would it work?

"Then why?" I press on and he lets out a sigh, like my questions are annoying him.

"Genali hunters put contraceptives in slaves to prevent them from bearing children," he says slowly, looking at me out of the corner of his green-eyelash-rimmed yellow eyes as if that should clear up some sort of issue between us.

I try to think of a response, but nothing bubbles up.

My elbow itches, and I scratch it absentmindedly, trying to ignore him. We can't be genetically compatible. I don't believe it. And this conversation has all kinds of weird layers.

Two days ago, if someone had told me my life would take this bizarre turn, I'd have laughed and asked how long they'd spent at the *hookah* lounge.

Although, come to think of it, there's no way I came from Earth to here in just one day. I shut my mind down before I can make any of the calculations.

We don't ride for much longer when Tehlmar rounds Roshan up around a tall rock, revealing a hollow cave protected by large, weather-beaten tree trunks. He gets down first and wanders inside for a few moments. "It is habitable and safe, and we will not be followed. This is where we will rest."

Too tired to argue, I nod. The cave looks decent and well hidden.

"I am going to gather firewood. It will be a cold night," he announces as he walks away.

A fire? With genali around?

I climb off the cart and move to Roshan's side, shaking my head. My hands move to scratch at his short neck, earning a soft bleat as he nudges me affectionately. His fur tickles my skin, drawing a chuckle from me.

"Stay still, Roshan. Let me get you out of this," I say gently.

The animal is too excited and doesn't listen, but I persist, finally separating him from the cart. When Tehlmar returns with his arms full of sticks, he dumps them inside the cave and collects dry leaves. As he emerges again, he chides me, "Don't spoil the beast with so much affection. It will make it less likely to be obedient,"

I narrow my eyes at him and scratch Roshan's nose. "I think affection makes it more obedient," I argue and I hear Tehlmar scoff as he reenters the cave.

The sound of rocks scraping against each other is followed by a flickering orange flame that brightens up the evening.

It is not dark enough that I cannot see at all, but I have to squint to focus on anything in particular. I hear Tehlmar walking off again, but I am too busy digging into Roshan's fur with my fingers, trying to figure out a way to get the reins off completely.

I lead him closer to the light and continue fiddling while giving him occasional pets to sate his endless need for affection.

As I fiddle with the reins, trying to undo them completely, my fingers brush against a rough edge. A horrified gasp escapes me when I discover a scarred, pitted hole in Roshan's snout, where the rope feeds through. "What did they do to you, poor baby?" I whisper, my heart sinking.

Roshan lets out a soft bleat, his head pressing against me as if answering my question. He's been harmed. The cruelty of it disgusts me. There is no need for such brutal measures. Ever.

Tehlmar reappears with a handful of green leaves. "These will be safe for you to eat," he says.

After a glance at the small bouquet of green leaves in his hands, I shake my head. "I don't think it's worth the risk."

I have had food poisoning from eating strange street food and unwashed fruit before. Having something like that while hiding away or on the run from hunters would be a terrible thing. Of course, I don't tell him all of that as I focus my attention back on Roshan.

The argila is all too happy to be the center of my attention once again, bleating playfully as his rubber teeth scrape against my hand.

I don't mean to ignore Tehlmar, but there are other things running through my mind, like why anyone would need to hurt an animal this way. I have known the argila for less than a day and even I see all the training potential in him and someone else just decided it was okay to put holes in his face?

"It is safe," Tehlmar insists softly, his persistence grating on my nerves. "I know you are afraid of being poisoned."

I heave a sigh and face Tehlmar. "How can you be so sure? We're not even of the same species, Tehlmar. I could die from a single bite of that."

"Why won't you listen to me when I tell you it is not poisonous?"

His voice is raised, and it scratches at my patience. "How do you know, Tehlmar? How do you know?"

"Because I just do," he says in a joking tone, but I have had enough.

9

Kuret

The walk feels endless, each step stretching time. As I move forward, a flash of silver catches my eye, a reflection, faint but unremarkable. My heart quickens. Certain it's part of something, I duck behind a tree, my movements deliberate and watchful.

Curiosity overpowers caution, and I dash toward the source, fully exposing myself to any lurking enemies. Laying in the grass before me is a flattened lump of gray and pink slime. A genali. Relief washes over me at the sight, though a small part of me is disappointed, I didn't get the satisfaction of killing it myself.

A gaping hole runs from its head to the end of its body, a familiar sight. It reminds me of the first weapon I found when I woke up on this strange planet. Nearby, I spot a container small enough to hold a youngling, matching Ree's description of the *cryo chamber*. I hurry to it, but my hope dims as I peer inside; it's empty.

I search for any signs of life, but only find more dead and crumpled up genali and nothing else. My search widens, moving in careful circles, my eyes fixed on the ground for any traces.

A soft grunt escapes me when I spot a print—three divots that look somewhat fresh.

My pulse quickens as my mind pieces together what might have happened. Ree had said the female in need of rescue was inside the *cryo chamber*. Does this mean she was taken?

Did the creature that left these tracks capture her? I follow the path, studying the ground for more clues. Relief flickers through me when I find another set of prints; smaller, faint but familiar. They match the shape of Ree's feet, which I was careful to memorize in case I needed to track her kind.

The realization strikes; the female must have been rescued by some other brave male, as Ree did mention that she had asked the same favor of others.

A sense of gratitude wells up in me. That's one less human female in danger, so I can scour this planet to find others who need help.

Yet, as I study the prints further, unease creeps in. The larger creature's feet are disturbingly large, indicating that he is tall. Even taller than I am. I look closer at the difference between him and the female and it is quite vast.

Something stirs within me—a pull to follow the trail, to ensure that Ree's friend is safe. But a larger part of me advises me to continue on my journey. If these women are such an important commodity among the hunters, other creatures will find them interesting as well.

The longer I stay without deciding, the more my conscience tugs on me until I turn on my boots and begin trailing the prints.

I justify my decision; I'll simply ensure there's no trouble ahead, leave the female a weapon, and perhaps warn them about the dangerously obvious trail they're leaving behind. I don't like it and I'm not sure if I should leave this human with such a reckless, stupid male.

I have to remind myself that I am only following to make sure there is no trouble ahead and hand them weapons if they need any. Even a large, stupid male is better protection than other females might have.

It doesn't take long to catch up. Their voices reach me first, faint but unmistakable. It seems like they are in a cart, from the tracks, but when I come to them, they are out of it. Facing each other and talking.

I stay crouched behind a tree, watching the human woman and the shiny male with her through a sliver between two leaves. Flashes of white from the woman's hair catch my eye as she moves around the bed of a stream. The parts of her body that come into my view are covered in the same black cloth that Ree was covered in.

I long to keep looking at her, to get more than a quick glimpse of her features, but it wouldn't be wise to linger.

There's no cart in sight, but they seem settled, and the male is certainly big enough to provide her protection.

I can't understand the language, though its cascade is soothing as they talk back and forth. It strikes me that this is the second pair of male and female I have seen interacting so closely.

From what I have observed, the male is lean and tall with skin of bright silver and green hair. With her shocking white hair and black body covering, it is almost as though he compliments her. A fitting donor, though not for one so young.

He looks at ease, a feeling I could never muster. The realization sits heavy in my stomach. Where would I even find such courage, and to what purpose? Still, seeing males and females interacting so comfortably shocks me, leading me to question whether I am the odd one.

On my planet, a male would need to be a female's donor to be so close to her, and their focus wouldn't be on conversation. That wasn't the case with Ree and Thivoll, nor does it seem to be here with Ree's friend and this shiny male.

In fact, the human females seem to adapt to their rescuers quickly. Is that a natural human trait, or something caused by the genali?

My eyes drift back to her. Those white eyes with the dark fur above them, that long cascade of pale hair, so unlike my own. Her brown skin, the way her lips move, it's all captivating.

A quick flash of her hair laying across my darker skin in lovely contrast makes my hearts race.

My body shudders, and anger flares at myself for being so focused on her. She's safe and seems comfortable with the male. His sparkling skin complements her brilliant features far better than I ever could.

My hand goes up to touch my skin and I feel the familiar ripple of my skin flickering. Parts of me are just as bright, aren't they?

I snort softly, my braids clacking against my face. This is ridiculous.

It is what Samke would call pathetic. I usually would not care for his opinion, but knowing I will never see him again makes me strangely nostalgic for the things I once ignored.

I need to go tell them about Ree, but it feels like I would be intruding. Yet, something about their interaction seems off.

Ree's body was always relaxed around her donor, and their interaction seemed easy and natural. These two are different, though I cannot be sure. I know little about females, not nearly enough to walk up and speak to one. What would I know about the intricacies of their donor picking?

But the way his face looks... he is far too interested in her. He shouldn't look at her like that. No one should.

The pair moves again, and I creep closer, weighing how to approach provoking the male to attack. The human and her protector are situated in a hollowed-out rock now.

The surrounding trees are strategically placed to conceal the cave, but an orange glow betrays the presence of a fire.

I watch the silver male walk off, leaving her alone, and frown at his carelessness. Lighting a fire at night in a forest crawling with hunters is reckless enough. Leaving the woman you're meant to protect? Foolish.

I keep my eye on her until he storms back in after a few moments. Their interaction is incomprehensible to me, but their body language is clear. The human is rigid, her hand raised in a gesture that seems to warn him away. I begin to wonder, are they arguing, or is it simply how they communicate?

From where I lay, I see the male straighten, appearing even taller than he formerly was as he takes slow steps toward the human.

10

Rin

Warning: Read the series content warnings in case you want to skip this chapter to Kuret's point of view.

I raise a hand in front of me and shake my head at him. "No, Tehlmar, you don't just know something like that about someone you just met. So maybe you should be telling me exactly how you know I can eat it. While you're at it, try not to leave out all the other information you know about humans so I can survive on this cursed planet," I hiss, my words coming out in a harsh whisper.

Tehlmar's back straightens and his expression changes from mild annoyance to completely stoic before rapidly deteriorating to a mask of pure rage. He strides toward me in a deliberately slow, menacing gait, like a predator stalking its prey, before stopping abruptly just out of my reach.

I can almost feel the tension rolling off his body. His fist is clenched so tight that I initially think he's about to take a swing at me.

I take a step back as my heart pumps faster. That expression, twitching eye, eerie calm just before the storm, I'd recognize anywhere. Trauma teleports me to a younger age, a million miles away, and the hateful looks I grew accustomed to—clenched fists and rocks thrown at my head by faceless mobs.

All because I wanted an education.

He is still silent as the side of his mouth stretches into a sharp-toothed sneer. He takes one step toward me.

I take another step back and he copies me. "Tehlmar," I try to call to him, stretching my hands in front of me in a useless attempt to stop him. But my gesture only makes him bare more of his sharp green teeth at me.

"Tehlmar, please." I attempt to make it a statement, but it comes out as a whimper.

"I am so sick of hearing you speak so much. Have you ever heard of silence?" he hisses at me. "I paid far too much to come to this planet just to have a mere slave question me. This ruse was fun for a while, but I've had enough of it."

I gasp in fear, missing a step and stumbling back, barely managing not to fall. My back presses against a tree and I whip my head around to search for any escape, but I am well and truly trapped.

Under my breath, I curse whatever bad karma led me to this moment.

My brain goes back to Bibi and hearing those exact words from her. 'Have you never heard of silence?'

I swallow the lump in my throat and clamp down on my tongue because there is no other way that I am getting out of this by running my mouth and speaking up about knowing my rights.

I am on an alien planet, about to get attacked by an alien who kidnapped and changed me. There are no rights here, just barbaric males. Everything is different, yet painfully the same.

He comes up to me and bends, looking directly at my face as his hot breath fans against me. I try to look away, but his silver hands grip my chin, pressing my mouth together into a painful O. "You have been so shy all day, pretending not to know exactly what I want from you."

His grip tightens, his sneer widening to reveal his sharp teeth.

A sob leaves my mouth, and he stands up to his full height once more, laughing at me. "You know, I had a good time playing savior because you were so appreciative at first, but you quickly forgot your place."

He wanders a few steps away from me and I attempt to run, but in an instant, his hands press against my throat again and he flings me back against the tree.

I know this behavior. It reminds me of a cat toying with its prey before the kill. A tear rolls down my cheek as I realize this individual that I have trusted for help sees me as prey.

My thoughts are interrupted by his fist ramming into my stomach. The wind is knocked out of me in a wheeze of pain, followed by a cough that leaves blood staining the inside of my palm.

Tehlmar presses himself against me again, holding me captive between him and the tree. "You forgot that you are just another slave species destined to wither to nothing. And I am better than you."

One of his hands grabs aggressively at my waist, and I scream, wiggling myself in desperation.

"No, please no," I heave, begging him.

It falls on deaf ears as he uses his body to keep me pinned to the tree.

He pushes me to the ground roughly, straddling my prone form.

I can feel his arousal pressing against me, so I intensify my efforts at self-preservation. My flailing arms don't seem to bother him until I jam a thumb in his eye and he roars out in pain.

For the first time, I'm thankful to the genali that my clothes work in tandem with my mind. I force myself to think of it sticking even tighter to my body than before.

Tehlmar pulls at the suit briefly before glaring into my eyes with raging fury. "If I can't figure out how to get this off, I'll just make a hole in it. That's all you are good for, anyway."

He leers at me like one of those lecherous old men in the marketplace, and all I want is to get as far away from this alien monster as I can.

Kuret

She backs up, he steps up, the distance between them closing until her back is pressed against the *tree*. She pushes out her hand, as if telling him to stay away, but he only closes in on her.

A part of me wants to look away. This is starting to look like an intimate moment between them, But I can't tear my eyes away; it feels like something is about to happen.

Something's not right.

I hope that I am wrong—that I'm overthinking these things, as I have no experience to compare these interactions. Maybe this nagging feeling is just a false alarm. An instinct from years of keeping an eye on females, making sure they were safe from predators while staying distant.

The male moves himself up against her rather roughly. One shiny hand pushes his hair back from his face while his free hand rises to grab her chin.

I expect a tender touch—some sign that I'm mistaken, just confused about females and donors. But I catch his hands pressing her chin with considerable force and I know there is no tenderness in his actions.

The human female lets out a shriek of fear. I hop to my feet and dash in a straight line toward them.

Rin

Warning: Read the series content warnings in case you want to skip this chapter to Kuret's point of view.

A twisted smile spreads on his face and I cry out in despair, realizing that this is probably how I'm going to die. My life starts to flash before my eyes, but then something knocks Tehlmar down, pulling me from him.

From the impact, I roll away, scrambling backward, catching sight of a wide-eyed Roshan.

Roshan rambles toward Tehlmar, but a flash of silver hits him. With a grunt, he reels back, crying out as Tehlmar's spiked foot hits him on the chest. Roshan whimpers, his spidery legs hitting Tehlmar in a furious flurry.

Then Tehlmar hits him again, harder this time, and Roshan runs away in fear.

The animal's cries enrage me and while the green-haired alien is down, I get up and drive my foot straight into his face.

I go for a third kick, but he catches my leg, yanking me to the ground. His elbow smashes straight into my side as I land on the ground. I had forgotten how fast he is.

I try to scurry away, but he grabs my hair, dragging me across the ground and against the tree I had just escaped from. His mocking laughter snaps something inside me; I know then—I won't be leaving here alive.

I can't die. Not like this. Not without a fight. Anger drowns out my fear, and I throw the hardest punches I can, each more futile than the last, twisting to break free. But it only thrills him. "Yes, struggle with me, you little pleasure slave. I love a fighter. They break so deliciously."

I want to scream again, but I know that would be of no use at this point.

"I will make you regret the day you ever set your eyes on me, *Ya Allah*," I curse, tears pouring out of my eyes.

"You can do nothing but take it like a whore."

He spits on my face. Presses his hand against my throat, he pushes me further up against the tree, cutting off all my air.

The wind is knocked out of me again when a heavy blow hits my stomach. Before I can recover, another strikes my eye, temporarily blinding me and sending a sharp pain shooting into my skull.

All I hear is a cruel laughter as this monster, my former companion, beats me relentlessly. As the pain fills my head, I feel myself slipping, thinking I am near my end.

13

Kuret

I am still too far from them, but running at full speed, my hearts pound from more than just the exertion. I only hope that I don't get there too late to help.

It's startling how easy it is to misread a situation. I have never seen a perpetrator actually harming a female, only witnessed their punishment afterward as a lesson to others.

The male has been her protector; he should've settled things peacefully without this brutish use of force. Anyone should be killed for daring to even raise his hands to a female in such a manner.

I don't care if we are completely different species. Even if he comes from an extremely barbaric and uncivilized planet, he should know that forcing a female against her will is a grave offense—a crime equivalent to murder.

Another scream echoes through the forest and I pick up my speed, ignoring the ache in my abdomen.

I cannot understand his language or what she just said, but I know it wasn't a sound of pleasure that she made.

The forest fades into a muffled whisper as my heart pumps loudly in my ears, metal tangs my tongue from biting down, but the pain is lost in a wave of fury. My vision is gray, and the *trees* are a blur as I wind my way through the thick undergrowth.

All I can think about is how I am going to rip him to pieces when I lay my hands on him. Out here on these lawless lands, I can take all the honor for myself.

The rage is a dull roar in my ears and a taste in my mouth—a taste I will gladly replace with that of this callous being's blood. Once I can reach them.

Another pained scream echoes, The male's harsh yell follows. The rage in my chest flares, and I curse myself for wasting time with my own discomfort and naivety.

As I close in on the male, I move in a half circle to give me the chance to pounce on him from behind. I must be quick and precise if I want to do this cleanly. The rage that's been building finally bursts out, focused into a sharp cry as I lunge forward, grabbing him by his hair to get a firm hold.

When I push him to the ground, his arms flail out in front of his body, but all he makes is a wet, gurgling sound as I tilt his neck slightly to the side for him to see who punishes him.

The sick cracking sound feeds my rage, but not enough. Getting on one knee, I drive the dagger from my boot into his chest, slicing through until the blade disappears into him before dragging it straight across his long torso.

His shocked face. It gives me a grim satisfaction, but it is not enough. Not nearly.

My hand moves faster than my brain as I butcher him, his dirt-colored blood spraying on my face and body. Every blow carves deeper; creatures like him do not deserve any part of them to be looked upon with a single shred of dignity.

I don't realize when my second knee comes down until it makes his head roll off.

Triumphantly, I kneel on his mutilated corpse, his blood soaking me, and I wish I could bring him back to life just to kill him again.

His severed head squishes in my grip as I lift it, driving my bloodied dagger into one of his shocked eyes. A barking cry leaves my lips as I yank the blade out and stab it into the other eye.

I throw the head aside and scream again—a raw cry of victory. I have carried out my mission and protected the human like I said I would.

I look down at the pieces of his bloodied body; every slice for a woman he has taken advantage of—predators like him don't just start hurting those they should protect.

My hearts are thumping loudly, almost like the cheers of my kin back home. There would be a feast in my name; I can almost hear Samke's playful laughter, teasing me how I cannot escape the donor ceremony now that females will flock to me, eager to make a titled protector their donor.

Thinking of females, I recall the reason I came here in the first place. To rescue the human.

I look down to find her dragging herself backward, desperately trying to get away from me. Her face is a ghostly mask of fear, as all the color is washed away from it, her bottom lip quivering and tears falling from her eyes.

I turn swiftly to check if there is something else behind me or if the male has magically risen from the dead, but there is nothing there.

When I take a step closer, her wide, pale eyes grow even wider and she scurries farther away from me, confirming my suspicion.

Confused, I wonder if I misunderstand the entire situation. Was all this consensual? Did I interfere when I shouldn't have? I swear I heard her scream out in pain. While I don't know much about the union between males and females, I know that doesn't sound like one is being attacked. I even saw him hit her a few times, so why look at me like that?

A cold dread settles in my gut; I might have upset a female for a reason unknown to me. I take another step and offer my hand to help her up.

She shrieks and collapses to the ground, her white hair falling over her face.

I reach out a hand to reassure her. "He can't hurt you now."

She grunts, wincing in pain as she tries to speak. "N-no, please."

I stand still and stare at her, unsure of what to do.

14

Rin

I brace myself for another hit from Tehlmar, my eyes tightly shut, but his body is suddenly ripped away from me. I collapse to the ground and suck in a breath, feeling pain in my stomach as I am heaving.

Directly in front of me, a big, dark thing doesn't give him a chance to struggle, grabbing Tehlmar by the hair and smashing his neck against the ground in one brutal, swift motion. He's dead before I can process what I've just seen.

I don't have time to process what I have just witnessed or even to scream. Frozen, shivering on the ground, wide-eyed as I stare at Tehlmar's lifeless form. My mouth opens, but only broken sounds come out—half-formed words stuck in my throat. I choke out a gasp, unable to look away as the monster pulls something from his boot and uses it to cut Tehlmar's upper body into chunks at a dizzying speed.

There's an animalistic look in his eyes as he does it, with a singular focus. Like a butcher at work on a piece of meat that he absolutely hates. He separates flesh from flesh in quick and fluid slashes of the blade.

Knees onto the ground, one hand still wrapped around Tehlmar's bright green hair, he separates the head from Tehlmar's neck.

At first, I thought he was just kneeling there doing his grisly work, but I realize he is making a low sound with every hit. It scares me; even with Tehlmar dead he continues to tear the body apart, ripping it into small pieces.

He looks as if he is carrying on a brutal ritual. I have never been more terrified in my life.

Tehlmar's brown blood bathes him, some of it spraying on me. It is a horrifying view from where I sit on the grass, frozen and watching.

Then it gets worse. He lifts the severed head and pushes his blade into one of Tehlmar's dead eyes, letting out a long cry when he pushes it into the second one.

Why is he doing this to the already dead body? He is no stranger to violence. No. He doesn't just embrace it. He is in love with it.

My mind starts to race. What if, after he's done with Tehlmar, he begins his work on me? I try to scramble away, but instincts cross in my panic, leaving me motionless on the ground.

He is kneeling a little straighter now, and he is much bulkier than Tehlmar was when he was alive. Although Tehlmar is obviously dead, this dark, massive beast is still not letting up on his corpse. It's almost like he has been so starved of violence that this is making him obsessed at the mere sight of it.

His efforts seem unwavering, as if he isn't tiring at all. When I look into his eyes, all I see staring back at me is cold deadness. The goat's green eyes of *al-Sheytân.*

No man who can commit such atrocities with such a cold, unfeeling set of eyes can be anything but a murderous psychopath.

I find myself being carried backward on the wings of memory and I start to succumb to its persuasions until another strange guttural cry brings me back to reality. I look at the monster to see that he has flung Tehlmar's head away from his body and is now looking right at me, his eyes wide and staring directly into my soul.

He takes a step toward me, and I scramble backward, small rocks digging painfully into my palms as I move. He looks behind him, his long hair whipping around, the bones of animals clinking together in his braids. Then he turns back to me, his expression confused and puzzled.

He steps forward again; reaching out, he makes another attempt to move toward me, stretching his bloodied hand out as if offering to help me up. The same hand that held Tehlmar's head, the blood still dripping from his three wide fingers.

I shrink back from his outstretched hand as if struck, causing a clear look of confusion to cross his alien face. It's as if he doesn't understand why I'm rejecting his help.

Then he speaks, revealing that he still thinks I am afraid of Tehlmar. I would be, and part of me still is, but now I am confused. Another savior has arrived, yet I just had one of those attack me.

Can anyone trust someone so clearly violent? My mind swims. No one in this terrible place feels trustworthy.

I yelp and try to get up, but the pain in my stomach reminds me how injured I am. I collapse to the ground like a helpless child, panic setting in. Then it hits me, I'm not actually powerless. If I keep acting helpless, I might make him pity me and use the chance to escape.

I sob, begging him not to come close. Peering at him from the corner of my eye, I fake tears, my throat aching as I speak. At least the pain my voice is real, it doesn't take much effort to sound desperate.

"Please, don't hurt me," I wail, hoping I'm not overdoing it.

I am terrified, the tears streaming down my face are real, and so is the pain. I'm simply giving voice to how I truly feel, praying it works.

The beast steps back, giving me enough time to brace myself. My instinct screams that this is reckless, but I can't stay here. I take a deep breath, push past the pain, and jump to my feet, rushing away from him.

He makes a sound of protest, but I run as fast as I can, ignoring the way my heart and lungs feel as if they want to collapse.

As I flee, I desperately search for Roshan. The darkening sky makes it nearly impossible to spot his coat. "Roshan, where are you?" I call out in a harsh whisper, terrified it will bring the monster to me.

I can't let either of us be the next to die, sliced to pieces and decapitated like Tehlmar.

When I call out again, it dawns on me that he probably doesn't understand his name. Calling for him feels futile. The darker parts of my thoughts wander when it feels like I have exhausted all the oxygen in my lungs from running and trying to call out to the poor, scared animal.

Black spots cloud my vision, but I push forward, stumbling through the brambles, squinting to see through the gloom.

He has to be here somewhere. Did Tehlmar hit him somewhere that would have killed him? I push the thought from my mind and simply focus on trying to find him.

"Roshan, where are you—AH!"

I misstep, tripping over a hidden rut, and crash into a dense, thorny underbrush. Pain stabs at my palms and the back of my hands as I struggle to untangle myself. Tears prick at the corners of my eyes, and my head throbs with pain.

Then I hear it, a low bellow and the rustling of leaves nearby. I rouse myself to my feet and take a step in the direction I heard the sound from, unable to stop myself from sobbing.

"Roshan, I'm coming."

I can barely see but cling to the trees like a lifeline, inching forward and praying he isn't too hurt. I'll need him to carry us both out of here before the killer catches up.

But suddenly, the ground vanishes beneath my feet. it seems as if I am watching someone else fall, a disorienting plunge down a hidden ravine. The undergrowth blurs as my body tumbles, coming to a jarring halt at the bottom.

At first, there's no pain, just numbness and sticky wetness coating my skin.

I wipe a hand across myself, realizing it's blood from countless cuts crisscrossing my body. The air swirls, and through the haze, I see my *bābā's* face in the leaves above me.

Is this the end of my life?

I blink sluggishly, my eyes heavy, but then I feel something soft brushing against my face. A gentle bleat follows.

"Roshan," I whisper, wincing at the effort it takes to speak.

His big yellow-brown eyes look much larger now that he's the one looking down at me. If this is how I'm going to die, I hope he comes up to *Jannah* with me.

15

Kuret

The human female startles me when she suddenly she gets up and runs in crooked, desperate steps. I stand there, momentarily frozen, my eyes rapidly blinking as I watch her get away. Why is she running?

I don't need her adoration or praise, but I didn't expect her to flee instead of letting me ensure her safety.

Ree never mentioned how vastly different her friends are from her in temperament. A part of my brain pushes back at the thought.

Ree was rescued by a manticorid and she feels safe. This poor human, however, has been through torment, first captured by genali hunters, and then confronted by that unspeakable creature. Its no wonder she assumes everything wants to harm her.

Yet, It's baffling. She seems more afraid of me than of the green-haired male, and I can't understand why.

Grunting in frustration, I start walking in her direction, wiping the thick, sticky blood off my body. His blood is thicker and much stickier than mine. Its musty smell fills my nostrils with its disgusting stench. While I typically take pride in wearing the blood of my enemies, this particular smell is terrible, a true reflection of the filth he was.

I spot her wobbling ahead in the distance. She's in visible pain, yet still desperately trying to escape me. I decide not to chase her outright, fearing her panic might lead her to harm herself. I simply stalk behind, keeping a steady pace.

Her white hair and loud movements act as a beacon, impossible to miss.

She calls out, her voice strained and desperate, and I glance around, alert for anything her cries might attract. She shouldn't be making this much noise in a place like this, where hunters might still be lurking. If something does come, though, I'll deal with it.

Moments later, she teeters and stumbles into a bush, falling out of my sight. Alarmed, I quicken my steps, only to see her rise shakily, looking around, as if checking whether she's being followed. Does she think I can't hear her calling out?

She cries out again, and continues dragging herself forward. I watch her pitiful movement, unsure of how to approach her. I feel like I'm a predator stalking its prey, even though I have no intention of harming her.

Perhaps I should explain myself once I catch up. But would she even listen? She had screamed for help earlier, so why is she running now?

Her white hair disappears from my view again.

I hear her let out an agonized sound, and I pick up my pace and run in her direction. My hearts pound, not with exertion, but with the fear I didn't expect; the fear of killing a woman I was only trying to save from a rapist.

As I approach the spot where she disappeared, I see it is a rocky edge. My stomach tightens. It does not look like a big fall, but the injuries she has already sustained from the aggressive male might be the thing that sends her to her death.

I carefully pick my way around the jutting edge of the rock so I don't end up in the same situation she is. No one will help the both of us if I find myself wounded at the bottom of the ravine.

Peering down, I spot her. Her small, frail form is pinned beneath a hideous creature. Six spindly legs protrude from its body, its broad head hovering over hers, its large blue lips parting to reveal terrifying teeth.. That is all I need to alert my sense of danger, running toward her with my knife in my hands.

From this angle, I can see a hideous creature open its mouth over her head, its large blue lips and large teeth going to gnaw at her even though her hands are covering her face. She is uncharacteristically still for somebody being attacked by a large animal.

My chest constricts with the realization that she might already be dead, but then I notice faint movement.

Relief surges within me. I have a chance to save her. Maybe I can redeem myself by saving her from a wild animal, and she will trust me. At least I hope that's what will happen. I must be careful not to harm her further or let her harm herself out of fear.

The human woman raises her head as she hears me approaching. Her half-lidded, bright eyes lock onto mine. Her eyes widen when they spot my weapon. I want to tell her that the knife is not for her and that she will be fine if she just stays still and lets me kill the animal before it hurts her.

"Stop!" she yells, her voice trembling.

Do humans from her planet pride themselves so much on independence that they'd rather run into danger than accept protection? Her reaction baffles me, but I know what I must do.

The creature glances at me for a moment before crouching lower, pressing protectively over her. Stupid animal, offering its back to me to directly hit. I will strike at it with great violence and save her from herself once more.

I close the distance in three strides, my knife raised, ready to strike. I will end this creature and prove that I am here to help.

But just as my blade is about to connect, the creature shuts its eyes and makes a low bellow toward the wailing female, and it dawns on me. I pause. The realization hits me like a blow, it's not trying to harm her, it's protecting her.

The swing of my blade lands despite my attempt to pull back. Though I manage to divert the strike slightly, the blade cuts deep into the animal's back. Bright blue blood seeps out of the injury as the animal makes a sound of pain but does not move.

I take a step back. The wound is deep, but hopefully not deadly.

The animal bleats again as the human female wails louder, a long keening sound that causes my hearts to constrict painfully on either side of my chest. Her cry cuts through me more painfully than any blade, filled not with physical agony but an emotion far deeper.

Her hand goes around the short neck of the creature, her tiny fingers digging into the fur of its head as she pulls it closer to her.

The creature's legs are so low that it is nearly sitting on her midriff, but she does not seem to care about that in the slightest. She continues to howl, and I take a few steps away from them. She soon runs out of breath and all I can hear is panting, interrupted by a low whine from her and quiet braying from the animal.

The creature turns its gaze to me, protective and fierce, with its large dark yellow eyes and lurches forward aggressively, hissing at me.

The human female mumbles something to it and it turns back to her, crouching even lower than I thought it could. How has she managed to inspire such loyalty from an animal who can't even speak?

Its legs tremble visibly, yet the creature remains steadfast, its body a protective barrier around her. As it turns to face me again, its large dark lips curled into a snarl, I take another step away from them and look down at my blade, watching as the blue blood on it starts to dry against the brown from the male.

I can see the fear in its eyes mixed with a sort of determination, intelligence clear in its gaze.

It dawns on me that this animal is the one whose tracks I saw earlier, then I notice the rope tied looped around its neck. It's what was pulling the cart, I realize.

"I have no honor," I mutter to myself as my dagger falls out of my grasp and lands on the ground.

The creature hisses at me again, but I do not pay it any heed.

I drop to my knees before the human female and her unwavering protector, the sting of a sharp rock slicing into my left knee going unnoticed. I do not deserve to feel pain or even speak of it. My judgment has led to harm, both to the woman I vowed to safeguard and the loyal creature that stood by her side.

Any honor I gained from saving her from the rapist is gone, and I do not know how to get it back. At this rate, she will never put her trust in me.

Maybe Ree is wrong to trust me too, and I am wrong for thinking I could do this. Why did I even think I was capable of such a task? They should have found someone better suited for this. What do I know about females that I thought I was qualified for such a delicate mission? I am ashamed.

The pain in my knee is nothing compared to the burning shame in my chest as I gaze upon the scene before me.

I should have known better.

16

Rin

"Roshan," I mutter as the boring story of my life plays behind my eyes, unrolling as an empty chasm of unachieved dreams and begging for the right to exist.

The argila brays softly, its cool nose nudging me, as if it can see the thoughts going through my head. Tears start to prickle at my eyes. In this hostile, unforgiving world, the only kindness I have received on this forsaken planet has been from an animal. A precious, spider-legged blue not-horse creature that is the only reason I am still alive.

A lone tear rolls out of my eye and Roshan sticks out his wide, black tongue to lap at it gently.

It tickles and the movement hurts, so I raise a hand to my face to stop his ministrations.

It's almost like he is determined to continue until I stop crying. The pain in my stomach stops me from laughing, but Roshan does not let up. The poor animal is only trying to help, but I could do without it.

I try to roll over and out of reach, but the agony puts a firm stop to all of that.

A rustling sound from somewhere above reaches my ears, followed by a low grunt, sending a chill down my spine. My breath catches, and a small whimper escapes me as dread takes hold; it's the big, angry alien, and it has found us.

Roshan stops licking and makes a concerned sound. His head tilts in a way that feels almost inquisitive before he turns around, positioning himself protectively once more.

I peek out from underneath him and see the alien bounding toward us with the same thirst in his eyes. Fear grips me. I've seen firsthand what he can do when sufficiently motivated. We aren't safe.

I recognize the blood-covered blade in his hand. The same one that he used to tear Tehlmar apart. He wants to do the same to

Roshan, and I muster all my energy to scream through the pain in my throat.

"Stop, please!" My voice barely escapes, a squeak lost in the air. It's far too weak to stop the freight train of an alien barreling straight toward us.

He will not hear me, and Roshan will be dead shortly. Despair grips my heart like a vise. The alien doesn't even glance at me as he approaches, his focus completely on hurting Roshan.

The argila turns to look at him before lowering himself over me and angling his body toward the alien. My heart hurts again, and I raise my hands up to Roshan's neck, digging my fingers into his fur.

Roshan's yellow eyes meet mine, filled with a strength I didn't know was possible. I burst into a fresh round of tears when I realize he is actually willing to die for me.

"I'm so sorry, Roshan," I sob quietly when the alien reaches us and prepares to strike. I cannot bear to watch him shred another thing to pieces before me. Not after the last time, so I close my eyes tightly.

The sound of the blade against the argila's body sends a chill up my spine and his injured cry echoes in my ears. Then I find my voice, letting out my grief.

When I pull in a breath, I expect his lifeless body to fall, but all I can feel are his legs shaking on either side of me.

He opens his eyes and turns, a fierce snarl directed at the terrible alien, then glances back at me. I poke my head out, unable to resist checking on him, needing to make sure he's alright.

"Oh, Roshan, you're okay," I whisper, my voice trembling. But the relief is overwhelming, and before can stop myself, I break down completely, sobbing loudly. My hands wrap around his neck. I bury my face in his fur and cry shamelessly with relief.

"You're okay. *Alhamdulillah.* You're okay."

The argila envelopes me with two of its free appendages as if to return my hug, the agony of the movement almost worth it. I feel liquid dripping on my leg and blink the tears away to see that it is Roshan's dark blue blood on me.

I know the alien meant to kill him, so why didn't he? I have already seen that he is capable of brutality, so what changed? What stopped him?

I would have thought it was another attacker swooping in to save Roshan and me if not for the utter lack of sound and evidence of a struggle.

I can hear babbling from behind Roshan, and my heart skips a beat in fear that this might be some kind of ritualistic killing, with him now praying to his god or something like that. My fright almost makes me miss the fact that I can still understand what he is saying, which, to my relief and slight confusion, is not a prayer.

"I have no honor. This is a loss of honor," he continues to mutter, his face twitching and the bright lights along his nearly black skin flickering as he stares at Roshan and me with dead eyes.

He just keeps saying it.

I don't want to say anything to risk triggering his anger again, but something tells me that if I am not already dead, then he either didn't want to kill me at all or has changed his mind.

Although it causes enough pain to make me grind my teeth together, I move from under Roshan, hoisting myself up to a sitting position with great difficulty and supporting my back against a small boulder.

Roshan is incredibly protective of me, standing by my side and glaring at the alien whose eyes have followed me the entire time.

The alien's dark lips continue to move as he babbles about his loss of honor.

I don't want to be anywhere near this creature anymore, but neither Roshan nor I are in any condition to move. I listen to him for a few moments, growing more uneasy, before I realize he may have nothing of importance to actually say to me.

"Please leave us," I choke out, wincing as my throat constricts over the switch from Farsi to his language.

His head shifts up at the sound of my voice and some life returns to his eyes when he stops mumbling. The silence suggests he didn't hear me, and he attempts to lean in closer, which makes me gasp and try to roll painfully to the side.

Roshan makes a braying snarl at the large alien. His feelings for the guy are obvious. I can't argue with him because I feel the same, but I don't want to lead the alien into another frenzy where he kills us.

"Leave us alone, please."

All three points of his ears twitch and he shakes his head furiously, the trinkets in his long braids clinking against each other.

"I cannot do that," he refuses, rubbing his three-fingered hand over his cheeks, causing glowing green patterns to ripple brightly in the dark.

His hands slide down the armor of his chest and he continues to look at me, well, in my general direction, unblinking.

I don't know what the gesture means, but I don't ask because, honestly, I don't care. He killed Tehlmar like a complete savage, and the only reason I am not running for the hills is because I am far too weak to move, as is Roshan.

I scratch at Roshan's head, trying to soothe him, but he doesn't make any pleased sounds because his eyes are trained on the alien. "Please, we don't want any trouble. You have hurt us enough. Go away."

I try to sound confident, putting as much metal into my voice as I can muster, but instead I sound like I have been crying for weeks. "Just leave us alone."

"I cannot," he says in a sharp bark, "not until I have restored the honor I lost."

His language is rough, with a lot of hissing barks, clicks, and guttural undertones.

"What honor are you talking about? There is no honor here," I spit at him before I can help myself and his eyes meet mine for a split second.

I expect him to lurch at me or hit me, but all he does is look away and bow his head. "I wasn't sent here to bring harm to you, but I have. The honor I gained is lost."

I tilt my head to the side, wincing. "Did you know of me before all this? Were you following us? Is that it?"

He just continues to stare, looking dejected. "Ree would not have wanted this."

The male makes no sense. "Wait. Who is Ree? What honor have you lost?"

He doesn't answer and I cannot help the rage that squeezes at my chest.

"Say something," I hiss out, feeling faint as my head throbs in the same rhythm of my still-racing heart.

I moan in pain and Roshan nibbles at my hair, his eyes concerned.

The alien lets out a long breath and speaks again. "I met with Ree, another like you. She told me to take you somewhere safe where you could be with your other friends and that is all I was trying to do."

I nearly laugh at how preposterous it sounds, though my heart leaps at the mention of there being other humans around.

"Help me? You tore Tehlmar to pieces long after you killed him, and you are speaking of helping? I want you to go away forever and let us be. Your violence is unacceptable, and I don't want to spend another moment in your presence."

He doesn't leave, and I finally take a good look at the alien.

Kneeling down, he is almost at my full height, and he glows, his dark skin littered with bright green luminescent patterns. The first thought that comes to mind is how terrible he would be at a game of hide and seek.

My second is that he's beautiful, despite how odd he looks. The bright green patterns on his skin cast a glow across his features in a mesmerizing way. His green eyes, with their black horizontal pupils also glow, pulsing each time he blinks. He doesn't have eyebrows, or a beard, only seeming to grow hair on his head. As far as I can tell, he doesn't have a nose, just a wide space that follows the same curve of his broad forehead down to too-wide, thick, nearly black lips. Like Tehlmar, his teeth are sharp, except they are white, not green.

A quick search for where he breathes ends when I spot two holes just in front of his pointed ears. The braids near them shift in a rhythmic way, matching the movement of his chest. It's broad, tapering to a small waist. His arms are enormous, with well-defined, corded muscles visible beneath his skin where I can see his forearms. His skin is rough looking, but in long striations. Almost like you can see the muscles right underneath. It makes my stomach queasy, reminding me of medical images of skinless humans.

He has long, thick black braids that start farther back on his skull than where human hair begins. There are primitive trinkets woven into them. He's wearing some sort of brown animal hide armor, which I assume is hiding more glowing skin, since the undulating green veins and dark gray skin disappear under it midway up his forearm. The armor covers all but his lower arms, part of his neck, and head.

His hands look strong, though odd with their three thick fingers instead of four. The green marks on them shift as his hands twitch and it's mesmerizing, a welcome distraction from the pain. But then I realize I have the same warmth between my legs for him as I did for Tehlmar and rage overtakes my brain for a long moment.

Clearly, the genali did something to me. More than just my hair and the translator, but something deep inside my body. Or my mind?

Because nothing explains this odd attraction to two males who are so obviously not even worth a single glance, let alone this unwanted arousal.

It sickens me.

The male continues to look downcast, and I feel the urge to throw a rock at his face to get him to move on. I won't feel safe if he is nearby.

I want to tell him to kill me off before I die of hypertension, but he mumbles again. "That was the only way to save you from him. Is that not what all females want—a male who can protect them?"

He catches my eye again and my jaw drops open. He thinks that is what a woman wants? To be splattered with blood as he looks like an enraged animal?

No.

"Cutting up a man like that is—"

He cuts me off and speaks. "I know there wasn't a tribunal, but we couldn't call one. He clearly didn't know how to respect autonomy."

"No, he didn't. He was a terrible person, but what you did... it was far too violent."

He exhales deeply. "No. It was over too quickly. He hurt you and would have forced your donor choice. Among my people, a rapist is stripped naked, spread, and tied to a large rock. Their victim is given a dull knife to carve their names onto the rapist's body and cut off whatever body parts they see fit. Afterward, they are left there to the mercy of the elements and whatever animals happen to pass by. Usually, by that time, their voice is broken from all the screaming, not that anyone would bother listening."

I'm in shock, completely appalled for a long moment, and then another part of my brain takes over. The one that has spent far too long huddling inside a house because someone wanted to silence me. If that was what happened when someone was raped... there would be far fewer people carrying around the scars. Especially the scars of having people disbelieve them.

What would that world look like?

I don't get to think through it before Roshan brays at me and stands up, shaking out his fur before crouching beside me. His eyes don't leave the alien.

"I was only trying to protect you, looking out for you. I was only doing my duty."

I cock an eyebrow. "Your duty?"

"Yes. Protecting you."

I rub my temple, feeling a headache coming on. "Your job is not to protect me. I don't even know you. I can't be around someone capable of that much violence. It taints everything they touch."

He looks confused, perhaps even insulted, as his hairless brow lowers. "Violence works best for people like him. I know. I have seen it. It is all I can offer to protect you."

I chuckle dryly. "Violence is the last thing I want from anyone, especially someone who claims that they are trying to protect me."

"It is what all females want, what they expect."

His tone is disbelieving, almost as if he can't understand what I am saying. I understand his point to some extent, but it isn't what women want, even though I can admit that it might be necessary in this situation. But that doesn't mean you have to embrace it, or make it your entire identity, like he seems to have.

I want to groan in frustration. "If there is a list of things that women want, violence is at the bottom of the list."

Maybe if I use a different analogy, he will understand me. I don't come up with one before I am distracted again. He moves, alerting Roshan, who hisses at him again.

I look down and see dark green liquid around where he is kneeling, indicating that he is bleeding. I look away quickly because the differences between us are too jarring. In the past day I have seen four... no, five different colors of blood. In just one day. It makes me question what I said to him about violence, but I can't sound weak right now. It might be needed here, but it goes against every one of my beliefs and my instinct is screaming at me to not trust him.

He looks at Roshan first, then at me. "Violence saved you back there, when you were in danger."

His words shift my perspective slightly, though it still bothers me. Why am I sympathizing with Tehlmar? He pretended to be on my side when all he truly wanted was to take advantage of me.

Sure, I don't appreciate this person's methods, but I saw Tehlmar kill the genali and if this alien had not killed him, I would most likely also be dead.

I groan softly and shut my eyes. Even though I know he has a point, I will not acknowledge it because I never want to see anything like that again. Ever. It will haunt my dreams.

He speaks again. "Let me get you somewhere safe and you will never have to see me again."

I look up at him questioningly.

Will this last? I have seen violence before, and I know that it never really ends. However, it is only a matter of time before some other twisted person finds me, and I have no fighting skills whatsoever to protect myself.

If there truly is a safer place, then I am willing to take the risk, especially if it involves seeing humans again. "I will only come with you if you agree not to be so needlessly violent. There is protection, and then there is... whatever you were doing."

I shiver as I remember the look of bliss on his face as blood splattered everywhere.

He opens his mouth to speak, but I raise a finger to silence him "I'm not done. If you show any sort of behavior that scares me, I will run very far away from you, and whatever happens to me will be on you and your honor. Understood?"

I am out of breath by the time I reach the end of my sentence, and I watch him mull my words over.

17

Kuret

This human woman is... strange, to say the least.

Even now, injured and barely able to stand, she still holds a lot of anger in her voice. I truly do not understand how she has such energy for it, though she lays prone on the ground. I want to go help her up, but I know it won't be appreciated.

It would have been admirable if it weren't so vexing.

Her blue creature that I nearly slaughtered looked like it was about to eat her, and I had made it my duty to make sure that she is always safe. I have done my best to explain my reasoning to her, but she is quite adamant about not understanding my motivation.

I am taken aback by her demand. No violence? It's almost like she has no idea how horrible most of the residents of this planet are. You are either an ally or an enemy and all enemies should be killed, lest they kill you.

The way she spat out the word honor wounds me, almost as if it means nothing to her. I am completely befuddled because she doesn't know what she is asking of me. Protection without violence?

If there is a way to keep her safe and never have to kill another hunter until we reach a safe point, I can't imagine it. This whole planet is basically stocked with only enemies. Besides Ree and her protector, the only ally we have is this animal she clings to.

These hunters are the reason she is here in the first place. Surely she has not forgotten that?

Agreeing to her absurd terms means that even when I try to protect her like I did today and there is an altercation, she will fight against me and leave. If anything happens to her after that, I will be completely responsible for whatever takes place? Madness.

I can feel my face screwing up into a mask of frustration, but I cast it off, not wanting to scare her further.

I clear my throat and hope that whatever I say does not make her change her mind. "This planet is dangerous. I know you have seen evidence of that. There is no way we are making it to a safe place without hurting others who are actively hunting and trying to hurt us."

She shakes her head. "Of course we should defend ourselves, but I stand by my words. A single needless exchange or you looking like violence is what you live for and I am heading in the opposite direction from you."

I want to tell her we are still living because of violence, but I bite down on my tongue. How will she define 'needless exchange'? She must delight in exasperating me.

It is the only thing that would explain her insistence. Or she's seeking revenge for the cut on her blue creature.

She holds my gaze with a piercing one of her own and I look away immediately. I have no idea what to do now and I think back to Ree. Surely she allowed Thivoll to be her donor because he is a proven protector. The way he stood between us like a solid barrier, his eyes hanging onto my every move with a threat in every line of his body.

There's no way Ree gave him such a stifling rule as this when they first met, and there's no way that beast would have agreed to it.

I thought it would be easy like it was for them, but nothing about this situation seems similar. I force myself to think back to what stood out to me about Ree and Thivoll's connection.

They met on this planet too, so he was rightfully intimidating at first, just like I am to this small, scared, stubborn female. The most annoying part of this is how fascinating I find the whole thing, in large part because of how she is challenging me.

It's exciting and infuriating all at once.

What did Thivoll do to make Ree trust him like that?

I look at her and the large companion by her side, and I realize that I need to get her to trust me before anything else. If she trusts me, I can kill enemies, and she will not see it as a senseless act of violence, but as a necessity in order to keep her safe.

Maybe I went too far with that male, but that's no excuse to ban me from killing.

I try again. "Let me see if I understand. You are comfortable being in danger, but not comfortable with the idea of me saving you from danger?"

She huffs out a breath. "Of course I don't like being in danger, and you keep making it sound like I said you can't protect me. I meant—You know what? This conversation is ridiculous. We're all injured. Let's focus on that."

"Alright," I concede.

I glance at her and her eyes are still trained on me, keeping watch on every movement my body makes, as if she expects me to attack her at any moment. It makes my hearts constrict painfully.

Why does she not see that my intentions are only to help?

I look away from her and wonder whether I am wrong about all of this. It would explain my difficulty in talking to females and all the issues that follow, as well as the knowledge that I was never chosen as a donor or wanted to be a part of it.

The words stall at the back of my throat, then try to spill out in a jumbled mess that only ends up as a noncommittal grunt. I shift on my feet and feel the shooting pain in my knee again, which reminds me why I am here in the first place.

I give myself a mental slap and force my head into focus. Self-pity after losing my honor makes it a worse loss for me and I am not taking defeat that easily, not after how many hunters I have vanquished within a few hours of being here.

Raising my afflicted knee, I pull the shard of rock from it and rise to my full height, relieved it's not a serious wound. I'm annoyed that something as simple as a rock found the weakness in my armor.

Taking a slow step forward, I reach a hand out to the woman and she flinches, alarming the odd-looking creature. It stands tall and places itself as a barrier between her and me once more, its big black lips pulled back as it hisses at me.

I can appreciate its goal, but now is not the time. "I know it is protective of you, but I have to get close enough to help."

She shakes her head up and down before placing a hand on one of the creature's legs and petting it. Her voice is low when she speaks to it, scratching at the sides of its head and under its chin in what I assume must be her language.

The animal responds to her, but doesn't take its menacing yellow eyes off me. I find it both endearing and agitating because things would go along much quicker if it just let me help.

It is getting rather late and I need to find somewhere safe. This area is good for hiding, but there are far too many rocks to be able to find a good place to rest.

The woman's voice takes on a higher pitch as she scratches somewhere it must like, and its eyes flutter shut when it lets out a quiet sound. I decide to use this opportunity to pick up my knife, but when I bend forward, the animal immediately opens its eyes and lurches forward, hissing at me.

It's more intelligent than I had previously thought. It obviously does not speak, although if it did, it would be easier to settle whatever problems it has with me. Maybe then the female wouldn't be so terrified.

I hold my hand out to the animal as some kind of peace offering and watch it flinch away, almost like it expects me to hit it again. I kick my dagger out of the way and take a tentative step closer, but it brays and steps back, its eyes locking with mine.

It bares its strange teeth at me and I take a step back and pointedly look at the female.

She is still talking quietly to it, but my presence obviously disturbs it. If this creature continues to stand in my way, I may have to get rid of it. I see how much she likes it and it seems like they have a great partnership and killing it will make her even more upset, but it seems like that might be the only way to even help her up from where she's laying.

The creature is calm once again, but its eyes don't leave me. I keep my eyes on it when I pick up my blade, clean it off, and shove it in my boot.

I need to get her to Ree. I could easily throw her over my shoulder the entire way there and withstand whatever weak punches her small, five-fingered hands might throw, but I don't want to do that. Those sorts of decisions shouldn't be forced.

I look at her and see how she is gazing at the creature with tenderness. My chest constricts again. I want her to look at me like that, without disdain and fear.

Dragging her the entire way against her will won't get me anything more than anger.

I have never felt the need to struggle for the affections of anyone before, mostly because it came naturally. It is uncomfortable, to say the least, this nagging feeling in my chest that discourages me from taking the necessary steps to make sure that she is safe.

It is rare for one female to be alone with a male, and it grates against my skin to constantly feel like I must be doing something wrong. Maybe she is feeling the same, and that is why she is so defensive. It could be that she is just as new to being around males as I am females.

I try to think of a way to comfort her and then remember the blue creature. "Neither one of us is alone with the other as long as your animal is with us."

The nagging feeling continues in my chest, its bitter taste traveling down my throat, something like guilt, but not quite.

I shake it off.

Nothing should be in the way of protecting a female.

18

Rin

Fear is an emotion I am well acquainted with.

At first, I was scared of the dark. Then, as I got older, I became afraid of my immediate surroundings and eventually, that fear grew into feeling scared for my life every time I stepped outside my door. After that, I tried to cover it up with conviction.

It was still there, just buried beneath something more important.

If you had asked me before I was brought to this alien planet, I would have said I had conquered my fears and could face most situations with my head held high.

Still, nothing compares to the kind of fear that has gripped me in the chest since the moment I found myself inside that silver cage. Every moment since then has been a terrifying, spine-chilling experience.

My heart is pounding so loudly that I can hear it in my ears, and tips of my fingers are growing cold. My body still hurts all over from that fall, leaving me in no shape to do anything—let alone defend myself if the situation calls for it.

Then I think over his words instead of just letting fear take control of my wandering mind. He talked about Roshan as if he was part of our group—not just some dumb work animal, like Tehlmar saw him.

Maybe that's a good sign? But then I see another rivulet of blood drip from him and am reminded that he is clearly insane.

The only one I can trust is Roshan. I shudder and twine my fingers in his fur. Roshan seems to feel the same, except he is more angry than frightened. I'm pretty sure he's trying to figure out a way to chase him off.

I can't blame him. No one that violent, that cruel, could be anything but trouble personified.

When he stands up, his height and massive size intimidates me, but I don't show it—or try not to anyway—and move to stand as well.

First, I slowly sit up, placing a hand on the boulder behind me and wincing as pain radiates throughout my body. I grunt under my breath before I settle back down, breathing hard. Everything hurts but I don't think I have broken anything.

Ya Allah, I hope, anyway. Who knows where would I find any sort of medical attention here?

I look at the man and see that he and Roshan are in some kind of intense staring contest. I want to lash out at him again, but I know that it could make things worse, especially considering how confused I am about being around Tehlmar and now this guy.

I don't understand the difference between alien cultures, and I don't want to get my throat cut. I shudder when I remember the way he dismembered Tehlmar like some sort of demented surgeon.

Roshan snarls; I tap his side to get his attention as the alien catches my gaze. He is looking directly at Roshan, his face blank and calculating. Whatever he is thinking about, I already know I don't like it.

I need to get up. I repeat this to myself, biting my lip as I look around for something sturdier to hold on to.

Roshan's body is in front of me and I decide he will be my crutch. I hold on to one of his fuzzy legs and push myself up, pressing my lips together when the pain rushes through me, making me feel lightheaded. It creeps up my legs and shoots through my body as I exert myself.

I want to scream and collapse back to the ground, but I shut my brain off, screw up my face, and pull myself into a standing position. My elbows are scuffed and raw, my joints groan, and I struggle to stay on my feet.

Now is not the time to show weakness.

The corners of my eyes burn with tears and my entire body feels raw. I suck in a breath and adjust myself against Roshan, opening my eyes again. Black dots cloud my vision and my hands feel cold.

"*Keke...*" I huff out.

Roshan pushes his mouth against my side and nibbles softly, making me suck in a quick breath at how painful the normally gentle gesture is.

I rub his head and put a hand to his mouth so that he can nibble at it while I search for a spot on his vast body to lean against. My eyes catch the long cut on his back, open and clotted blue, and it reminds me why I don't want to go anywhere with this alien.

I face him, imagining my eyes to be guns and my glare bullets. His broad shoulders slump and he looks away from me, guilt flooding his features.

That's right, he should feel guilty for hurting such a sweet animal.

Looking at the cut again, I wonder how I am going to treat it. I know he is an animal, and they get wounded all the time, but this was from an already bloodied and maybe even rusty knife. I don't know what kind of diseases they have on this planet and because Roshan is not native to the place, it might turn out even worse for him.

My brain feels like it is being stomped on, but I focus on Roshan, while trying to figure out how I can help him.

My unwanted companion notices how worried I am about Roshan. "I have something to help with his wounds," he says, his voice low.

I snarl at him, and he averts his gaze. "Is it another weapon?" I hiss at him, not feeling any remorse for my tone.

His brow lowers again, his skin moving differently than a humans, and on a different arc because of his rounded forehead, but instead of saying something back, his shoulders slump even further.

He shifts the buckle, which I didn't notice before, to the back of him and a large stuffed pack appears in front. He opens it, pulls out a weird, slim silver tool and tries to hand it to me.

Roshan didn't like this and bleats loudly as his head pushes my hand back. He is such a good boy, looking out for me, but right now I need him to be still. I put my full weight against him and try to distract him by grabbing on to his muzzle.

I stroke my hand over the surface of his fur to calm him, then go back to holding his mouth, pushing it gently to the other side. While he's distracted, I stretch my other hand to collect the silver item, but Roshan interrupts again and this time pushes the man away from me and snarls out a warning.

"He is very protective," the man says, but I don't respond to him.

My only concern now is Roshan; this alien can go stuff himself.

Instead, I try to pull Roshan's large head toward me and my throat tightens. "You are such a sweet boy, aren't you, Roshan?" I coo in Farsi.

I can see that he is still suspicious of the man and the thing in his hand, so I muster strength and pull his head a little harder. It strains my body, but it works.

"Oh, my sweet little angel. Well, you're not little," I chuckle painfully mid-sentence. "But you sure are a cute little weirdo, my sweet little star. You'll stay still for me, won't you?"

He doesn't understand a word of my babbling, but he loves it, shaking the fur on his head and bleating softly.

I wonder if he understands any languages at all because he did not seem to respond to Tehlmar, whose soul I hope is suffering in the deepest parts of *Jahannam*, when he spoke his language to me or mentioned certain phrases, not until he hit him with that whip.

I have to work hard to keep rage out of my nonsense babbling, which seems to be working, but I can't get the image of that whip out of my mind.

The thought of it stresses me, remembering how he hurt the poor argila. I should have known then that he was complete filth. I shake the thought away. There was no way to know the plans that the *haroomzade* schemed in his dirty mind.

I can't start blaming myself for another person's untrustworthiness. Considering no one can be trusted, I'd be drowning in guilt.

While Roshan is distracted, I take the tool from the alien and sigh in relief.

Roshan nudges against me a little too hard and I grunt in pain as I take a step back. Thankfully, the pain seems to be lessening, because the argila isn't making this easy. I can feel the alien's gaze on me as he watches me struggle to get Roshan to stay in one place and try to close his wound. Roshan is more interested in playing with the tool and my fingers than listening to my pleas to stay still.

"Roshan, please. I can't struggle with you so much. It hurts," I plead with him.

"I don't know what you're saying, but it doesn't seem to be working."

I refuse to dignify his words with a response. I bite down hard on my tongue as a punishment for being too weak to do this by myself.

I try to take a deep breath to settle my pride down before I ask for his help. It hurts as bad as the words' taste coming out of my mouth. "I'm a little too battered. Can you do it?"

There is not an ounce of politeness in my voice when I ask, but his ears shift up and the patterns in his cheeks glow distractingly.

When Tehlmar was pummeling me against that tree, I promised myself that I would not speak to another male on this planet unless it was absolutely necessary and that I'd only look for allies among females. But now, I revoke that promise because I just have to ask him later whether those are natural or tattooed.

My stupid curiosity.

"If you can find a way to get him still, I will do it."

I stare at him blankly and my voice is monotone when I speak. "That is what I have been trying to do."

The alien reaches for the tool while Roshan leans on my hand that's digging into his fur. "Distract him, like you are doing now. I can stitch him up quickly if he is calm."

I nod my head and place my hand on the other side of the creature's face. "You will stay still for me, won't you?"

Roshan lifts his head from my hand and looks at me questioningly.

I look up and see that the alien is about to use the tool. I try to watch closely and see how he is using it, but the second his fingers touch Roshan's back, he growls and kicks out at him.

The alien dodges it swiftly and then darts toward us, grabbing the tool from the argila's back.

"Roshan, stop it," I say in a sharper tone. "He is trying to help."

The shift in tone startles him and he freezes. I refuse to coo at him, and he tilts his head to the corner, his nose going to nudge my shoulder when I continue to look at him sternly. The alien works swiftly while I try to keep a straight face with the creature nuzzling me, its soft fur tickling against my neck.

"I am finished. Does he have any other wounds?"

I start to say no, then I remember that Tehlmar speared him in the chest with his weird, pointy feet. It was the first time that Roshan left my side, in fear of his own life. I'm glad he saved himself.

"Yes, on his chest. Tehlmar hit him."

He looks at me, confused.

"The male you killed," I spit out, my tone venomous.

"He deserved it."

That is something we both agree on, but I refuse to admit it to him. I inspect the wound he just stitched and appreciate his neat work, then scoff. A skill learned from a life of violence, no doubt.

"Will these have to be removed by hand when the wound heals?" I ask, my tone still stiff.

He crouches to look under Roshan, but the animal is not having it, shifting his body and snapping out at the alien.

"They will disappear."

The alien hisses, and we struggle for a few more long minutes until he can get a few stitches in.

"That will have to be good enough," the large male grunts out and the aching in my body once again agrees with him.

My mind seethes at the mere thought of that agreement, but holding a grudge never helped anyone, as my *māmān* always said. I nod my head and kiss Roshan's nose.

"Thank you," I say hesitantly.

I know that I don't have to, but I do it anyway because my parents raised me right, which is more than I can say for him.

19

Kuret

I wouldn't have imagined her ever thanking me for anything, especially not after how our interactions have gone so far. Judging from the look on her face, she didn't expect it either.

I do not know if it is the lack of disgust on her face or her thanks, but I feel like a bit of my honor has been restored. She might trust me a bit more after this.

It will definitely be a different story with the animal, though. I can see its yellow eyes still filled with distrust and anger, staring daggers straight at me. I ignore it. My priority is the female and her safety.

As if to mar the calm sands between us, she turns away from me. "Do you go around wounding innocent people and animals just so you can fix them up and earn their trust?"

I frown and turn to her to insist that I would never do anything like that again, but the look on her face tells me that it is no use trying to change her mind... for now.

A surge of loneliness and regret rises. I have lost everyone I care about. All my friends are gone, just like that. Now, I am left with a female I'm supposed to protect, but I have a feeling she is going to make it very difficult.

My mind's on fire, aching for someone to talk all this through with. Samke's face with those big ears, keeps popping into my mind, then that large manticorid. I need another male to help me make sense of this female. I have so many thoughts in my mind about this place, but I must maintain the proper boundaries as her guard.

It will be a long journey back before I can talk with Thivoll about them. Even then, there is no guarantee he would welcome my friendship, and it hurts my hearts to have yet another reminder of the bonds I have lost.

I realize she is still looking at me with distaste, wondering about my motivations. "No," I reply. "It is a tool I reclaimed from the

hunters I killed. I learned how to use it from Ree, a woman like
you."

"Yes, you said that. Tell me more about her."

The animal pushes into her a little, causing her to lose her
footing.

I reach out a hand to steady her, placing it at the small of her
back so she falls on it instead of the ground.

Her protective companion lunges at me, but I dodge it., It snaps
at the air and then bare its strange teeth at me.

It doesn't stop snarling at me, even when the woman tries to
keep it calm, so I take a step back and start to make a clicking
sound, hoping that will work. The same one we use to help calm
young males who have just been pushed out of the cloister.

"He has a name," she says, supporting herself with a boulder
now instead of the animal.

I can't blame the animal for its attitude, but it needs to stop or
she is going to get injured... more injured.

Is it the animal's language she was just speaking? It would
explain the loyalty I have seen from this animal, which should be
as alien to her as it is to me.

"A name. He told you this?"

"Of course not," she says with a huff in her voice. "I can't talk to
animals. I named him."

Once again, I am left feeling foolish. "What did you name him,
then?"

Her eyes sparkle with pride as she turns to look at him. "I call
him Roshan. It means bright in my native language."

The sparkle leaves her eyes as quickly as it came and I feel sad
for her. Perhaps being taken from our homes and everything we
used to know is something we can bond over... but, no. She is
female.

My stomach feels tight, but I push the thought aside.

"Rooshun," I stammer, wondering why it does not sound like
what she said, considering that she is speaking my language.

She lets out a mocking trill. "Roshan, his name is Roshan."

The creature looks round at her, probably wondering why she
is calling its name.

I watch her mouth move in hopes that it will help me say the
name better. "Rashun."

Her eyes light up again. "Close but not quite. Ro-shan."

She drags out the syllables and I repeat it, getting it right this
time.

"Greetings, Roshan. Will you stop trying to bite me now?"

It does not respond or seem threatened by me anymore, simply turning away.

With the animal completely distracted, I turn to face her, still keeping my distance so it doesn't get alarmed and charge at me. "My name is Kuret. What is yours?"

She looks warily at me, as if considering whether or not to trust me with her name. "Nasrin, my name is Nasrin."

Her name is intriguing, and I find myself rolling it around on my tongue—enjoying the way it tastes—before I try saying it out loud. My first attempt at saying her name is horrendous, but I ask her to repeat it.

She does and I try again a few more times, failing every time.

"What's so hard about saying Nasrin?" she mocks and I frown. She seems to delight in mocking me.

Her name is not native to my language and the syllables feel different, especially the last part of the name. It sounds elongated and almost musical when she speaks it, but it translates to something else on my tongue.

If I can't do something so simple, how can she trust me to keep her safe? I must do better.

I go over the name again silently until it sounds close and then try once more. Her name is a pleasant song coming from my mouth this time and I know I have said it the correct way this time. Pride blooms in my chest.

Her eyes widen slightly and the edge of her mouth starts to lift into a smile. I mirror her, but the smile quickly drops off her face, and she pushes her bright hair behind one of her ears, a tiny appendage I wonder how she can even hear with.

Did I do something wrong? Surely I didn't mispronounce her name to that degree. "Have I said it right, or do I need to keep trying?" I ask in an attempt to lighten the very somber mood we seem to be stuck in.

She shakes her head. "No, you finally said it right."

She turns back to me, her voice flat and face set in a displeased scowl. I find myself thinking about how many women's names I knew before I was abducted.

Even as a cloister guardian, I never asked the women their names. I didn't need to know them personally to protect them, and it's not like they would tell me if I did.

The sun has not risen a second time and I know the names of two women now: Ree and Nasrin. I enjoy how Nasrin's name tastes on my tongue, the foreignness of it, and the way the last part comes out as a gentle, melodic whistle. I want to continue to call it out as much as I can.

I like the way it feels in my mouth and I like the way she forces herself not to smile a little every time I say it. Too bad she will find it strange if I begin to repeat her name over and over until I slumber. It is beautiful, like she is.

But I need to stop being strange. I simply want her to like me, as much as I like her name. More, even.

The lustrous black cloth covers most of her, but I can see her smooth brown skin mixed with small silvery patches behind her hands. Her eyes are beautiful, yet strange, with small black circles in the middle of a brilliant white. Nearly as white as her teeth, which I only see when she snarls at me.

Her laugh is a soft tinkering that I have not heard nearly enough of and her voice, at least when she is speaking softly to the animal, is a gentle melody.

I remind myself not to stare too long. My mind and eyes start to wander to the rest of her body as I wonder what the silver patches might look like under her clothes, but I stop myself, recalling how uncomfortable Ree felt when I did it to her.

Instead of just staring, I decide to tell her what I think. "The pattern on your skin is quite unique," I express and her frown deepens.

I point to the hand that is still scratching at her Roshan's fur. I can understand her not noticing such markings as those she had been born with. It would be like me noticing my dark gray skin.

She looks down and squawks, sounding similar to an avoid, and the sound nearly makes me laugh. Her eyes are as wide as sand disks as she stares at her hands, eyes flitting from side to side. The long sleeves of her clothes recede until they are around her elbow and she gasps softly.

I appreciate the thought, but I don't say anything. I'm still being careful, trying not to ruin the mood that seemed to be getting slightly better between us.

She pulls a face that I can't quite discern and her lips move in a wordless chant. I watch her, continuing to appreciate how the silver coloring spreads over her skin in small, strategically placed patches.

Nasrin's chanting gets more audible, but I can't understand the language she is speaking. It is smooth and pretty, with no clicks or whistles like mine, but it sounds worried. Her dark furred brows, such a stark contrast to her white hair, are furrowed and there is no hint of joy on her face.

I must have done something wrong again. Maybe I said something disrespectful to her, which could easily be the case, as I do not have a single idea what her customs are like.

I curse silently and wish I had never mentioned it. Have I insulted her instead of complimenting?

Maybe being unique is not a compliment for her people, so I wrack my brain for some other way to express it to her. "Nasrin," I call out and her head whips around to face me, the worried look still prominent on her face.

I gesture my apologies to her before I speak again. "I am sorry if I disrespected you. I just meant to say that your skin is beautiful."

She still looks horrified when I say it and I feel annoyance creeping up my spine, not at her but at myself. Females have always been confusing to me and it seems I will mess up with them no matter the species. I silently curse my inexperience and lack of tact.

Instead of giving up, I strengthen my resolve to learn. I am not sure how long it will take for Nasrin and I to get to Ree and the others. But in the meantime, I will make sure to learn everything so I don't get an appalled stare from her the next time I try to pay a compliment.

20

Rin

I can't believe those hunters would do something like this—actually, yes, I can. If they can kidnap me from my home and bring me to an entirely different planet, then why wouldn't they be comfortable to continue violating my body in this way?

I almost don't notice the pinching in my throat as I start to quietly freak out. Will this happen every time I want to switch languages? It is getting old fast.

"*Ya Allah*, what is this? Am I reacting to something or am I dying? I knew something was up with this *khar* planet when it seemed too good to be true."

Who knows what else they did to me? I had just started to accept the new long fall of white hair and the translator in my throat, but this new development is terrifying.

What am I turning into?

Kuret says my name again, and it pulls me out of my panic.

Kuret. I say the name under my breath to distract myself. Even in the most absurd of films that I have seen, the characters will usually share their names before going on life-changing quests or even try to kill each other. However, this is real life and Kuret only let me know his name after he's done patching Roshan up.

It is not as strange a name as I expected it to be, and it is easy to say even in Farsi.

It was kind of funny watching him try to say our names. He messed up few times, but he eventually got it right.

When he calls my name, the end of it sounds like the start of a song, which fascinates me because his language is made of soft clicks, guttural sounds, and whistles that don't sound very musical to my ears when I'm the one saying them.

It makes me want to ask him to call me Rin, but I shake myself out of it. We are barely even acquaintances, definitely not friends, and I've just recently been taught yet another invaluable lesson about trusting people.

I turn to face him, hoping he has some answers. Dread dances in the pit of my stomach, making me feel sick.

What does he mean by beautiful? My arms resemble a shakily done collage, and I am too scared to even think about what the rest of my body looks like.

If modesty wasn't so ingrained in my moral fiber, I would have stripped down right now and inspected every inch of my body to discover what else has been added to it—perhaps a tail I haven't noticed till now?

I feel like my body is foreign, even to myself. Is this the cost for calling him *the alien* with such venom?

I look down at the skin he called beautiful again and tears prickle at my eyes. I need answers, and the only person I can ask is him. "I-I don't understand what's happening," is all I can mumble in his language, but he does not hear me.

My knees buckle and threaten to fail me, but I fight to stay on my feet. I can't be weak right now.

"I don't understand what is happening to me," I hiss out in a stronger voice, looking to make sure Roshan is not perturbed.

I know Kuret doesn't have any answers for me, but there's no one else to ask. Not that I have any intentions to lean on him, regardless of how unsettled I feel. He is far too hot-headed and, in my experience, people like him are never dependable.

My mind flits back to Tehlmar for a second. I think about how calm and mild-mannered he seemed the entire way, just to turn into the worst kind of beast. Is this an opposites sort of situation?

Kuret tilts his head and his hair swings with him. "Is this not natural for human women?" he questions, peering closer at the new silver patches on my arms as I shake my head vigorously.

I want to strangle him, but I remind myself that he doesn't know what humans would naturally look like. His only points of reference would be myself and that woman, Ree.

I stretch out my hands directly in front of my face. "I have never seen a human grow skin like this. I am an anomaly and it is all because of those terrible aliens," I groan, rubbing both my hands on my face.

I can see tenderness in his eyes and it makes me do a double-take, but the change it makes to his features—and how much I like it—won't help me figure this out. I hiss under my breath, annoyed with myself for being so easily taken in by a pretty, glowing face.

Or that I'm letting it distract me from figuring out how to stop all of these changes happening to me.

Understanding my body as a woman is hard enough, especially growing up in a place like Afghanistan where silence is celebrated. At least I had *māmān* to teach me the basic things I needed to know. But now, I'm on a foreign planet, with even more foreign things happening to me.

"What caused this?" I ask again, with a huff of breath and an aching stomach.

I chew on my bottom lip worriedly, but his eyes flare a brighter green and he speaks. "Ree mentioned getting her black scales from her magnificent orange donor."

He is looking at me like he just gave me some profound information, but I am just left confused. What black scales? And what is a donor?

I shake off the last question as unimportant. "Can you describe Ree to me?" I ask, suddenly unsure if he knows what a human is and we've been talking in circles the whole time.

He could have been deceived by another creation of the genali hunters. Was he sent to get me back for them? No, that seems unlikely, though the thought of being captured by those things again makes me shudder.

"Ree is small like you and her hair is purple and orange. She has scales up her neck and down her arms as well. Her donor is a large orange manticorid beast," he informs me in a hushed voice, probably sensing my discomfort and trying to put me at ease. But it is having the entirely opposite effect.

With every word that comes out of his mouth, I am left more and more confused. "I don't know what a manticorid is, but Ree does not sound like a human."

I find myself back to square one all over again, stranded on this alien planet by myself, probably headed straight into a trap. I sigh softly and rub at my temples.

"Maybe I have gotten it wrong, as I was badly injured when I came across her. Do human females look more like you?"

"Yes, but no scales."

"Well, you didn't have those silver marks before and they look like the skin of that waste of breath male."

I whip my head around to glare at him, but it strikes me he is right. I freeze, looking back at the new silver patches.

If I can get a reaction that turns me silver, then something similar could have happened to countless other humans as well. The genali might have manipulated Ree's DNA somehow, just like they did mine. I can only hope there's a way to reverse this.

"This is so unfair," I muse, only realizing that I'm thinking out loud when the words leave my mouth. "Women don't deserve having their autonomy taken away from them like this. It isn't right."

The realization that I sound like a whiney teenager shuts me up. Nothing makes sense to me right now, but I need to just move on.

Kuret makes an agreeing sound. He clears his throat and I look up at him, realizing again how much taller than me he is. "Ree did mention that the hunters made changes to the bodies of all the women they captured, like you and your friends."

There is a great sadness in his eyes as he speaks, like he really cares. Still, I'm not moved by it. I convinced myself Tehlmar cared, despite my intuition, so it's clear I'm not the best judge of character.

A flash of anger crosses my mind at the thought of us being treated like commodities, but I am more focused on figuring out what the hell is going on with my life.

From my conversation with Tehlmar, I know that we were going to be used as sex slaves. If they modified our bodies to please their target market, it would make sense that they gave us traits from the donors who purchased us.

The thought of Tehlmar reminds me of how much he dodged around any conversation about women's rights and it occurs to me to see how Kuret responds. "Many women I have known have had men suddenly betray them."

His face contorts and his eyes narrow. "I assume those males are now dead."

I blink. What is it with him and death sentences?

I decide to try again on a more neutral topic. "Women from all over Afghanistan are protesting the rights—or the severe lack thereof—that women are supposed to have. Since the power changed hands in the country, women have been banned from going to school or doing any jobs. In a country with as many women in the workforce as men, it really affects things, especially farming. What do you think about that?"

His head is tilted now. "A lot of those words were not in my language. What kind of labor can you not do?"

"I used to be a grade three teacher. I taught children for two years before the ban. Since then I have used the only thing I have to stand on the side of justice: my time and the risk to my life."

He's staring intensely at me as I finish speaking. My cheeks blaze with warmth as I open my mouth, but he beats me to it.

"I know that staring is unacceptable. Thivoll made that clear, but your face is so delightful to look at I cannot help getting lost in it."

The compliment takes me by surprise, and I can't tear my eyes from his. When did his eyes start to look interesting instead of like he was *Iblis* in the flesh?

My childhood best friend, Laila, and I had a theory that men give the most compliments when they think you are dissatisfied with your appearance. I think the same of Kuret but his cheeks and arms distract me by glowing in a different pattern, making me realize he is blushing.

A blush to match my blushing cheeks. How cute.

Cute? No. Another flash of his face as he eviscerated a person washes that thought away and makes my stomach ache even more.

I close my eyes for a long moment and open them again, but he still seems softer to me now and I'm once again staring into those huge bright green eyes.

"I do not understand your words fully, but I do know that you should never have had to risk your life to have control over your own choices. There should be protectors. I will be yours, though I am not very good at speaking with females and so please do not take offense."

His markings flair again and he fidgets. He is a fierce warrior, I can see, but he is also a bumbling mess, which makes me find him a little endearing. It's an odd mix with how annoyed I am. He's barbaric, not charming.

Something flutters in the pit of my stomach—arousal again, that reminds me it is always there lurking beneath the surface. I catch myself and quickly pull my eyes away from the staring match. The familiar feeling shocks me again and I gasp softly, taking two steps away from him.

I can understand why this arousal was there with Tehlmar. He saved my life, and he was an attractive male, so it made sense. I don't even find Kuret attractive. He's weird and blurts out things like "you're so pretty" right after injuring Roshan and nearly killing me.

Interesting, maybe, but not attractive. And, I remind myself, not someone I can trust, but at least he seems open to having Roshan along. That will have to be enough for now.

I stretch my arms above my head, feeling a numb pain in my stomach and the spots that were blazing with pain not too long ago. It's not natural—I know it is the work of the genali, but I have to count my blessings as they come.

The wind picks up slightly and goosebumps line up my bare arms, reminding me that I still have them exposed. I look down at the silver sheen in disgust and attempt to wipe it off.

The strangest thing about it is that I don't feel any different. It blends seamlessly with my skin, but I can't stand it. I picture how much worse the rest of my body must look, and the jumpsuit shrinks immediately. I yelp, quickly imagining it covering my body again, ignoring the concerned look from Kuret.

I can't stand the idea of being exposed for even a second longer.

Hate burns in my chest at the flimsy piece of clothing. I shut my eyes tightly, imagining it covering my body even more than it did before. With my eyes still shut, I imagine as hard as I can that it is a floor-length dress with an attached hijab.

When I feel the cool fabric sliding up my neck and chin, I almost jump for joy. It covers my forehead, lips, and nose, tightly wrapping around my face and cutting off my air supply.

Panic immediately sets in, and my heart races as I think of it as a regular face covering. It saddens me I can't even achieve a skirt, no matter how hard I try, and I feel tears prickle in my eyes.

My body is sinking back down onto the ground before I can stop it and a moment later my arms are around my knees.

I hold tears off because if a single one drops, I am going to become a sobbing mess. I still feel naked and I hate that I don't have the ability to change it right now. I hate that everything I have ever known has been taken away from me and I have no idea how to get it back.

Hate. That evil word my *bābā* worked so hard to expunge from me. To help me realize it is a sharp thing to hold too close to you. Just as willing to tear you to pieces inside as it tears apart the world around us.

In the name of religion. In the name of culture. In the name of countries and claimed homelands.

But it's rattling around inside me, nonetheless. There hasn't been this much of it threatening to explode out since they locked me away. This alien isn't cute and endearing and I need to get those sorts of schoolgirl thoughts out of my head.

He is a vicious killer, exactly the thing I hate most.

21

Kuret

Nasrin's discomfort is obvious and I can tell there is anger coursing through her as she questions the fairness of life.

I want to tell her that life is never fair. Things just happen to us and the best we can do is find a new purpose, but I know she will get more angry at it, so I say nothing and try to comfort her with my silence instead.

It doesn't work.

She becomes silent and covers herself with her clothes. I watch in sadness as it crawls over her body, covering the exposed parts of her arms and tender fingers, her light brown neck and finally her beautiful hair.

I decide to speak and risk her anger. "We will return to Ree and maybe she will have answers. I... I am glad I found you. That it is you I get to protect."

She lets out a long breath and glances over at me. At least I can still see her expressive eyes.

Right now, they are still angry and she doesn't reply. Doesn't say she is glad I found her, too.

This is more than enough evidence to me that males and females should indeed remain separate because we are not compatible with each other. At least I am not.

All I have been trying to do since I caught up to her is assure her that I am not the enemy. I thought we had an understanding, but the moment I speak up, she creates a shell over herself.

It is because I stared and complimented her. Ree told me and I didn't listen, and this is the consequence. Samke would know what to do, and I find myself longing once again for someone that knows what it is like on my world, in my culture.

With a start, I realize she must be feeling the same. I am used to females trusting me, but it was something that had been earned by all the cloister guards before me. I just have to earn her trust instead of continually making her angry.

Knowing that I am the direct cause of this reaction does not sit well in my stomach at all, and before I know it, I am seething quietly. Not at her, but at the fact that I have ruined... something.

I'm not even sure what.

I keep making these childish mistakes and I wish again that I could remember my time in the cloister. Surely they taught me something about how to interact with females?

Nasrin's bright eyes are still trained on mine, with only her lips and nose visible. I have to hold myself from blurting out how she cannot hide her beauty no matter how much she tries to cover herself up.

An avioid squawks in the air above us and it reminds me that predators will soon be attracted to the smell of the male's dead body and we will need to be far from there by the time they arrive. If we are caught by them, I will have to fight for our lives, and her dislike for violence might make her take off from me.

And then she would hiss at me for following her.

I force myself to pull my eyes away from her and dig through my memory for any nearby places we could rest.

I don't like the silence between us, so I try to fill it with neutral topics. "I scouted a few clearings and caves we could head toward tonight."

Maybe that one hidden behind large, leafy *trees* would be the best option. I had meant it to be a resting place after I shared my information with Nasrin and that terrible male.

It is strange how your plans can get interrupted without warning. The day I was captured, I hadn't expected to spend my time fighting genali. I would have offered myself to them without struggle to save the rest of my people, had they only asked.

I suppose life makes its own plans. It certainly gave me no sign whatsoever that I would become the protector of this female who seems to loathe my very existence. Yet here I find myself.

When I turn back to Nasrin, she is still looking at me, but it feels like she does not actually see me. I realize she is lost in her thoughts and while I would like to take advantage of the opportunity and stare at her pleasant face, we need to leave this place.

I clear my throat and she focuses on me, her face devoid of any emotion. "We should start moving. The stale blood will soon attract unwanted visitors," I say and she looks away from me as if she didn't hear me or didn't care.

"I don't know if I feel safe going anywhere with you," she tells me, scratching at her blue guardian.

Her words are daggers going straight into one of my hearts. What have I done this time?

The large animal makes a noise before getting up, not even sparing me a glance.

I hope she doesn't remember that I have not yet promised not to shed blood the entire time I am accompanying her. She might not understand the repercussions of such a promise, but I do.

"Please, Nasrin, we have to leave this place. We must find somewhere else to rest and recuperate. It has been a long night," I beg, my voice strained.

Surely she has to understand the urgency of our situation. What if the genali are hunting or tracking us?

I can tell she agrees with the last part of what I said when she doesn't argue and lets out a deep sigh instead. "It has," she simply agrees, and I exhale in relief that stirs my braids, glad that she is not fighting me anymore.

I look up at the ridge and note that we will have to climb back over it to resume our journey.

Nasrin is looking up at Roshan, then glances over to me. "We will have to go up there," I tell her, pointing.

She moves her head up and down in agreement.

She starts to speak to the creature beside her in a different language and tone of voice.

I assume she is telling him about our next move, and I fight back the urge to laugh. It is an animal that cannot understand a single word that she is saying, regardless of the language she is speaking, but I find it beguiling that she feels the need to involve him in everything.

Everything she does fascinates me. She's fragile but so strong inside her mind and her will. Unfortunately, that strength of will is holding onto a grudge.

After she has spoken to him, she faces me. "He should go up first and I will go after him."

Now her guard is back up, the switch in tone between when she speaks to the animal and when it's me clear. There is an edge in her voice when she talks to me that just melts when she's cooing at the big animal.

I'm more than a little jealous, but I force my mind to focus.

"He will not agree to go up if you do not go first," I protest and she opens her mouth to say something but decides against it.

As I hold my arms out, offering to help her up, I can see her struggling with the decision.

Then she glances in the direction of where I carved up the male and shudders, then uses my hand to steady herself as I pull her up. She barely weighs anything.

I make a mental note to make sure she eats more, all while trying not to stare at the tantalizing curves of her body.

She hobbles toward the ridge. Roshan follows right behind her with no persuasion.

I take a moment to appreciate the movement of her thighs and rear, wondering if all of her would jiggle like that if she were properly fed. I shake my head with a sharp click of my tongue, annoyed when I have to adjust myself so I can move to catch up.

I make myself look at her annoying companion, catching a glimpse of the gash I caused on it. The reminder of her anger is more than enough to crush my errant arousal.

"Where are we headed?" she asks when she hears me coming behind her.

"I'd like to move back into the heavy *trees* right away, but for tonight we should go toward known shelter."

"You mean go back into the *forest*?"

"Is that what it is called?"

I roll the foreign word around on my tongue as she makes a snorting sound. "Life has become very strange, Kuret. I just realized you spoke an *English* word, and I understood it. A word I didn't know, somehow translated by an alien *technology*, after spoken by an alien who doesn't even know what a *forest* is."

I'm not really sure I understood what she means, but I'm relieved to hear the humor in her clicks and the undertones of her whistles.

We are on the edge of the *forest*. The *trees* are sparser here with more grassland and outcroppings of rock like the little cliff face she fell down.

Maybe now that her mood is better, she will take part in the larger mission and I decide to share it with her.

"The plan is to take you to Ree. She is currently putting together a cloister of all the other women that she can find a way to rescue."

She whips her head sharply and I miss the way her white hair would flow around her face when she had it out.

I want to ask why she has covered it, but the stormy look in her eyes stops me.

"I am not joining a cloister."

Her words are firm and don't seem to have any space for argument.

I am extremely confused. I open my mouth to ask why, but she answers my question before I can ask it.

She squeezes her knuckles tight and the animal at her side visibly tenses up in response. "I have lived my entire life confined to a place. I don't want to do that again. Ever."

I'm not sure how to respond, especially the way her narrow eyes are directed at me. But I don't understand why she has had such a negative reaction.

"A cloister is the best way to keep you and the other women safe, especially with the knowledge that the hunters are especially after your kind." I try to explain, hoping that she will understand that it is a matter of safety.

Nasrin is adamant, and she shakes her head at me. "I can't live the same life on two different planets."

Her eyes are glistening fiercely, and she has not relaxed her stance.

If she wasn't being so unreasonable, I would find the movements and pose noble and beautiful. I don't know what she means by that, but I decide I it's best to not argue anymore.

It is all we have done since the moment we met and I don't want to continue like this.

I want us to start over. To meet each other for the first time again so that I will not be the violent killer she sees me as, but I know that I cannot have everything I want.

Or anything, it seems, judging by how she's once again looking at me like I'm the enemy.

Maybe there will be a chance for that when we get to the cloister, but I will have to get her there first. "It is acceptable if you do not want to stay in a cloister with the other women, but we have to get to Ree first. She is soft-spoken and will listen to your requests so you can take them to her."

Ree will know what to do and say to get her on their side. I am terrible at explaining things to other people.

And especially terrible at saying anything to this small female.

I would probably only make everything worse if I tried to explain further.

Her shoulders droop as she loosens when I mention this, and her frown drops slightly. I can tell she still has thoughts running through her mind, but at least this is enough until we get to Ree.

I am conflicted on whether I want the journey to be quick or not.

Part of me wants us to get to Ree as soon as possible. So that I can make sure she and Roshan are safe and not have to worry about them any longer. While the other part of me thinks that now that Roshan is not trying to bite me every time I move, I don't think of it as an enemy and Nasrin is pleasant to be around when she is also not verbally attacking me.

In those brief, blissful moments. My lips quirk up.

It's nice to share the experience of being confused on a new planet with someone else, though I can tell she thinks I have more experience here. I hope I can tell her I am just as confused as she is about why she is here so we can talk about it more openly, but first I need to figure her out.

That means getting her to safety faster than this crawling pace, though I haven't heard anyone else so far.

"Roshan, he can carry your weight, yes?" I ask her, eager to change the conversation.

She shakes her head up and down and I take pride that I understand what it means. "There was a cart and Tehlmar and I were on it while he pulled it, to I believe he can."

I click my tongue against the roof of my mouth gladly. "That is good. You should get on him to see if he will carry you."

She frowns and shakes her head left and right. "No. He's hurt," she says. "I can walk on my own."

Her resolve is so strong that I nearly believe her, until she takes a step forward and squeaks painfully, nearly falling over. I dart forward and catch onto her hand to stabilize her, hovering until she at last puts some of her weight on the animal.

It nudges her with its nose, as if it is trying to find out whether she is fine.

"He might be injured but you are far worse than him. He seems to want to help. I think you should let him."

As if agreeing with me, Roshan nudges her again and bleats quietly.

She chews on her brown-pink bottom lip, thinking. Watching the movement, I first wonder why she isn't bleeding, then get lost wondering how it would feel if she bit me like that. She can pick where.

"We can try," she says. "But if it looks like it hurts too much, I'm getting off."

I blink for a moment, trying to remember what we were talking about.

That's right.

I make a sound of agreement and help her get on his back, only part of my mind paying enough attention to avoid jostling her painfully. Mostly, I focus on how her waist feels under my hands. Easily two finger-widths of softness before I feel her sharp bones and flexing muscles.

Nothing like the thin skin covering the corded muscle of my body. I hold in a groan as my cock swells again and I imagine how it would feel to hold her against me.

To hold on to her there as I...

It takes a sharp bite to the inside of my mouth and the taste of blood to get myself back under control. She's even younger than Ree and not that long ago I was judging Thivoll for this very thing.

My chest tightens with shame as both hearts thump.

I watch as she puts space between herself and the marking of his injury. I start to feel guilty again about the injury, but I shake it off. The creature does not seem bothered anymore, so why should I?

After steadying her on him, I take hold of the reins and pull him forward slightly.

He lets out a braying sound that I can tell is from pain and I look to Nasrin to see if she has any complaints. She looks down worriedly at the animal and rubs her palm against it but it does not protest so we start moving.

I lead us back in the direction we came from and toward the cave. I don't know how she'll feel about being so close to her former companion's remains, but I'll just have to endure her rage.

22

Rin

Roshan's complete compliance with Kuret's plan to ride him makes me feel worse than I had expected. I direct all of it into annoyance for the tall alien. Why does he have to be right? It's annoying.

I lean forward to place my hand on Roshan's furry head and he crosses both of his eyes so that he can look up at me, and it elicits a giggle. He bleats softly, like that was his initial plan, and his warm yellow eyes focus back on the road.

I can feel Kuret's eyes on me, but I don't acknowledge them. Although, the rest of my body seems to be healing up nicely, my ankle still hurts a lot from that nasty fall over the rocks, and I would only slow us down if I insisted on walking.

So, yes. I know he is right, but it doesn't stop me from being upset with him.

We need to get to shelter fast, not loiter around and possibly come across another group of genali. We wasted enough time arguing already.

I don't realize we are heading back toward the cave Tehlmar spotted until I notice the bright orange embers of the fire we lit in the makeshift hearth.

"Why are we coming back this way?" I ask him as we approach the cave.

I intentionally keep my head down so that I don't make eye contact with any of the pieces of Tehlmar's dead body. As glad as I am about the fact that he is gone, his death was more brutal than anything I have seen before.

"The cart," he points. "It will be useful if we find any other women."

I nod in agreement and try to imagine what the other women might look like. A purple-haired woman, he said.

"Do you have an idea of what these women look like?"

He adjusts his hold on Roshan's reins. "Ree mentioned they all have colorful hair, lovely like yours."

The cave looks far more intimidating than I remember it, and a shudder runs through me. I look away from it and directly at Kuret.

As he says this, his dark skin glows in beautiful patterns around his face and avoids my gaze, looking like he is searching for some imaginary lost item on the floor. There is hesitation in his voice, as if he is expecting me to take offense at his words.

I pretend not to see the patterns on his cheeks or feel the warmth in mine as I ask him if there are any other defining features besides colorful hair.

I think about how many there are—maybe seven, like the colors of the rainbow?

The rainbow idea makes little sense as my hair is white. Unless I am the cloud?

What would psychopathic aliens like the genali know about the rainbows of Earth? Does light refract the same here? I keep forgetting how different everything is now and my mind keeps going on ridiculous spirals.

I need to fix that.

"They are supposed to be in silver containers called cryogenic chambers," he stumbles over the English words, then continues, "and if we find any that are still inside, we will need to keep them there."

I nod in understanding. He must mean like the one I woke up in. I still remember how cramped I felt in mine, and it makes my throat close up a little when I think of other women in them.

Why leave them in? And why were we in them to begin with?

Another quick flash of anger at the genali blends into the background din of annoyance. Mixed in with this nagging feeling that maybe Ree can't be trusted if she plans to start a cloister.

My heart aches for allies and to have other female women around me, but I trusted Bibi and she sold me. Women can be just as prone to oppress other women, after all. Often, they are the instruments of continuing it, actually. Too worried about keeping things the same and pleasing those around them and more than willing to betray women who don't agree.

Kuret reaching for me breaks me out of another loop of anxiety. He gingerly helps me down from Roshan's back. His hands splay on either side of my stomach and my heart pounds, and I'm not sure it's just relief I feel when he lets me go. Then he goes to steer the cart closer to the cave.

The surge in my arousal leads to an equal surge in my already peaked irritation. Tehlmar was handsome too, and look where that led.

As much as I try to reason with myself, the arousal just keeps surging. Even worse than with Tehlmar, but he was horrible, so I was fighting it.

Wait, so is Kuret, I remind myself.

He immediately starts attaching the reins to the vehicle, leaving me standing there feeling useless. I try to ignore how much better he treats Roshan, but I can't help but notice.

I let out a long breath and pinch the bridge of my nose. I never thought I would wish for the confines of my brother's house, but I also never imagined... this.

The events of the last time I was there replay in my mind and my hands start to shake. Shutting my eyes, I take a deep breath and scratch at Roshan's cheeks, distracted when I touch his scars. When you can't even trust your brother...

But I push that aside. So far it sounds like it is just human women. If some women can't be trusted as allies, since they have taken on male ideals, then how do I recognize them on an alien planet? She clearly spoke English, since Kuret has been speaking words of it, and that name suggests maybe she is American.

Every terrible thing I've heard about Americans mixes in with the ridiculous things I have seen on television, then my mind pushes back that it can't all be true. Can it?

The feel of Roshan's scars pull me out of another mental spiral. I quietly gasp in Kuret's alien language when my fingers connect with the pitted holes in his cheeks once more.

Limping over in front of him, I squint and focus on undoing the knot inside the argila's mouth. He stays still for me, occasionally scrubbing my hands with his rough tongue and making me smile. It doesn't take much time to undo it, and I let out a sigh of relief.

So, not completely useless.

"Was that painful for him?" Kuret asks me, and I look at him for a moment.

He's in front of the glow of the fire, blocking it, and it makes him look much darker and his shadows look more imposing, which doesn't match his tone.

Almost like he actually cares. My heart lurches, longing to do what I know it shouldn't. Trust.

When will it learn? But do I really have a choice? And could I live such a bleak existence, anyway? Surely there is someone who won't betray me. Will I recognize them? Can I even trust... myself?

What a terrible thought. It sits like a stone in my chest, making each breath hurt. As usual, there are no answers.

My shoulders lift in a shrug. "I don't know if it is right now, but I know it was the worst pain he experienced when they did and that is enough to make it cruel."

Roshan pushes his face into mine. I adjust my weight to my good leg and scratch the place behind his ears.

Kuret is silent and staring at me again, clearly processing the weight of my words.

I am silent too. The only sound comes from Roshan fussing.

He starts to make a soft sound, and I lower my hands to the thick fur on his cheeks. I rub my fingers against the pitted scars and scratch at them softly, not wanting to go too hard in case I end up hurting him. However, he seems to enjoy it the harder I scratch, his body twitching violently.

Kuret looks surprised, and he steps away for a moment, probably for fear of being kicked.

"Hey boy, are you feeling better?" I say in Farsi and the sweet creature nibbles at my hands some more.

Somehow, his adorable little gesture wipes my irritation away, and I feel a lot better. I look at Kuret and although I can't see his face, I can tell that he is waiting for me to decide whether I want to get back on Roshan or not.

The bright light from the fire makes the velvety blue and brown of Roshan's fur shine in a weird, ephemeral way and it hits me—I am really on another planet, friends with a horribly cute argila, with an extremely violent warrior alien at my side.

I am living in a science fiction movie.

Stranded on an alien planet protected by an alien guardian and alien animal, while being hunted by an entirely separate alien race. It's almost laughable.

It's like all those movies I would never agree to sit down and watch, except this time I'm living it.

Kuret sees I am looking at the fire. "Is all well, Nasrin?"

I nod. "Well, no, but I'm fine. I'm just thinking that it might be a good idea to douse the flame so nothing can follow our trail."

As soon as I say it, I realize I had the same exact thought with Tehlmar, but didn't feel comfortable saying anything, but I just blurted it out to his killer.

I don't get a chance to think it through when Kuret speaks again. "Yes, the fire is a beacon."

"There is a bag with some supplies in there. It has some water bottles that we took from a genali camp. You can use one of them to quench the fire," I suggest and he flicks his finger on top of his other hand.

His hand glows brighter for a moment as he walks into the cave. I am confused for a minute before I decide that it must be an agreement, just like my nodding.

He holds out the water, then pauses, instead feeding it more fuel.

I open my mouth to protest, but he speaks. "I'll get you settled and then come back here to cook something, then douse it then."

My stomach tightens painfully as a reminder of my hunger, and I see the wisdom in his plan.

He secures the bag in a little nook inside the cart and walks out in front of Roshan and me, but I immediately notice that Roshan does not move an inch.

When I take a few steps, he trails behind me slowly, pushing his nose into my back playfully. Apparently, Roshan will only follow my lead.

It makes me giddy that I have been able to win the loyalty of a creature so quickly, but I also feel a burdensome responsibility. As the last child of my parents, I never really had people look up to me. When I lived with my brother's family, his wife did her best to make sure I didn't interact much with her children.

Me being the bad influence that I am, of course.

I shake off the fear and decide that I like Roshan and everything that will come with him, regardless of what it means for my own comfort. My ankle still hurts, but I limp ahead of the argila, pleased that I can hear him walking behind me.

Kuret is a small distance in front of us, turning around every few minutes to make sure that we are still there.

Kuret finds us a place to settle down before I run out of breath, and I am astonished at how many places like these exist. From the front, I had no way of knowing, but after pushing through a few prickly bushes, it looks like a small cave surrounded by an even smaller oasis.

It's beautiful. The cave is warm and tucked directly into the ground, such that we almost have to climb into it. There is a variety of flora growing everywhere with what looks like this planet's version of flies hovering soundlessly around them and a small babbling brook sprouting out of a rocky outcrop that hopefully contains drinkable water.

I don't know how Kuret found such a perfect place, but I won't complain.

We settle in wordlessly and Kuret announces that he is going to patrol around us. I make a sound of agreement and wait until he has left to pee in the bushes and wash my face. The wind blows against my hair and I decide that I will not put the makeshift *hijab* back on.

I don't like the way it covers my ears and makes me feel less alert here, though I do admit sometimes I love being covered.

Thankfully, Kuret is more confused than anything at the head covering, and I can be at peace with the knowledge that he is not seeing something unspeakable when he looks at me.

It's freeing, actually. To think of being able to wear *hijab* or not, based on my own preferences and beliefs instead of the expectations of others.

He returns when I am nearly done with removing the argila from his reins and have convinced him to enter the cave, grateful Kuret already checked it for animals.

Kuret has something roasted in his hands, wrapped in leaves. Closer inspection tells me it is some version of a bird, but I honestly don't care all that much. I just scarf it down hungrily.

I murmur my thanks to Kuret for the food, and then move to the back of the cave and put Roshan between us.

Thanks to Roshan's large body, the cave feels warm and after Roshan settles on the ground, I lay close, using his wide, soft body as a pillow. My heart pounds at the idea of spending the night in a cave with someone I don't trust, but I gradually calm myself by running my hands through Roshan's fur.

Roshan will let me know if something is wrong. Before long I am completely exhausted and fall into a restless slumber, hoping morning comes soon.

23

Kuret

I do not realize how tired I am until I have filled my belly with the wild avioid I killed earlier.

Nasrin and Roshan are settled comfortably around each other and fall asleep as soon as they rest their heads, but I stay up a little longer to wash myself in the stream.

I scouted the area thoroughly, so I am hoping to enjoy the time in the water leisurely, cleaning every bit of myself to get rid of the built-up grime. Though I was excited at the novelty of it, being submerged in water isn't quite as pleasant as I imagined.

The temperature of the water helps ensure I spend as little time in it as possible, which is best anyway because of how vulnerable a position it is.

It is far too cold, which none of my kind tolerate well, but when I rise from the water, I can't deny that I feel better.

Nasrin won't need to give me any more pointed looks over the brown blood, especially once I take the time to wipe off the animal hide; once again I am grateful that it sheds stains so easily.

It was worth the long nights of hunting and the harrowing fight with the multi-horned beast. I even take a moment to re-braid my hair, the task soothing and familiar enough to ease some of the nagging worry that I have harmed something between Nasrin and me.

Maybe there are signs that she is not as angry, though.

I noticed when I returned from cooking that she let her hair loose from the black covering and it sent a victorious surge through me, nearly the same feeling as a well-fought battle.

My breath huffs against my hands as they complete the intricate looping around my left ear.

It has been a battle.

I set out to rescue as many women as I could while getting my honor back. While there have been many unexpected hurdles, the serenity around me, the satisfaction of Nasrin being safe, and the lulling sound of a cool stream more than make up for it.

If she continues to warm to me...

I'm not even sure what comes next, but I'm excited about the possibilities. About the mystery.

After catching myself nodding off a few times by the stream, braid still in hand, I decide I've made enough progress on refreshing them for now. I make sure that the wound on my stomach is healing nicely before putting my leg armor back on.

I leave off my torso cloth to give the wound space to breathe. It'll also help illuminate the cave in case Nasrin wakes up before daylight.

My lips quirk up and my hearts quicken at the idea of being a beacon for her.

I wander slowly back into the cave, my ears twitching and alert for danger, but I hear nothing. Everyone is just as I left them, and I'm put at ease.

I let my eyes roam over Nasrin's sleeping form and allow myself to say her name out loud in a soft whisper. She does not stir, softly snoring with her light hair splayed against Roshan's darker body.

My hands twitch toward her and I picture myself moving back to her, fitting myself up against her soft curves, but fling the thought away.

The universe truly is not fair at all because something as precious-looking as she is does not deserve to endure a reality such as this. She is fragile, yet firm and powerful. She should be in a cloister surrounded by females.

She does not deserve the horrors that have been visited upon her.

Once I find myself wanting to place my hand against her smooth face, I push those thoughts out of my mind and find the corner nearest to the entrance of the cave to settle in.

I can't see her from here, which is probably best.

The distance between this place and the main path is the primary reason why I chose it and I am confident that we will be safe. Still, I have to make sure that I am the closest to any danger. Since there is no one to relieve my watch, I shouldn't sleep, but I am too exhausted to stay awake.

Sleep finds me fast and before I know it, I am swept up into a restful, dreamless sleep. It is peaceful until I start to hear scratching noises coming from around me. I crack an eye open and look around, but I see that it is only Roshan adjusting himself.

I yawn noiselessly and make sure Nasrin is still resting before allowing myself to fall back to sleep.

The scratching noise rouses me again, but this time I am sure it is coming from outside the cave.

I get up and cautiously start to walk out of the cave with a hand over my knife handle when I feel something sharp pierce into my thigh.

Whoever my attacker is, they are quick and silent. I hadn't even heard anything before there was a short spear stuck nearly midway through my left thigh.

I let out a grunt and stumble backward before falling on my back as I watch a small green creature scurry toward me and jump on my chest.

It is smaller than a genali hunter and its sinewy, thin arms reach out and grab at my neck before I can pick it up.

Its eyes are black, pointing so far out of their sockets that I think they might reach my face like his smelly breath. It's small but strong and wiry for its size, so it is difficult to get out of its grasp, but I struggle against it.

I growl at it before I land a blow to its face, but I find that its grip is tighter than I thought, so I go for the obvious weak spot—its eyes. I jam a finger into its closest one while simultaneously trying to rip its hands off my neck, and it works.

The assassin lets out a yelp of surprise and loosens its grip enough for me to get him off my back and finally get a proper look at my attacker. It is a small creature, half my height, with a large bulbous head from which protrudes piercing black eyes full of hate, a slender trunk-like body, and long, spindly arms that end in stubby clawed digits.

It doesn't spend much time on the ground before it lunges at me once more, spewing what must be obscenities in its alien tongue as it flies at me at top speed.

I manage to dodge its advance by a slim margin and throw a punch wildly in the direction I thought it would have been in, but my fists meet nothing but air as the creature has launched itself directly off the wall and at me once more.

This beast is fast—too fast for me to fight in such close confines, where it has the advantage.

With a frantic roll, I move out of the cave, as I try to dislodge it from my back. It only grips harder. My mind flashes over to Nasrin and the animal stuck in the cave with her. If I fall here, they will not be able to fight it off and will die shortly after.

I hear Roshan's scared bleating as I struggle with the disgusting thing, just managing to get my knife in what I hope is a vulnerable spot.

24

Rin

I fight my way back to consciousness in stages, feeling sick, images of Tehlmar mixing together with other memories of violence into an appalling, jumbled nightmare that has my heart racing. I go through my usual mantras to help me release the fear, the pounding in my ears steadily decreasing. As I fully awaken, there's a hissing click that could only be Kuret.

I open my eyes to see Roshan pacing around the small cave, looking as agitated as usual when Kuret is around. It's surreal for a moment as my groggy brain tries to process where I am.

We are still in the cave that Kuret scouted for us earlier and it is still dark outside. I struggle to gather myself mentally.

The only real difference to me is some very curious itching in and around my ears that I hadn't noticed before. Maybe I'm having a reaction to something in the cave? I don't really know, but it's extremely uncomfortable and, honestly, rather distracting.

Then I remember the changes in my skin. My heart skips a beat, then skips another when I realize that the sounds aren't just rustling and Roshan is far more than just agitated.

It's dark in the cave without Kuret's glowing. Wait. Why isn't he glowing?

I shoot up, my ankle protesting the movement. The pain is sharp but is gone almost instantly, leaving only a dull throbbing and the familiar aches from my misadventures earlier in the day.

Roshan is still moving erratically, and I can hardly see in the dark, but the odd sounds and Kuret's hissing continues. I want to call out to him, but I clamp my teeth down on my tongue.

I move toward Roshan, pushing him to the side, searching for Kuret's green glow. I finally get Roshan to move enough so I can move forward in the cave enough to look out the entrance.

My eyes widen when I see a strange-looking creature pushing something sharp against Kuret's face with a devious, wide grin on its face. I move a hand to my mouth to keep a gasp from escaping.

Its head is far too large for its body, which is much smaller than Kuret.

How did it gain the advantage on him?

Kuret is calm, so still he's not even blinking, the only movement the thrumming of his green glow, but his eyes are alert and his muscles tense. A quick glance down reveals he has his own knife poised and ready to strike.

Both must be unsure they can move fast enough to survive.

My heart is roaring in my ears, and I hear all my inner voices screaming at me to do something. One part of my brain is telling me to run before it notices me. That I have enough time to make it past them while Kuret grapples with it.

But if Kuret loses, I have no idea what this new alien will do to me.

I look over at Roshan to see if he is big enough to hurt whenever this creature is, but he looks even more frightened of it than me. He must have encountered it somewhere before.

The two aliens are still in a weird staring contest, neither one looking frightened. They are clearly insane.

I glance back to the forest, but no, I can't leave Kuret. I might not have liked that look on his face when he killed Tehlmar, but he saved me.

The other alien's body is coiled around Kuret like a shadow, its sickly gray-green skin an ugly contrast to Kuret's dark gray. It's head is so much larger than it should be, it's nausea-inducing.

Even though they seem evenly matched, their sizes are so different that it doesn't make sense. From the look on its face, the monster is getting ready to strike him down. It's just enjoying itself in the meantime.

No. Kuret might have weird views, but my *bābā* taught me better than to abandon an ally.

My eyes frantically dance around the cave for a weapon or anything I can use to attack this monster. There are only packs, a water bottle, and of course lots of rocks. There might be more, but it's hard to make out much in the muted light.

Without any idea if it will work, I pick up a rock that looks closest in size to the balls I used to play with as a child.

After a moment of agony wondering if I'm about to get Kuret killed, I toss it at the creature's head with all the strength I can muster. My skills haven't diminished, and I hit it hard on the side of its head.

It's a flurry of movement after that.

Kuret stabs upward into its chest, but it twists to the side enough he only grazes it. Next, Kuret darts his other arm out, grabbing the knife and twisting it out of the creature's hand, yelling out in pain as he does it. I instantly feel better, assuming with the blade out of the way, Kuret will destroy the thing.

Instead, it screams at him, then raises a booted foot and kicks him in the side. My jaw drops as Kuret flies through the air and collides hard with a nearby tree.

What?

My heart is in my mouth as it races toward me, pure hatred in its ugly face.

If Kuret had no chance, I don't either. I suck in a breath, shut my eyes tightly, and say my last words to *Allah* before I fight for my life, then open them wide again.

There is a promise of death in its large, crazed eyes, then it starts speaking. "I'll kill you slowly for that."

I clench my fists, ready to kick out, but I don't get a chance. It suddenly shudders to a halt, then falls, a knife sticking out of the back of its head.

My heart thumps painfully as a surge of relief rises and I let out a breath, thankful to still be alive. Kuret is propped partly against the tree, panting.

He saved me. Again. I'm still reeling when Roshan moves up against me, seeking reassurance. I pet him absently as my mind races.

Everything here really is going to try to kill me, isn't it? I hate violence. It has been the cage that has defined my life... but here... here it isn't about just violence. It's about survival.

Maybe I need to trust Kuret. Something in me surges in anticipation at the thought of not being alone, but then the ever-present fear surges back up to crowd it out, replacing that deep longing to feel safe and settled with the hard truth of reality. Life has taught me that safety is an illusion, and people usually abandon their principles to cling to the lie.

I shake my head, my mind finally screaming out to me that there is a spear sticking out of Kuret's leg and he's bleeding.

25

Kuret

Nasrin stands her ground and my heart swells with pride as the brute darts toward her. I take my time to line up a throw before sending the knife hurtling into his head.

It falls to the ground soundlessly, a small distance from Nasrin. Its blood reminds me of her former companion's hair, and I feel elation starting to erupt in the pit of my stomach.

Both of my hearts are thumping violently in my ears and I can feel patterns flickering across my face, but I keep my face stoic.

I won't make the same mistake I made when I first met her.

Nasrin is shaking as her eyes go from the creature to me. I must be a sight, holding onto the large plant behind me for support, blood dripping from the hand holding the thing's knife.

I just killed something in front of her and both hearts ache as I wait to find out if she will leave now.

The pain from the spear still lodged in my thigh is radiating through me. I move to a more comfortable position to catch my breath. I make sure my eyes keep scanning around us in case there are more of those deceptively weak-looking aliens.

I have a feeling that even if there are, they would not want to face the same fate as their friend, but I've been reckless enough as it is. If only Samke was here with me... but no, I wouldn't wish this on anyone.

Roshan makes a sound that snaps my attention to him and when I look to make sure he is not hurt, I find Nasrin holding tightly onto him.

Her eyes are still stuck to the dead body of the creature, and I am torn between celebrating my kill and asking her whether she is still going to leave.

I do neither.

I can still hear her threats echoing through my brain, the rage and fear in her eyes as she stated how quickly she would walk out if I was violent like I was before. I cannot help but wonder if the only reason she has not left is because she is still paralyzed by fear.

I want to celebrate my victory and roar triumphantly from the mountaintops, but I know how she feels about bloodshed and I would rather not make her uncomfortable, so instead I sit quietly and pull the spear out of my thigh with a wince.

Although I made no promises, I really did intend to keep my hands blood-free until I reunited her with Ree. The night had different plans.

"You're bleeding."

I barely hear her whisper with how hard my hearts are beating but I am sure I would be able to pick up the sound of her voice anywhere now. I look down at the source of pain in my leg and swallow thickly.

"Yes, but it will heal."

She scoffs and circles around the dead body to sit a short distance from me, visibly shuddering when she looks at it.

We sit beside each other in silence for a moment before she pushes away the hand that is doing a terrible job of covering up the wound. "It looks bad," she says. I want to argue with her, but her piercing gaze makes me keep my mouth shut.

"We will have to patch it up to avoid infection," she concludes and I slide my pouch out from behind me, opening it up to pull out the tools that I think we will need.

Nasrin lets out a dry, throaty sound that I decode as some kind of laugh when I look up at her face. "You slept without a shirt but left your weapons close," she notes and I make a sound of agreement.

"For times like these," I say and she smiles shakily.

I pull out the spray canister and stitching device Ree used on me earlier when she patched me up and pass them to Nasrin.

Her hands are shaking when she reaches out to grab it and guilt envelopes me like a thick blanket. I should not have let her come that close to danger. I was complacent in my efforts at guarding Nasrin; that's the only explanation for it.

I curse myself silently. How I long for the high walls of a cloister.

She gets up and grabs a water bottle from the bag of supplies and waits for me to stretch my leg out.

I do so and clench my jaws firmly together when she pours the water and then sprays the liquid on my leg. It burns, but I grind my teeth and look at the wall of the cave.

She reaches her hands out again. "Now your hand."

Nasrin quickly patches me up, washes my blood off her hands with the remaining water, and sits down again—this time a little farther away. I don't mind it at all. She can sit as far from me as she likes, as long as she doesn't leave.

I wouldn't even blame her. She had only one request, and that was no more violence. If I had stayed vigilant, I wouldn't have given that creature a chance to strike.

It would have been dead well out of her sight. I'm still not sure how I didn't hear it, or that I was so confident in our position that I decided it was safe to sleep.

Stupid and reckless.

Roshan has moved close now, his eyes still staring at the dead creature, fear evident in them. Clearly he can't always be trusted to protect her.

I've never had to work alone before. I have always had my brothers to rely on, and we made certain that no woman had to defend herself. I can't provide that for Nasrin. In fact, I think I will need to start teaching her how to protect herself.

If she'll even let me.

I am not sure she understood when I explained that I don't have control over whether or not I kill, as there will always be enemies but I am glad she is not gone yet.

"I'm glad we took the cart. I can't walk far with this inconvenience," I mutter to myself as I stare at the wound.

We will need to get moving soon, but my injured leg will slow me down and leave me almost completely incapable of protecting Nasrin and Roshan.

They are both injured and have no way of protecting themselves and I let myself get a leg and a hand wound. The worst possible locations.

"I think I know what that was," Nasrin says as her hand absentmindedly strokes at Roshan.

I look at her questioningly and notice that Roshan has its eyes on me, staring at my wound.

"A braceaaer. They're hunters, like the genali. Tehlmar told me about something that is stronger than it looks."

Being reminded of that male makes my marks flair.

Roshan gets up from where he is pressed beside her and wanders to where I am. He holds my gaze for a long moment before settling beside me, not touching, just hovering.

"I thought he hated me," I say and her shoulders jerk up and down.

Her face is more relaxed. "I thought so too, but he did just see you defend us."

I place a tentative touch on the nose of the animal, and it leans its face into my hand, taking me by surprise. "You must be right. He's a smart animal."

Nasrin's eyes light up and her brown-pink lips stretch into a smile.

I've only seen her direct it at the animal, not me, and now I know why Roshan bleats at her and pushes in for pets. She's as beautiful as the rising sun. I want her to always have a smile on her face when she looks at me.

I'm still enjoying the glow of it when she turns back to Roshan. "He is the smartest ever."

She keeps on talking about the animal, and before it would have made me jealous, but now I have some hope that she will some day give me the same regard.

Hopefully, I'll do less bleating than Roshan, but I'm not too proud to do what must be done.

If she had not told me herself, I would have been convinced that they came from the same planet and had been together most of their lives. It makes me feel a lot better knowing that Roshan has warmed up to me, almost like I am a part of the loving relationship they have.

I know that I will not be fully a part of what they have, as we will have to separate when they unite with Ree, but I am willing to enjoy the affection while I have it.

After she is done doting on Roshan, Nasrin looks up at the sky. "No sign of dawn yet?"

"The days seem to be abnormally long and the nights must be the same," I tell her. "We should start heading out before we gain more attention or this blood attracts predators."

We glance at the dead braceaaer and then at each other, a strained silence falling on us. "We will have to go a different way than I planned, and you will need a weapon."

She shakes her head with vigor, her long white hair whipping against her face. "No. I understand why you have to do it, but I don't want to. I... I can't."

Her hands are shaking now and once again I wonder why she is so opposed to protecting herself with a weapon when she just used a rock as one.

It makes no sense.

"I understand that, but I am injured. If we come across something more dangerous and I am killed, you will have to protect yourself. You cannot do that without a weapon."

She's still shaking her head and I remember how she looks at the blue beast. "Roshan needs protection, Nasrin. Use a weapon or you put him at risk."

She closes her eyes, then lets out a long breath. She scrambles over to the dead alien, like she has to move fast before she can change her mind.

After a retching sound, she pushes him over. "What?" she says, her voice confused. "He has a *gun*, Kuret."

"A what?"

"Oh, that didn't translate," she tells me as she wipes green blood off of her hands, her face screwed up into an expression of what I assume is disgust. "It's a weapon that kills from afar by... well, that doesn't matter right now. It makes no sense why he was fighting you like he was. He could have killed you from way over there with this thing."

I look to where she is pointing, confused. He doesn't have a spear or bow.

It doesn't matter. "Whatever that is, you need it. Take that and the knife."

She turns to me, her eyes wide. She's shaking harder now. "Kuret... I'm... I can't. I'm afraid of *guns*."

The need to comfort her rises up, but I push it back down. "Do you want Roshan to die, Nasrin?"

I don't let her continue with her argument as I lift myself up into a standing position and move toward the corpse. He has a dagger better suited to our hands than the ones I took from the genali hunters and I pluck it from his body and hand it to her.

"I will do my best to make sure you never need to use it," I promise her.

She gazes uncomfortably at the weapon before taking it from me and putting it away. "Alright then. Let's get out of here before something else shows up."

She pulls an odd-looking metal device toward her, treating it like a wild animal that is about to bite.

There's liquid building in her eyes now. I don't know what it means, but I know I have to keep pushing. I open my mouth to say more, but she starts speaking.

"You're right. If they have *guns* here, then if we don't use them too, we're going to die. I can teach you how to use it, Kuret, though I hate them and would prefer to never even touch one."

"If we find another one, then yes, you can teach me. That one is yours. Also, I know you won't like that I say this, but you need to also learn how to use a knife. Not right now, I will need to heal a bit more first but consider it."

She swallows hard but doesn't argue with me and I take that as a good sign. With a grunt, I push myself to my feet again, sucking in air through my teeth in pain.

The wound isn't as bad as I expect, and there is less pain. Strange.

I strip the body of anything else useful, pleased to find another kit with the tools Ree showed me how to use, plus more of the disgusting rations. After hooking Roshan up to the cart, she fills up the empty bottles by the stream and loads them into the cart before climbing in herself.

It is slow progress, but we move toward another cave. As much as I would like to simply move quickly through the night back toward Ree, I don't think we will make it with me injured and Nasrin unable to defend herself.

Rin

The gun in my hand feels like a giant weight. Like I am becoming part of the very thing that I hate, but I remember the look in the alien's black eyes and it helps harden my resolve.

Roshan pulls us along. It is going to be difficult to push recent events out of my mind, but we don't have the time to waste dwelling on that now. Who knows if there are more on the way?

Kuret takes control of the reins as we move back into the clearing, his face extremely focused on the road.

I put the gun in a place it can't accidentally be fired, but keep the knife. I fiddle with the weapon in my lap, turning it every which way, and allow the events that just took place to play through my head.

He is taking an entirely different route than the one we had planned earlier and the forest has started to change. The most obvious difference is the abundance of what looks like mushrooms peppered here and there on the previously smooth barks of the trees we passed.

I still can't believe that we were attacked in our sleep like that. There truly is nowhere safe.

Kuret believed we were safe and by association, I did too, too exhausted to question anything. I'm sure that if Roshan had not stirred, I would have kept sleeping the entire way or gotten up when it was too late.

I don't want to begin thinking about all the things that could have happened if I didn't toss that rock when I did. I'm still surprised it worked at all.

Roshan is moving quicker than he ever did with Tehlmar steering and it warms my heart that he is now seeing the good in Kuret.

I believe in the judgment of animals, and I was determined to keep my distance and stay on alert around him as Roshan had.

Then he proved to be more than a senseless killer and the events of tonight have shown me a different side of him.

There was not enough time to think, but I could see that during the struggle, he tried to fight without killing. I can see what he meant now by having to kill or be killed off first. I'm caught between a fight of morals and survival, but I know what side I am choosing now.

It seems that Roshan has chosen as well, or he would be resisting Kuret. I was afraid I would have to keep shuffling along in front of him with my ankle injured... wait, now. I just realized I've been walking on it just fine since I woke up.

After a quick rotation, I confirm that it isn't hurting anymore. Quick checks on my other injuries let me know they've healed as well.

I glance over at Kuret and notice that his wounds are also closed up. He's using his hand without favoring it and I'm not sure he even realizes it yet as focused as he is on our surroundings. The glow from his chest gives me a clear view of his leg wound.

Our quick healing is a mystery, but not one I can solve just by staring at him... though I can't seem to stop following the long, hard muscles in a V pattern, leading to somewhere that makes me press my thighs together.

Kuret has a body type I am not used to seeing in the men back home, not that I have much experience. He is big and well-built but made of mostly lean muscles. As far as I can tell, he has almost no body fat, but I highly doubt it's from special exercise regimes or diets like it is for humans. It's just the way his species is built.

His muscles and markings follow patterns that would scream *alien*, even without his dark-gray skin, sharp teeth, and the nostrils on the sides of his face. Then there's his long braids, which at first terrified me when I saw animal bones woven into them.

Now I notice there are other things woven into them. Beautiful little sculptures of animals I've never seen before, rough beads, stones, even a few feathers. They tinkle together in a soothing sound when he moves.

I'm still staring when he pulls us to a stop, my face flaming when he catches me at it. I'm about to comment about his braids when he starts speaking.

"This should be far enough for us to rest again for a while."

I shake my head to fling off my, quite frankly, disturbingly erotic thoughts, then look around. He's found another cave. The region must be teeming with them to have seen so many in such a small area.

He gets out of the cart, his hairless brow furrowed as he looks down at his leg. I assume it must feel better than it should.

"I'm healing far faster than normal here, Kuret. Are you as well?"

He looks back up at me, his large eyes with their horizontal pupil communicating his puzzlement. "Yes," he confirms. "This happened with another wound, and it isn't natural. Why would they make me heal faster if they just brought me here to hunt me?"

My own brow furrows as I try to get into the mindset of a species that traffics women and brings people to a planet to hunt them. Then I realize it must take a lot of resources to capture, contain, and move people as dangerous as Kuret.

"Well," I say, drawing the word out, "it's just a guess, but maybe it's because you are expensive... uh... prey. If a hunter wounded you, but didn't kill, and you got away, they wouldn't want you to die holed up somewhere you couldn't be found."

He blows out a breath that makes his braids shift and his large hands clench, sending ripples of light through his marks. "That makes sense, in a terrible sort of way," he grits out.

His hands unclench and he opens the injured one to look at it. Then he shifts his weight on the ground, clearly testing how much he can rely on it.

"I am not quite healed enough to fight, but enough to teach you some ways to defend yourself. Will you let me?"

He's staring at me intently and a surge of fear passes through me. I hadn't thought the decision would be quite so soon.

He lets out another breath and starts speaking again. "If another one of those creatures was about to attack you, what would you do? What if next time there is a whole group of them? They aren't always solitary, Nasrin. What would you do?"

My hands shake. I would defend myself. I would defend Roshan... and Kuret. I glance down at the gun, remembering the burn of the barrel in my mouth, which sends a shiver of fear snaking along my spine. I need to put those memories aside. They were from a very different life in a different world.

Before coming here, I would never have considered it, but that terrible green creature, Tehlmar, the leering genali... Who knows what other amoral people are out there. Defending myself doesn't make me anything like them.

Learning how to use weapons just means I'll know how to keep Roshan and me alive. It would put some of the power of taking care of myself in my own hands. I glance down at them. Not being able to use weapons meant I was at the mercy of terrible people on Earth. It will mean the same here, but even worse.

Defense doesn't make me evil.

The thought sends a shock through me, and I tear my eyes from my hands and look at Kuret. Defense didn't make him evil, either. I think back to the fight with the green creature and realize he listened to me when I told him how his extreme violence disturbed me.

As much as I long to, I still don't trust him, because that would be stupid. But so far, he's done exactly what he said he would do.

"Alright," I say, clearing my throat when it comes out in a weak whisper so I can speak more decisively. "Yes. I want you to teach me."

His eyes open wider, and his lips stretch out into a large smile, sharp white teeth making divots in his dark lips. I swallow hard, tamping down the instinct to run from the intense gaze of a predator. A moment later I feel the fear transition to increasing tightness in my belly and I nearly groan at the pulsing between my legs.

No. I will not find such a thing as him looking predatory a turn on. I will not.

Neither my mind nor my body listen to the small part of my brain sending out vociferous protests.

When he speaks again, it startles me out of staring at his lips and wondering if they are soft. "Excellent. Let's get started, then."

He reaches inside the cart to grab water containers and heads to a small stream that's bubbling out of the cave entrance. It must be an underground spring. I try to focus on it, but my eyes keep drifting back to him as he moves away, the growing light in the sky allowing me to greedily take in every detail.

When he walks, all the muscles in his back ripple in the most deliciously seductive ways.

I can't take my eyes off him.

I'm thinking the most indecent thoughts, and I don't know how to stop them—or if I even want to. I want him to use those rough hands to touch me. What? I do? I press my thighs together. Yes, I do. A wicked shiver runs down my spine and into the wet hidden spot between my thighs.

I blush. I need to focus.

My body feels unsteady as I climb down, my heart racing and a kind of anticipation I've never experienced before rushes through my veins. It's something I never thought I would experience, truth be told, since the best I could have hoped for was an arranged marriage with someone old or desperate enough to ignore my activism.

They would have held me captive for it, of course, and I would have hated them. I never let myself think of feeling something like this, and though part of me is saying I'm being stupid and that I don't trust him; the other part is screaming that this might be my only chance to find out what it feels like.

From the sounds of it, this Ree person is making a new version of containment and another ache shoots through me at the idea of recreating the same sort of injustices on a new planet rises, but I push it aside.

I'm going to die here. If I want to feel the pleasure my body is promising I will feel with Kuret, this is the time. Visions of how appalled my family would be try to bubble up, but I force them down, rubbing at my aching eyes as I do it. They lost the ability to comment, even if just in my mind, when they sold me.

So what if I don't trust him? If he wanted to kill me, he would have. It's like all those American shows I've managed to sneak watching. None of them trusted each other, they just got their pleasure and moved on.

Should I have other things on my mind right now? Of course. Am I likely to die tomorrow? Yes.

Resolves tightens in my belly right along with arousal. I will learn to defend myself.

I'm also going to get Kuret to touch me. The thought of it makes me groan, whatever the genali did to me surging along all my nerve endings as soon as I stop resisting it.

Now that I've decided to do both things, as usual, I can't make it happen soon enough. I push myself away from the cart, feeling like the predator now as I stalk behind Kuret.

27

Kuret

I refill our water, in case we need to flee quickly, then turn back to Nasrin. My breath stops midway through pulling it in when I see the look on her lovely face. She's no longer avoiding my gaze.

She looks... I don't know how she looks, but it is so intense my markings flare. I haven't felt like this since... ever. I have never experienced whatever this is, and I'm not sure if I like it. My head feels light and I blink rapidly.

What I said had an impact, and she's ready to learn to fight now. I swallow compulsively, almost feeling sorry for the hunters she will soon be decimating.

I feel tense as she approaches with a knife, my hand almost reaching for my own. My instincts are screaming out at me that there is heavy danger in the air right now, but I force myself stay still.

She holds it up toward me, her grip awkward. "Teach me how to hold this. Use your hands to move my body how it should be. We don't have much time, Kuret."

Her breathing is elevated, and it makes me realize mine is too. Those images that I keep trying to suppress of her white hair moving against my skin surge up again and my hearts start pounding.

I swallow hard, then move to do as she asks, hoping she won't notice the ever-increasing bulge of my erection, which I have to start ignoring or I'm going to have to adjust myself and all of this is awkward enough as it is.

I take the knife from her, listening carefully to our surroundings. A glance over to Roshan reveals that he's napping, which makes me feel a bit more settled. If I had to guess, he has a better sense of smell than I do. We've been downwind of where I killed the green hunter—the braceaaer—since we left. He was tense for a while, sniffing the breeze, before finally relaxing.

I turn my attention back to Nasrin. She still has that intense look that sends shivers down my body and makes my armor even more uncomfortably tight. She's much smaller than the females of my kind, and softer. My fingers twitch, longing to touch her waist again, and then I realize I've been given an invitation, and a good reason.

But, first, she needs to know where to strike. "The best places to slice are here and here," I tell her, pointing at my neck and wrists. "If there is no armor, make quick stabs for the chest and belly if you are standing, and the back of the ankles or knees if you are on the ground."

She moves her head up and down, which is her way of saying she agrees, and I assume must also mean she understands.

"If you are behind someone, the base of the skull is good for a stab or you can reach around to the throat to slice... if you are tall enough."

She wrinkles the small structure between her eyes, and I smile. I was initially taken aback by humans breathing from there, but now it's just endearing. Especially now that I know that it can convey emotions, though I'm not sure which one yet.

I take in a deep breath, and then move my body behind hers, still pulling in the air as I settle myself behind her and so her personal scent invades my senses. I take a moment to enjoy it, then bend my body down so I can place the knife in her hands, carefully rearranging it so she can take it in a firm grip.

I bite down on my tongue and taste blood when I imagine her with something else in that hold. I have to keep my hips away from her so I don't announce my struggles by pressing into the middle of her back as I move my arms so they are positioned to the outside of hers.

She shivers as my braids engulf her and my fingers wrap around her wrists, but she doesn't complain. I hope it doesn't mean she is still afraid of me. My hearts constrict at the thought, but then I get distracted for a moment, enjoying the way my braids have mixed with her long hair, before pushing all the unhelpful thoughts aside.

It doesn't work and I'm right back to looking. Light mixed in with dark, soft waves caressing war braids. The glide of her hair against my skin makes me ache to run it through my hands.

This is about our survival, I remind myself, not about how much I want to touch her soft body.

It's hard to remember that admonishment after I get her arms in the correct position and then move my hands to her hips. She's just as delicate as I remember, and now as I move her, I also realize just how flexible she is.

I clear my throat. "Keep your hips shifted this way so you provide a smaller target. Good, now move your body a bit lower and shift your weight this way so you can move more nimbly."

As I shift her to keep adjusting her stance, I move my grip up from her hips to help her feel the difference between her balance in different positions. "Does that make sense?" I ask as I tilt her weight a little too far forward, then reposition my hands to pull her back.

When I do, the heavy weight of her generous breasts pushes against me and she takes in a sharp breath. I let go of her, appalled that I have frightened her, but she grabs me with her free hand, moving it back to her body, once again right under her breast.

"Like this?" she asks.

It takes me a moment to understand what she's asking, since my world has narrowed to the feel of that soft weight, then I realize that she has moved her body back into the exact position I had her in.

I swallow thickly again, then answer. "Yes, that is correct. Then you can shift like..."

A groan tries to rise up when I realize I will need to press her up against me to best demonstrate how she can move from one stance to the next. My marks are flaring with my embarrassment as I pull her close, but she's right. We don't have much time.

28

Rin

Now that his hand is brushing the bottom of my breast, the only thing that's keeping me from turning around to see if he will let me kiss him is the unfortunate reality that learning this could save my life.

When he pulls me up against him, I almost give in anyway. It takes me a moment to remember that he is a lot taller than me, and then I register what I'm feeling between my shoulder blades. He's aroused... and big.

I'm panting as he takes me through different scenarios with his body, somehow still moving me gracefully through it despite how much smaller I am, but I force myself to focus. Even though his rough hands send shivers when they slide along the thin fabric of my black suit, or when his long braids brush against my face as he bends to rearrange my limbs.

It's easy to image how much my heart would beat in fear during an actual fight as it tries to gallop out of my chest with each new place he touches me.

By the time he stops and steps away from me I don't exactly feel like I know what I'm doing, but at least I have some idea of what to do. I'm no longer holding the knife like a complete amateur.

"That is much better, Nasrin. We will keep practicing."

I turn to him, just in time to see him rearranging himself, confirming that I didn't imagine that I made him just as hot and bothered as he did me.

It makes me even bolder than usual and I move toward him, closing the space between us again. His glowing eyes widen as I get close. I'm disappointed when I realize I would need a step ladder to try to kiss him. Instead, I reach forward, taking one of his braids in my hand, marveling at the difference in texture.

It reminds me of horse hair. Straight, thick, and even longer than the hair the genali gave me. I move my gaze back to his face. His eyes are locked on to where I have a hold of him.

"I like when you touch me, Kuret."

He takes in a shocked breath, eyes darting back to my face and his dark hairless brow furrowing. His marks are undulating and I'm convinced it means he likes what I just said. Really likes it.

He puts his hands on my shoulders and my heart leaps, hoping it means he is about to bend down and kiss me. Instead, he holds me in place as he takes a step back, then moves his arms back, tapping the back of his wrist with the fingers of his opposite hand.

"No, Nasrin. You are too young."

I narrow my eyes, then move my gaze down to where he is clearly trying to burst out of his pants. "I'm an adult. You want me, Kuret."

He taps harder this time. "No."

I open my mouth to ask why, but he whirls, his braids flying over my head, and he takes long strides away. If I didn't know better, I would swear he's the one afraid of me now.

A grin spreads across my face. His movements were saying one thing, but there was a question in his tone. As if he was trying to convince himself as much as he was me. He's being hardheaded, and it's... hot. I'm not used to thinking that about people, and it takes me by surprise, but I don't dislike it. Not in the least.

I let him stew, my lips stretching wider and wider as he walks around, moving things from one place to another, clearly off center, carefully not looking at me the whole time.

I settle next to the spring, practicing the slices and stabs he taught me, increasingly entertained by his antics. I've never had that effect on anyone before, and it makes me feel powerful. I just wish my eyes didn't ache so much so I could better appreciate it.

I keep practicing, deciding to give him space, while he fusses over Roshan, making sure he is comfortable and free of the harness for a while and packs and repacks our few supplies.

A sudden piercing light distracts me from my latest footwork practice and I wince. It's been steadily getting brighter, but the sun just now made its way through the canopy.

He must not be ignoring me after all, because he notices. "Are you hurt?"

"My eyes hurt. It's too bright."

"Really?"

There's a concern in his voice as he walks back over to me. There's another surge of pain and I double over, rubbing frantically at my eyes, then blinking rapidly, then rubbing again.

Then I feel his big hands cupping my face. "Let me see, Nasrin. You're going to harm yourself."

I groan as he tilts my head back, unable to open my eyes to look up at him. He gently feels around my face and as he does, the pain steadily lessens until I'm able to carefully open my eyes.

He slowly comes into focus. He's frozen, his big green eyes open wide, staring at my face.

My heart skips a beat. "What?" I ask as I raise my hands to feel for new patches of silver skin there.

"Your eyes changed."

My hands are shaking as I feel around for differences, but everything seems the same shape, though my face is wet with tears. "How?"

"They are fully black now instead of mostly white."

My stomach clenches, then I try to look up at the sky and hiss. "Is it brighter today? There seem to be far more colors and the light hurts."

Kuret glances up, the light clearly not affecting him. "No. It is still morning, so it is actually muted light."

I let out a huff of breath and rub at my newly sensitive eyes, longing for easy access to sunglasses, and annoyed with the reminder of how much harder everything is here.

How much I miss and might never see, touch, or taste again.

Tehlmar's eyes weren't like this, so I assume I'm changing because of that terrible creature who attacked Kuret.

It makes me feel sick. How can I have parts of such terrible people within me?

Kuret opens his mouth to say more, but we are both distracted by Roshan shifting uncomfortably, staring off into the trees.

"What—"

I don't get to say more before Kuret's hand is over my mouth. I instinctively squirm at first, but then stop myself. They both have better senses than I do and so I just relax into his arms, my heart beating for a much less pleasant reason than the last time I was in them.

He repositions himself so his wide mouth and sharp teeth are right next to my ear. "I can hear a hunter," he whispers. "The green one. Stay here."

I shake my head and point to where he left the gun near me. "Nasrin you—"

He doesn't get to whisper more because I deliver him a hard blow to the top of his thigh so he knows I mean it.

After a growl, he lets me go and I spin to face him. He's still bent over, so I position my mouth next to one of his three-spiked ears, my lips brushing against one of his many pieces of jewelry when I speak.

"They are as strong as you are, Kuret. We'll need a gun and you don't know how to use it yet."

I tip back, assuming he will whisper something in my ear now, but all he does is wipe a hand down the back of his other one. I'm surprised he agreed, but I don't say anything; I just move to scoop up the gun and follow behind him as soundlessly as I can. My hands are damp, but with a knife in one of them and a gun in the other, I can't wipe them off.

Roshan is shivering, his eyes wide and he doesn't follow us, which is another surprise, but also a relief. I hold my hands out to him, signaling for him to stay and feeling silly as I do it.

I'm not sure if it's the gesture I made or his own fear, but he doesn't move.

I follow Kuret as quietly as I can, periodically taking time to study the gun, wishing I had tested it when we first found it, though it seems to work the same as I expected. The shape is different, but not so much that I don't think I can use it.

Thoughts about how wrong it is that I'm even thinking about using it crowd my mind, but I keep following Kuret. He has his braids gathered in one hand and twisted so they don't make sound and a knife in his other one.

He stops periodically, tilting his ears for sounds I can't make out, then we keep stalking forward. Eventually, he motions for me to stop and then waves his hand downward, which I take to mean I should crouch. I want to protest when he keeps moving forward, but I bite down on my tongue.

He knows what he's doing. I hope.

A few minutes later, I hear the hunter. They are tramping along the underbrush, breaking sticks and muttering about insects and mud. I listen closely to anyone responding to them, but it only sounds like one person speaking.

Kuret moves through the underbrush and my heart leaps when I can't see him anymore, but I know I can't follow him. The sounds are much closer now. When I see a movement, I aim my gun, but it's so quick I can't be sure if it is the hunter or Kuret so I don't fire.

The gun Is trembling in my hand and I'm holding my breath when I hear an undulating cry and a thumping sound.

After a moment frozen in position, I scramble toward the sounds of the fight, hearing a bunch of thumps and hissing curses in the alien's language.

When I push through a thorn bush to get to them, they are grappling, the thing's gun is on the ground and neither one has the advantage on the other. I raise the gun, but they are moving so much that I can't be sure I won't hit Kuret.

After a moment of indecision, I tell my black suit to make a pocket, pleased when it actually listens, and stuff the gun in it, moving the knife I was holding to my dominant hand.

Allah protect me, I mouth, then I run at them, knife held up as Kuret taught me, headed toward the creature's back. Kuret sees me, eyes wide, and he strains to hold the braceaaer in position.

I don't hesitate, taking three quick steps and bringing the knife down in an arc, striking the base of the alien's skull. The impact sends a stinging pain up my arm, but I don't let go. Instead, I pull it back and stab three more times in quick succession before stumbling back, suddenly realizing I'm covered in blood.

I'm not sure if it is already dead, or if Kuret kills it by taking advantage of its surprise by ramming his own knife up into its chest and dragging it until entrails pour out.

I stumble back farther, my mind screaming out at me for doing something so... terrible.

My heel hits a root and I fall backward, landing hard enough to knock the wind out of me. Once I get it back into my lungs, I keep breathing faster and faster. Then I notice the blood-covered knife still in my hands and I fling it away, frantically wiping at my body to get the blood off.

I flip over just in time to start heaving, then startle when I feel a pressure on my back.

"You did well, Nasrin. Your first kill is always the hardest."

He pulls my hair back, twisting it behind me, taking the time to carefully detangle it from around my limbs before twisting it so it stays out of my face. Then he rubs my back as the heaving subsides. Once I am calm, he pulls me into his arms, pressing me against his chest and tucking my head into his broad shoulder.

One arm holds the back of my head, the other runs down my back as he makes a hissing sound through his teeth. It's odd at first, but quickly starts to soothe me.

"He was a worthy foe. So small, but so strong. Just like you."

I laugh mirthlessly. "I'm not strong, Kuret," I tell him with a raw throat. "I just totally lost it."

"I'm not sure what you think you lost. All I saw was someone doing what had to be done. What you gained was even more of my respect than you already had."

I let out a long breath, my shaking starting to subside. He's right. It was what had to be done.

There's a braid next to my hand and I shift so I can hold on to it, using it to help ground my mind, much calmer by the time he speaks again.

His body is stiff now. "I held you like a brother comforts another. It is a loss of honor," he tells me as he starts to move me off him.

"What?" I protest. "No, it was exactly what I needed. You didn't lose any honor. I thought we had moved past that."

He doesn't listen, just keeps moving us until he can place me on my feet. Then he takes a step back and my heart drops. I don't understand him, but I'm still too rattled to try to work through where I lost the thread of what was going on.

He didn't do anything wrong.

I shake my head, wishing for the comfort of human companionship and things making sense.

Instead, I watch a glowing alien rummage around the pack of another alien I just killed. Or he killed. We killed. *Ya Allah*, this place is going to drive me insane.

My mind is still scattered when I follow him back to Roshan and the cave, this time at a near run, though, unlike Tehlmar, he is careful not to outpace me.

When we get back to Roshan, I breathe a sigh of relief that he is unharmed. He initially runs to greet me, but shies away when I hold out a blood-soaked hand.

It makes my stomach roil again and I head straight toward the stream, no longer caring about modesty. I lie down in it and tell my suit to recede, then frantically rub my hands all over my body, desperate to get the green blood off.

Once again, I feel Kuret's hands on me, this time pulling my own away from my face and positioning himself over me so he can hold up my head with one hand and use the other hand to gently wash my face and hair.

The stream is just deep enough that I can mostly submerge myself and I spend another few minutes rubbing my hands together as he finishes washing my hair. Finally, reason comes back, and I realize that I'm naked and he's stripped himself down to just some rough woven not-quite-pants, which are currently getting soaked so he can help me.

The pants are odd, not covering the outside of each thigh so I can see the thrumming patterns, and I'm distracted by the leather lacing down his calves that lead to his bare feet. Now that his boots are off, I can see why they are domed in the front. He has thick black claws on them.

He's barely clothed and I just stripped myself naked. I might be bold, but such a sudden loss of modesty is too much, even considering my plans to get him to take my virginity.

With a hiss, I rise from the water, the suit covering me as I do it, then turn to him. My mind is panicked over what he will think of me now, even as I tell myself I'm being ridiculous. I had already thrown away all the rules.

29

Kuret

Her eyes are wide, their dark coloring a beautiful contrast to her white hair, which is very distracting.

I realize I have been kneeling here staring at her, not saying a word since she scrambled out of the water, so I clear my throat and avert my eyes from hers. The only thing I seem to excel at with her is making her uncomfortable.

Her brown-pink lips are pursed, and her eyes look a lot larger from this angle.

It causes an inconvenient stirring in my loins that makes me swallow thickly. I should not be thinking like this about a woman I am supposed to protect. I have tried to keep these intrusive thoughts out of my head, but all my efforts have been in vain.

She consumes my thoughts.

"We should keep moving."

Luckily, she doesn't argue, but I don't move yet, feeling weighed down in the water.

As much as I tried to not look, the memory of her naked body is seared into my mind. As I suspected, she has none of the hard planes and defined muscle of my species but is instead large stretches of soft flesh. Just waiting for me to press myself into it.

Then there was the patch of white hair at the juncture of her brown thighs, letting even someone as clueless as I know where to pleasure her. Males talk, and I have ears. One of their favorite topics late at night is how different it is to pleasure a female, compared to the pairings many of us have formed with each other.

I hadn't yet found my pairing among the males, though many assumed it would be with Samke. He was just a brother, though, and this... this is something far, far different. Something, if not forbidden, at least unattainable.

She said she liked when I touched her, though. I long to do so again. And again, and never stop. But it isn't right.

I make myself turn to the task of cleaning my own body, aware that she is still looking at me. Still standing there with that look on her face that I don't know how to interpret. Except that it seems like she can't decide about something.

"Kuret?"

"Yes, Nasrin?"

"I don't... I don't normally just undress like that."

I'm not sure why she feels the need to say it, especially since she has been more likely to cover additional parts of herself than necessary since we met, but I try to soothe whatever she is struggling with anyway. "I am sure that is the case, Nasrin. Though if you would like to undress, it is alright."

I bite down on my tongue, yet again, not sure why I had to add that. It has the desired effect, though. She is no longer looking so lost but is instead smirking.

"Is it? It seems to make you uncomfortable, but I could..."

As she trails off, the material creeps away from her wrists and I groan out a protest for leading us to this point before deciding it is best to simply get away as fast as I can.

As I move to get out of the stream, she shifts forward. I accidentally bump into her, and she loses her balance.

She lets out a yelp and falls toward the ground, but I am quick and I catch her in my arms long before she can get there.

Something is building and I don't know what it is or how long it will stay suppressed.

Rin

We stay there for a moment, uncomfortably close to each other while staring into each other's eyes.

I know it is a bad idea before I go ahead with it, but I allow my brain to be fogged by the moment and the longing look I think I see in his eyes.

One of his big hands is holding my back and I push myself forward in his arms and move my face slightly closer to his, then I get too shy to close the remaining distance.

The heat coming off his body is spreading to mine, radiating off from his body in waves and seeping into my pores.

Kuret is completely still for what feels like a full minute before his eyes widen dramatically and the warmth of his hand leaves my back.

I lean my face forward and I see him doing the same; our lips are a breath away from each other when Kuret stops and jerks back.

His eyes seem thick with passion. I shut mine and look away, heart aching from the rejection.

How am I reading this wrong?

I am a terrible mix of appalled and ashamed as I pull myself away from him and wrap both of my arms around my torso. I want to speak up and say something to let him know my actions don't mean anything, but whatever words I have are stuck in my throat. Embarrassment turns itself into a metal ball and sits deep in my stomach.

He speaks up first. "Do not take this wrongly, Nasrin. You are just too young, and I will lose honor if I do not stop this now."

His words hit me like heavy bricks, one at a time. Painful each time. What does he mean? Too young?

I could swear that he wanted this too. I know it in my bones. So why make up things about age differences?

Is he like those vampires people are swooning over lately? Thousands of years old while looking like they are twenty?

He looks just as young as I am.

I frown at him, annoyance replacing my shame. "Too young? What do you mean by that, Kuret?"

The words slip out with more anger than I intend, and he turns away from me. I have to know why his so-called honor requires him to kill things and make decisions based on my age. Why does he feel like he has the authority to tell me who I am old enough to kiss?

If he doesn't want to, he should just say it. Not blame it on something about me.

It reminds me too much of the oppressive regime I have spent my entire life living under, and I don't like it one bit.

"We don't know how much daylight we have."

He has his face turned away from me, like he can't bear to look at me for too long.

It makes me start feeling a little dirty, but I push it aside. There is nothing dirty about the way I feel or the things I want to do. I won't be made to feel that way ever again.

It's my choice, just like it has been any woman's choice, and I always hated when people judged it.

I know he is only trying to avoid me and that makes me a little more annoyed. I am not a child; I am an adult and I find it completely disrespectful that he is choosing to reject me based on something I'm not.

"Don't call me a child, Kuret. Just say you don't want me."

"I didn't call you a child and I... can't say that."

What? He makes no sense, and it makes me so mad I whack him as hard as I can on his shoulder.

It surprises us both when he stumbles, but then he looks back at me with a hiss before whipping an arm out and yanking me to him.

Kuret pulls me close, his hands wrapping around my waist as he squeezes me to him. I can feel the strong beating of.. two hearts? I shake my head, then let out a squeak when he lifts me up off the ground so I am face level with him, my legs wrapping around his waist without thought.

My heartbeat quickens to match his, and time seems to slow down around us.

I start to pull myself away from him, but he is still clinging to me, his eyes staring into mine. Our faces are in such close proximity that I can see the black striations in his bright green eyes.

His face lowers onto mine, and my entire nervous system starts to misfire.

I freeze as my brain recollects all the information about kissing that I have ever known. It is one thing to attempt to initiate it and not know what you're doing and another to actually do it.

He notices the apprehension on my face and sets me down immediately. "I am sorry, I forgot myself," he says after he has cleared his throat and starts to walk away, but I decide that I have had enough of the back and forth.

"What if I want it, but I'm just not very good at it?" I ask softly behind him and he stops in his tracks.

I expect a response, but I watch his shoulders drop with defeat when he decides against it and makes his way to the cart. I chase after him and repeat my question, louder this time.

"You are too young for me, Nasrin. Please understand," he finally says when I catch up to him.

I let out an annoyed grunt, and this seems to catch his attention. "I think you are using this age thing as an excuse instead of just outrightly saying that you are not attracted to me."

He turns around, his hair whipping in the wind, the ornaments clacking and tinkling. His brilliant eyes are wide, the marks against his dark skin flaring to show his shifting emotions.

I almost can't believe there was a time when I didn't find him attractive.

"That is not true, Nasrin," is all he lets out.

I stay locked on to his gaze, afraid to break the connection I feel between us.

I can see that he has more to say but will not unless I force the words out of him, so I speak again. "So what is the matter, then? Surely I am not that much younger than you, Kuret. I would say that we are pretty close in age."

His brow furrows in the middle, creating a wrinkle on the sides of his face that I have come to associate with him being annoyed, insulted, or confused. "How long into your life are you?" he asks me.

I want to say about twenty or thirty percent but can't bring up the words to properly translate it into his language. When I don't find a suitable word, an idea comes to mind and I dart out to pick a long blade of grass from the ground, then turn back to him.

I hold it out between us. "This much is how long I have lived." I mark a quarter of the length of the leaf to show him. "And this is how much is left." I raise my hand and wave the longer bottom of the blade of grass in front of his face.

He shakes his head in what looks like a poor mockery of the human movement, and my heart speeds up.

I plead with it to slow down, thankful that he cannot hear my heart going crazy over the fact that he has just mirrored my actions. Surely that means something? That he would study my movements and mimic them.

You don't do that if you don't care.

He points to the bottom of the blade. "This is when you are ready. You are still too young."

Hearing him say this again feels insulting—like he is infantilizing me—but I try to figure out where we are miscommunicating.

Because that's the only explanation once I push aside my pride. He has never lied to me.

I shake my head vigorously and throw the blade of grass away. "I am not living my entire life being aroused like this and unable to even touch you, Kuret."

He lets out a breath. "I want to hold you tightly against me and make you happy for as long as I possibly can, Nasrin. You do not know the torture it has been watching your beauty and not being able to say the things that I really think and—"

I don't let him finish. "Then why don't you say them? Why do you continue to pretend like you don't feel all the tension between us?"

I raise my hands up to my cheeks as I talk, exasperated, and also embarrassed that I have been so pushy with him.

My family would be appalled to see me acting so shameless.

Can't he see we can't go on ignoring this?

"Because you are far too young for a donor, Nasrin! You will die after it, and I couldn't live with it. I will live as far away from you as possible if it means that you get to you live your life and be happy."

I take a deep breath. "You have spoken about donors before, but I don't know what they are. Can you at least tell me?"

There is still so much I don't know about him, but I genuinely don't care about all that; I just want to know why he is torturing both of us this way.

He swallows thickly and I watch his throat bob up and down. Why am I finding such weird things about him attractive? Is this how these things work? I wouldn't know. I have never been around men outside my family I felt anything but anger and disgust around.

I have never had any crushes, and I told my family I would never marry and become one of the greatest teachers our country had ever seen.

Bābā would joke about how it saved him the stress of having to kill any man who looked my way. *Māmān* was much less happy about it, scolding *bābā* for encouraging my silly words and telling us that she wants grandchildren from me.

The memory of them saddens me again, but Kuret speaks and I divert all my attention back to him.

"There is one time in a woman's life when she sees a man. The donor is the man who she sees."

I frown. "I am seeing you right now, am I not? And you can see me, so what do you mean?"

The patterns on his cheeks start pulsing, which means he must be embarrassed, and his eyes meet mine for a split second before he looks away nervously.

This seems hard for him to talk about, I realize, but it is a conversation that must be had.

One of his hands goes to rub against his shoulder and I watch as the same green patterns dance over the skin of his exposed arms. "That is not what I mean. They touch each other," he places emphasis on the word *touch*, like I am supposed to understand what he means.

"You are going to have to give me more information than that, Kuret."

My hands are folded over my chest and my foot is tapping impatiently on the ground.

Kuret sighs again and presses his hands over his eyes. "It is the time when she wants his seed."

The words come out in a low grumble that I almost don't hear, but I piece together the words after a moment and it dawns on me that he is talking about sex.

I cannot blame him for having such a difficult time talking about sex like this, since my mind is trying to shut this conversation down, too.

But why would they wait their whole lives?

Sex education back home is nonexistent, and the best explanations of sex most women are given happen days before their wedding night, when the older women tell them all the ways to please their husbands. It is either that or they have conversations with their friends who were "defiled" before their wedding nights.

I step forward, reaching up to I place a hand on Kuret's face and he leans into it, his eyes finally meeting mine. "Kuret, at the end of my life, my body will have no use for the seed of any man. I will be too old then."

He looks down at me, his face a mask of confusion, but I don't care to clear it up. I just want him.

Kuret

Rin is gazing at me tenderly, but I am too distracted by the questions roaming through my head.

"I-I don't understand," I stutter and her gaze turns thoughtful.

I am extremely uncomfortable with this whole conversation but it's beginning to feel like it's not one that we can put off having any longer.

Taking a few steps away from me, she bends to pick up the discarded blade of grass. "Ideally, human women have children between these years—" She points out about a quarter of it and looks up at me to make sure I am watching.

I can tell she's doing her best to simplify the situation, but I am inexperienced in these matters.

Her gaze is averted quickly, and she lowers her fingers until they are at about half of the blade. "—and these years. After that, our childbearing years are over."

I don't tear my gaze away from the blade of grass because I am sure that she will see the sadness and pity I feel for her and the women of her race. My stomach tightens as I think of it. To be subjected to giving up such a large chunk of their lives to have children...

"It does not feel fair to give all of your life like that."

I too wouldn't want to be kept cooped up with others if my lifespan were that short. I feel bad now about having pushed the idea onto her with such consistency throughout our journey.

She shakes her head. "We don't all start having children at the same age. Some do earlier and some later. Eventually, the kids grow up and we get our lives back."

It annoys me how often I am disoriented by Nasrin's words, but she is always eager to explain, which helps take away the sting of ignorance. "Are human women capable of resurrecting from the dead?"

"What? No. What I am saying is childbirth doesn't kill us."

My jaw drops open, and then my mouth speaks before my mind stops it. "Does this mean that if you take my seed, you won't die?"

"I won't even get pregnant. There's a block in me against it."

We linger for a moment as the full weight of her words settles around us, both of us ignoring the steadily increasing wind as we stare at each other.

No longer running away from what's between us, but we are not bridging the gap.

There's no reason for me not to touch her now, but I can't seem to make myself move, my hearts hammering as the wind whips my braids.

I don't know how to pleasure a woman, and very few males have discussed it in depth, mostly just telling stories. Considering the act leads to a female's death, it isn't really something to celebrate.

No, that's thinking from a different life.

It's hard to believe coming here could bring any sort of blessing with it, but there she is. Standing right in front of me, just as beautiful as always, looking as scared as I am.

If she dares to face something unknown, then I can't continue to insult her by keeping myself away.

I'm taking a stride forward and pulling her close to me without conscious thought.

Once again my hands seek her waist, desperate to feel her softness again, this time letting them roam to her front and the lovely swell of her stomach, groaning when it's too much to fit in one hand, excited to know how it will feel to have my throbbing member pressed against it.

For now, I keep myself contained, afraid I will do something to embarrass myself.

Instead, I keep my hands moving, carefully watching her face to see if she doesn't like it. Her eyes are hooded and she moans, making me throb even harder.

I reach around her, pulling her close, no longer willing to wait to have her crushed up against me, grinding my hips forward into the softness of her chest as I reach behind her, quickly finding an even better hand hold on that delectable rear that has taunted me each time she walked by.

Jiggling and asking to be grabbed.

I squeeze each large globe, a groan rising, then I use my grip on them to lift her, and move my mouth to her own, just like she offered before and I was too hard-headed to accept at the time.

Not knowing what I know now.

Her lips are soft against me. Much smaller, just like the rest of her, but just as fervent in their movement against mine as my own.

When her tongue darts out to run against my lower lip, it surprises me, but then it sends a blazing surge of arousal and I want her to feel the same.

When I open my mouth, her tongue seeks entry, but I push back, not wanting her to get cut on my teeth, but enjoying the way her slightly rough tongue feels against the slickness of my own.

With gentle pressure, I invade her mouth as she tried mine, instantly understanding the appeal as the sweet taste intensifies and the hot opening makes me grind against where she has her legs wrapped around my waist.

Pleased to note how hot she is between her legs, I pull her higher so I can feel her against my stomach, her moist heat making my hips buck.

I accidentally graze my tongue on one of her teeth, freezing for a moment before I remember they are dull, then move a hand up from her soft backside up to the base of her head, using her long, thick hair to tilt her head back.

Then I explore her mouth, enjoying the vibrations of her moans against my tongue for a long moment before I lower myself to one knee, then the other, before tipping her down onto the grass.

I'm momentarily distracted by Roshan making a bleating sound and moving away from us and into the trees. Good.

I need to find out how she feels in other places. I take a long look at her face, pleased to see how swollen her lips are now, her eyes unfocused. When she tilts her neck to the side, I take it as an invitation, lowering my mouth to it, pressing my lips to it in different ways and taking careful note of which ones make her moan the loudest.

When I flick out my tongue, she writhes under me and it feels better than any kill I've ever made.

I need more.

Her hands are in my braids now, pushing my head lower as the black fabric disappears from her body.

She guides me to the large, soft swelling on her chest. I soak in the sight of her brown skin, and the much darker center of each before she pulls harder, guiding my mouth right to one of them.

A clicking laugh escapes and she huffs out at me in impatience, so I don't keep her waiting.

Remembering what she liked on her neck, I flick out my tongue and am rewarded with a high-pitched gasp I've never heard her make.

I keep going, growing drunk off the sound, but pull away. She growls at me, and I break into a grin.

"I love your softness, Nasrin," I tell her, and then give her other soft mound the same treatment, a hand reaching up to squeeze the other one.

Her hips twitch with each darting touch of my tongue, and I know where I am headed next.

I work my way down her stomach, pressing my lips into her, delighting in the feel of her under me, excited as I get close to the wet heat I felt against my stomach.

I push open her legs while I look closely at her face for any sign that she doesn't like this. All she does is pant, her eyes unfocused as she looks down at me, and I stop worrying about it.

She's more than willing to tell me to stop when she doesn't like something.

I take a moment to study her, appreciating the triangle of short white hair that points out where to go. Just like her mouth, her skin is pink and wet, just as inviting.

I lower my mouth to it, licking her, pleased when she makes another of her high cries of pleasure. She's just as sweet down here, though the flavor is more complex. Her wetness grows with each flick of my tongue.

No wonder the other males never fully shared what this was like. They probably spent the rest of their lives longing for it again.

Rin

I could have sworn he is just as inexperienced as I am, but there's no hesitation. Just an insatiable curiosity and a long black tongue that might kill me.

At first I was afraid of his sharp teeth, especially after I almost did something as stupid as pushing my tongue against them, but he has been so careful with me. Making me feel things I didn't think were possible.

Certainly not anything I heard about the few times other women spoke about sex.

I stop trying to analyze it when he pushes his tongue inside of me. Then he's back to flicking his tongue between my legs, each stroke becoming more and more confident the longer he spends with his head between my thighs.

A surge of embarrassment tries to bubble up at how large they look with his three thick fingers digging into them, but then he finds a place that makes me drop my head back and my world narrows to the quick movement of his slick tongue against me.

When he moves one hand down to hold me open, I lose all ability to reason. All I can focus on is how he is alternating pushing his tongue into my channel and flicking it up along my clit. His movements get faster and faster the louder my moaning gets.

Then something starts building low in my stomach. It's almost like a cramping, but far more pleasurable, but the more I think about it, the more it recedes. Kuret pushes my legs wider apart and I stop focusing on it, caught up in the thrill of his tongue entering me, my heart pounding when I feel the fronts of his sharp teeth against me.

He finds a place inside of me that makes my sounds turn into little inarticulate, high moans and twists his tongue against it until my legs are shaking.

A moment later, the ache in my belly explodes into pleasure that shoots up my body, stealing my breath as my body arches.

When I come back to myself, Kuret's looking down at me, pleased with himself. Like he just found the meaning to life.

Maybe he just did.

I try to speak, but nothing comes out. I clear my throat but realize I don't really have the words to describe what he just made me feel.

"That was amazing, Kuret."

He breaks out into one of his giant, sharp-toothed grins and my heart skips a beat. His patterns are glowing and I need to know if they extend over his whole body.

Plus, I want to make him feel that way.

I push myself up on my elbows, distracted for a moment by the way it makes my stomach look bigger, but then I dismiss the thought.

He seems to love my body, so what does it matter?

"Lay down for me, now," I order him, and he is quick to comply, his eyes wide and roving over me.

I leave his pants on for now, not quite brave enough yet to take them off, but I do straddle his stomach, and his eyes dart down to where my wet core sits against the hard planes there.

I run my hands along the sharply defined V that runs from his chest down to where our bodies meet, just as mesmerized to see the shifting flares of his marks as always as I run my fingers along each contour.

I lean forward, my long hair dragging against him, making him moan. I grab it in my hand, rubbing it over his chest until his eyes close, then lean forward so it's my breasts against him instead, putting my mouth on his smooth throat.

He hasn't grown a beard and I haven't seen him shave it, so I assume he only grows his long black braids.

I grab one of them in my hand, running the course hair through my hands until it reaches one of his ornaments, this one a small carving of an alien creature.

Then I put my mouth back to his throat, sucking until I get a moan from him, understanding now the look of triumph on his face.

How hearing one of those makes me want to hear many, many more.

I keep sucking, nipping at him, and running my tongue along the side of his neck, rocking myself enough that my nipples drag across his chest, moaning now myself.

His hands come up to grab my hips, taking over the speed of my movements, slowing me to an achingly unhurried speed.

I push against him, but he keeps the same pace. I bite down hard on his neck and feel a surge of satisfaction when his hip thrusts up toward me and he lets out a deep grunt, then a clicking moan.

Then I'm the one moaning when he shifts one of his hands and pushes a long, thick finger inside of me.

I tilt back into his hand, enjoying the stretch, though it occurs to me that it should hurt. Isn't that what everyone said it would feel like my first time?

Him pulling his finger out of me and pushing slowly back in makes the thought fly out of my mind and instead, I lock eyes with him.

I'm panting by the time he slowly eases back in the third time, then he moves his head up toward me to press those full, nearly-black lips to mine, the marks on his cheeks flaring in a mesmerizing sequence of flashing.

He moves his hand faster as his tongue enters my mouth, both keeping the same increasing speed until another orgasm washes over me and I'm moaning out into his mouth.

He catches me as I lose my balance. "That's right, my sweet Nasrin. Cry out for me."

He's holding me close now, stroking up and down my back, something about his bearing letting me know he'd be content to leave things here, pleased with himself to have given me pleasure.

Possibly still afraid he'll kill me if he takes his pants off.

Well, too bad. Because that's happening. I make my boneless body move, shifting myself down until I can pull at the ties to his pants, swatting his hand away when he tries to tell me I don't have to.

Finally, he stops resisting me and helps and I tip to the side while he takes them off, my eyes eating up the sight of his long legs. Once again, the muscles don't quite look right, but they are just as beautiful. Just as covered in the same bright green markings.

The striations seem to lead my gaze right between his legs, and I'm not sure what I was expecting, but I'm not the least bit disappointed.

He's big, of course, considering how much larger he is than I am, but not so much I think I might die.

When I reach out a hand and touch him, the markings there respond just like the rest of him, except here he lets out a hissing series of clicks that make me feel powerful.

Each stroke turns this huge male into a writhing, inarticulate mess.

Next time, I want to keep at it until I make him fall apart under me, but right now I want him inside of me more. I scramble back up to him while he's still moaning and then lean back so his nearly-black, ribbed tip is at my opening.

Then my hands start shaking and everything I've been told about how this will make me dirty and unwanted flits through my mind.

"Let's stop, Nasrin. You're scared," he tells me.

I shake my head. "No, I'm not scared. I just needed to let go of my former life."

"It's alright, we should just—"

I don't let him finish before pushing back against him, making him cut off with a long groan as my body envelops him.

I keep waiting for the pain, but it never comes, and after a long, slow slide I'm sitting on his legs, the full length of him twitching inside of me.

I look up to see his eyes glazed over, but still glued to where our bodies are joined.

Now that I have inside me, I'm not really sure what to do with myself, feeling suddenly self-conscious to be looming over him, so I run my hands along his skin, letting the pulsing patterns soothe my unsettled mind.

As I do, I start a slow grind against him, letting my body stretch to accommodate him at first, but then I realize just how good it feels to press him into my terminus, the slow movements of my hips building that feeling again.

Before long, my movements pick up speed, then pleasure bursts again as Kuret lifts his hands to my breasts, then holds me upright as I lose control of my body. Is that what an orgasm is like? Of course I had heard of it, but I had no idea it would be like this. From what women have told me, it isn't guaranteed.

Kuret

I will never tire of seeing that look of pleasure on her face and knowing I caused it. When she slid onto me with her wet heat, I thought I might die.

She stops shuddering and then her channel starts to squeeze me, and I lose that final bit of control I had that kept telling me to not spill my seed.

Before I think better of it, I'm moving her onto her back, spreading her legs wide and sliding myself out of her.

My body urges me to move faster, but I don't want to hurt her. I slide in again, my body shaking as I hold myself back, her body still tightening against me in waves.

She moves her arms up to my hips, digging her blunt little nails into me, wordlessly urging me faster.

I open my eyes, and look down at her, increasing my pace slowly, excited by the way each thrust makes her soft curves bounce.

I'm clicking out my pleasure in a long string as she moans.

"Yes, like that," she pants out.

I move the angle of my hips, searching for position that brings the most sounds from her. My pleasure grows as the harder thrusts send ripples across her.

Something is building in the base of my spine as I shift my body so I can grab each rounded globe on her chest in my hands, spurred on by her increased cries of pleasure at the contact.

The view of the flesh trying to escape the confines of my tight grip sends a thrill through me that pulls out that growing sensation from my spine and sends it rippling out, my hips pounding an erratic pattern as she lets out a wail of pleasure.

When I come back to myself, the guilt hits. "I'm sorry, Nasrin. So sorry."

She smacks a hand against my naked rear, shocking me into silence.

"Stop it. I'm not going to die, idiot. Now *kiss* me."

And so I do, at least for a little while before my instincts remind me that this place is deadly and we are naked.

She complains when I pull out of her, but lets me carry her to the stream so I can gently clean her, still enthralled by the softness of her body. Excited now that I don't have to hold back from touching her.

Rin

It doesn't take us long to get cleaned up. I enjoyed every minute of it, but once his hands are no longer on me, my mind starts to overthink everything.

I just had sex with him... and I'm not sure I even fully trust him yet. I mean, I guess I should, but when I search for that settled feeling of trust, it isn't there. Just like it shouldn't be. Right? From the way my chest constricts, my heart doesn't agree. The longing for trust might just be my undoing, but now I see my error.

Sex might not mean much for other people, and that's fine, but apparently I am not one of those people.

I don't feel guilty about losing my virginity, but it happening when there isn't trust makes me question if it was truly my choice—or if it was something the genali did to me. Suddenly, knowing that becomes crucial, but I don't know how to tell the difference.

I push the thought aside for now, following Kuret's lead to help us get out of the clearing, surprised that I didn't notice that Roshan had left or that I would need to call him back.

Hooking him back up to the cart helps calm my nerves and I'm able to put off thinking about what all of this means for now. What we are or aren't and if I am the type who can just move on now.

Before long, we are moving back along the path.

Roshan brays and steers us in a different direction. I turn to Kuret, wondering if he was the one leading him that way, but the expression on his face tells me that he is just as confused as I am.

I lean forward to talk to the argila but I hear a braying sound coming from a distance away, as if in response to Roshan.

Could it be another argila? That would be extremely unlikely given the circumstances, but with the way things have been going recently, anything is possible.

Kuret is doing his best to steer him away, but Roshan bolts in the direction of the sound, moving faster than I have ever seen, and we cannot stop him. For a moment, fear grips me—it could be a hunter or a predator with mimicking abilities, but as he starts to slow down, I realize that it was not a false alarm.

There is indeed another argila here.

Kuret helps me down from the cart.

I unhook Roshan before he tips over the cart in his excitement, then he scampers toward the lone creature, before halting nearby. Something about their differences and the way Roshan acts makes me think it's a female.

"Even bigger than he is. Interesting," he says, obviously amused by the situation, as he leans casually against a tree.

The strange argila really is much bigger than Roshan, on a general scale, but also has a more distended belly that makes her truly look like a furry spider with those odd legs.

Hopefully not of the type that eats males alive. Roshan seems to be entranced by her, though, rubbing his head against her short neck.

It makes so much sense why he was so eager to get to her. It's amusing to think about the way he bolted directly for the female. Seems like men are really all the same, regardless of species or planet of origin.

She seems to appreciate the attention until she catches me in her line of sight and starts to bray loudly. Her movements scare me off, and I take several steps back.

"Nasrin, be careful," Kuret hisses and I nod, chewing on my bottom lip.

I have a feeling that Roshan will not leave without his friend and I don't want to leave her either. He seems eager to help quicken the entire ordeal, so he pulls the cart toward me and nudges my hand with his nose, as if pushing me toward her.

Her bright yellow eyes are laced with confusion as she looks between us, but Roshan leads me to her and looks between both of us expectantly.

My heart swells with pride at how smart he is and I make a quiet promise to find him good treats as soon as possible. There has to be a reward for him being such a good boy. The female argila keeps its wary eyes on me the entire time. It is making me more than a little nervous, but I keep myself calm and maintain my composure.

"Hello," I murmur softly, reaching a tentative hand forward to pat her head.

Her eyes are glued to my hand, but the moment, I touch her head, her large eyes flutter closed and when I start scratching her she lets out a sigh of satisfaction.

Roshan makes a low squeal and stamps his many feet down on the grass a few times.

It's beginning to seem like I have a natural affinity for these gentle creatures. One time might have been a fluke, but this second occurrence all but confirms it for me. I chuckle lightly to myself.

I hear a sharp, hissing bark and turn around in fear, only to find that it is just Kuret, laughing.

It looks like something out of a horror movie, with his mouth wide open and sharp teeth jutting out. When he catches me staring, he stops laughing immediately, looks away, and clears his throat. "Roshan is really smart. That was admirable of him."

It sounds like he is trying to convince me that his laughter is not mocking, so I smile to let him know that it is alright. I was just surprised at how human, yet scary, that was.

As if to remind me that there is nothing normal about the situation I'm in. The alien spider-fuzz ball nuzzles her head against my hand and begins to nibble on my fingers.

She is encumbered in a way very similar to how Roshan used to be, with a rope strung through holes cut into her cheeks, then tied fast to a large tree. Being familiar with this, I quickly free her from the ropes and unhook her from the tree.

In a matter of minutes, I am done, though I don't want to risk removing the rope through her cheeks just yet. We'll have to build up some trust first.

The female argila bolts away from me, closely followed by Roshan.

I am standing there in shock, staring at both animals as they crash through the underbrush, and I don't notice Kuret moving forward until he is standing right beside me.

"Roshan will come back," he assures me.

Although I find his words reassuring, I can't help but feel afraid as I continue to hear them moving farther away. After the last couple of days we have been having, anything could happen at any moment. They could get attacked, trapped, or anything, but I swallow it down.

It's not like I can go running after them.

I sigh worriedly. "You are probably right, but I hope she does too. I would hate to leave her here for something much worse to find her."

Kuret makes a sound. "They will."

I stand there, staring into the dark forest for what seems like hours before I see the two argila skittering in our direction. I squeal excitedly and call out to Roshan, watching as he increases his pace, looking back to make sure the female is still behind him.

Even though I had no involvement in his sweet temperament, I feel like a proud mother watching him like this. Obviously, he loves me as much as I do him, and that is enough for me.

When they return, they nearly push me to the ground, demanding pets, and I giggle like a small child surrounded by puppies.

They seem completely enamored with each other and it pulls at my heartstrings.

While I am scratching the female argila, I confirm that the reins are disappearing into her cheeks, just like Roshan, and I bend forward and undo it. My fingers have gotten good at knots.

When I am finished, I loop the rope correctly and hook her to the back of the cart so she can follow behind us.

"She needs a name," I say to Kuret, and he makes a distracted sound of agreement.

I had forgotten how alien this behavior must look to him. I don't think his people are very familiar with the concept of using animals for anything other than work or food.

"Do you have one in mind?"

Looking at her, I notice that her blue coating is just a few shades lighter than Roshan's. If I had the patience to wait until morning before naming her, I'm sure I could find something more well thought out. I wouldn't want to be stuck calling her something I don't like for the remainder of the journey just because I rushed to name her.

Roshan can't seem to take his eyes off her, craning his neck to make sure she is well. This gentle gesture reminds me of a poem I once read about a man being lost in his lover's eyes like a sailor lost at sea. A name immediately pops into my head.

"Darya, I will call you Darya."

It seems to fit her perfectly. It makes no real difference to the argila what we call her, but I repeat the name, regardless, hopeful that she will start to recognize it like Roshan does.

Kuret's patterns dance on his bioluminescent body. "Darya," he tests the name on his tongue. "What does it mean?"

He seems mystified by the entire process I have gone through but is humoring me.

I see him still leaning a little to take the weight off his still-injured thigh, and my mood becomes more somber. It must be bothering him more after sitting for so long. He got that protecting us, and now we have even more responsibility.

I glance back at her. An even bigger target than Roshan. I'll need to figure out a holster for the gun, not just have it glued to my side with the weird black material.

The thought shocks me, but I know it's the right thing to do.

We climb into the cart again, with Kuret going first and then helping me up. As if I'm the one that got stabbed.

"Ocean," I respond with a proud grin on my face.

"That doesn't translate either, but it sounds nice. Gentle, just like they are."

I like how interested with the argila he has become over the course of our time together. I remember the animosity between them when they initially met. Look at them now, comfortable in each other's company.

Kuret steers the argila on the right path and our journey begins again.

We roll along in silence for a while before Kuret speaks in a quiet voice.

"May I ask a question?"

A surprisingly intense tone in his voice comes out of nowhere, considering the lighthearted tone of our conversation up till now.

I turn to face him, starting to worry about the sudden somber look on his face. I push my hair behind my ear in my usual nervous gesture.

"Yes."

"What made you decide to take off the covering from your head?"

It seems like years ago and I'm wondering why it's still on his mind.

I place my hands on my cheeks and stare blankly ahead at the swaying grass. The cool wind bites at me as I search my brain for an answer. Thankfully, I don't have to give one, as Kuret lets out a gasp.

"Is something wrong?" I ask, sitting up straight and he points to my ear.

There is no way to look at my reflection, so I run my hand up and down my ear, breath stopping when I feel three points instead of a rounded helix. I gasp and touch the second ear, finding out that they are the same.

Maybe I have been desensitized by all the craziness that has been happening recently, but I don't feel as bad as I did about the silver patterns on my skin, and definitely not as upset as when my eyes changed.

"They are lovely," Kuret says and I smile stiffly at him.

I can't say I like it, but it doesn't seem all that important in the big scheme of things, though I suppose this is the third change. Of many?

My mind is more weighted with thoughts of other changes that will start happening to me and what they will be. The more time I spend on this planet, the less I will look like myself.

That is frightening.

I hope I can look at my reflection and not hate what I see.

It isn't helpful, so I distract myself thinking about how good it feels to know I'm better at defending myself, even though what I want to talk about is what we did together in the grass.

I just don't know how to bring it up.

35

Kuret

Nasrin is lost in her thoughts, but her face doesn't look as upset as she did when I pointed out the silver patterns on her lovely skin.

I take it as a good sign she doesn't seem to hate these new traits, especially since they are from me. Still, she isn't pleased, either. As much as I want to tell her how much I loved touching her, there is a space between us now and I don't know how to close it.

Instead, I focus back on her ears.

Every inch of hers is asking for piercings; I wonder how much smaller each design would need to be for her dainty ears.

While she always looked beautiful to me before, now I find her stunning beyond all measure. I'm careful not to say too much so she doesn't become self-conscious and begin to cover up again.

Instead, I pick a neutral topic. "Does your species not have jewelry?"

She glances up at me, then to my ornaments. "We do, yes. I just never pierced mine. And I'm not used to seeing piercings on males, since it isn't allowed."

I touch one before I can stop myself. Does that mean she doesn't like them? It's hard to imagine something so important being forbidden.

Is any topic with her truly neutral? I grip the reins tighter, annoyed with myself.

"That sounded violent," she adds, noticing my expression. "I'm sorry. Wait. Violent? I'm trying to say something else, and it won't translate. What I mean is, I think your jewelry is really interesting, I'm just not used to seeing it. There's so many, all with different designs. Do they have a special meaning?"

My hands loosen on the reins. It's hard to stay upset when she doesn't even know what they represent. Odd, but understandable.

"They do." I turn my head and touch the rolled pattern near the top of my ear. "This one shows I am a cloister guardian. This is from my first kill. That one is the mark of my bond brother, Samke. That—"

She interrupts me. "Bond brother?"

"Our chosen brother."

She lets out a mysterious noise. "That must be nice. Getting to choose."

Before I can respond, her small finger lightly touches my ear, and everything narrows to that one sensation.

"What about this one? It's beautiful. I've never seen metal like that."

It takes me a moment to remember; the shiver makes its way down my body. And I have to clear my throat before speaking.

"That's for surviving my testing to be an adult."

"Surviving?" she says, her voice rough. I glance over and notice that the skin on her cheeks is darker than usual. "I just reached a certain age to gain adulthood."

"No test of strength? No time spent in the desert?"

"No, definitely none of that. Though, I suppose being called an adult didn't make me in more control of my life. So maybe it didn't mean all that much."

"Well, if you weren't tested then—"

She's back to touching my ear and I don't remember what I was about to say anymore. Her finger trails from the bottom tip up to the middle one, then up to the top.

"Why aren't these pierced?"

"I haven't earned them."

I open my mouth to tell her about the donor hoop and mentor cuff, but realize there is no one to grant them to me here. Or even make them. I suppose I just... earned one?

No, that doesn't seem right, although the memory of being inside her makes me swell again, but I ignore it.

I didn't think I'd ever earn a donor hoop, but this is the first time it's occurred to me that I won't ever be a mentor. My stomach feels tight for a moment, then I remember that I'm going to take Nasrin, and any other women I find back to a cloister.

Maybe I can mentor Ree's sons. Although, I suppose she probably isn't going to die either. The idea fills me with joy and the way I feel about Thivoll becomes far less complicated.

She strokes back down the outside of my ear, interrupting my mind trying to picture what they would look like.

I glance over to Nasrin. She's deep in thought again, this time while touching her own ear spikes. I hope we both live long enough to do her piercings.

That thought is enough to make my armor no longer seem too tight.

I distract myself by asking her to share what she knows about the argila.

Apparently it isn't much, but she lets me know that Roshan and Darya came from her former companion's planet; telling me all the horrible ways he treated the poor creature.

I am once again glad that I used much violence on him, but even more thankful that she does not see me as a brute anymore.

The day stretches on, and I measure the time until sunset using my fingers against the sky. Perhaps another six or so hours. The day is still young, but we still haven't gotten good rest. We are both tired, though I don't let it show; she doesn't need to waste her energy on me, even if I'd enjoy her attention.

The silence in the cart is peaceful, the argila communicate with each other in low bleats, as Roshan pulls the cart behind him. As if they have known each other for longer than a couple of hours.

I would have asked Roshan how he did it, got a stranger to trust him.

I wish it was not so tense when we first met. Now that we have gotten familiar, I can see all the warmth she is capable of sharing and it makes her mixed feelings for me apparent. She has been stiff since we climbed back into the cart.

Maybe she regrets it.

Then I think back to her fingers brushing my ear, and I feel hopeful.

We keep moving along and Nasrin moves closer and closer to me. Soon she is leaning up against me and I decide not to move, unwilling to interrupt something that is making both of my hearts pound.

The wind nips at my fingers harshly, and when we move past a small, rocky path, Nasrin falls against my shoulders and doesn't stir.

I adjust her sleeping form properly on my shoulder and will the patterns on my skin to stop dancing around so much. The green radiating from me looks beautiful against her sleeping form, and it's difficult to tear my eyes away and focus on the path.

I wonder who put these paths in and why they aren't in the area where I met Thivoll and Ree.

The cart rides on and in my peripheral vision, I catch a silver sheen. I make sure all my weapons are close, but when we get closer, I realize that it is a chamber like the one I saw in the ruins of the hunters' camp.

"Nasrin," I mutter, shaking her awake softly.

"Hm?" she says, yawning and stretching her arms above her head, half turning to face me as she does so.

I point in the direction of the silver chamber, and she turns to look at me with wide eyes. "It's like mine. A woman could be in there."

The excitement in her voice is reflected in my own chest and I slow the cart down a small distance away from it.

I hop down from the cart but hold a hand out in front of her when she goes to follow me. "Hold tightly to your weapon and stay close. This could be a trap."

She nods. I place my hand on the hilt of my knife cautiously. And we move ahead, her trailing behind me.

I scout the area ahead to make sure we are alone before walking to the *cryo chamber*. I am able to breathe a little easier after seeing that there is a person inside, although I am not sure if she is alive.

Nasrin pushes me aside, crouches in front of the chamber, and starts fiddling around with it. "We need to get her out. What if she's hurt?"

She is chattering to herself as her fingers look for a way to open the container, but I place a hand on her shoulder. "Ree mentioned it might be better to leave them in their chambers until they are in a safe place."

I relay the information given to me by the other woman, cautious so I don't somehow tamper with the pod or the woman inside.

Nasrin whips her head around to look at me, annoyance in her eyes. "Leave her? She could be dead!"

I sigh, wishing we were back in the cart with her warm, soft body pressed against me. Things are easier that way instead of constantly saying things she doesn't like.

I squat beside the pod and slide my hands over the glass top of the chamber to get a better view. "She is breathing fine. She is alive," I try to assure her, but she is not eager to listen.

Her face screws itself into a disapproving frown and my hearts beat faster in unison. We are about to have another one of our disagreements. Again.

She shakes her head vigorously. "When I woke up inside this thing, I couldn't breathe. I thought I was going to die, Kuret. Do you understand that?"

Her face is a deep red, and the hair on her brows is down.

"That does sound terrible, but Ree seemed to have more experience with these sorts of things and I wouldn't want to mess anything up. Maybe you are not meant to wake up while you are inside of it."

It would explain why the woman is sleeping peacefully. Her green hair is splayed around her hands, covering a good deal of her naked body. Clearly another woman like Nasrin or Ree who has been brought here against her will.

I don't let my eyes linger on her form, uncomfortable with how vulnerable she looks and not wanting to be disrespectful.

Nasrin sits on her legs and stares hopelessly at the chamber. "Why did Ree say that, then?"

I rub my hands along my marks, thinking. "I only recall her telling me that it would be best if the women who have not already gotten out stayed inside."

She stays silent and I start to get increasingly worried. Regardless of the fact that we are not directly in the way of danger, I need to find somewhere for us to rest soon.

"Nasrin, we need to leave."

She turns to look at me with great sadness in her eyes and I feel my hearts drop. If I could, I would take all this pain from her and bear it myself.

When she speaks, her voice is low. "I know why Ree asked them to be left in there."

I open my mouth to ask why, but she beats me to it. "So that they don't end up like me."

I crouch beside her again. "What do you mean, Nasrin?"

She points to her ears and her sleeve slides up. "We are not supposed to leave the chamber until we've been sold. Once we leave it, we start changing. I guess based on who we are around."

It all starts to make sense to me. The first trait she got was the silver skin, like her dead companion Tehlmar, and then eyes from the dead hunter, then her ears started to look like mine. It also puts into perspective the reason why Ree got hers.

"All this because of the genali," I growl out.

I love her qendi traits, especially that they come from me and not another male of my kind. Though what is happening to her is a terrible thing to do to another person.

I get on my feet and help Nasrin up. "We should head out, find another place to rest for the night, and decide when we are not so exhausted."

She agrees as a yawn leaves her.

I carry the heavy chamber, glad I don't have to move it far, place it in the corner of the cart and climb in. I help her up and we settle into the cart.

Roshan and Darya start moving and I steer ahead, keeping my eyes out for a good place to rest.

Nasrin stares at the woman inside the chamber, her hands resting on the glass.

I can only imagine how she feels. It can't be easy—she understands all too well what this other woman has endured and what she'll face when she wakes up. It must feel like looking at a mirror image of herself.

It is dark and there is a nagging pain behind my eyes. Desperate for rest, I search for a spot with enough cover then divert off the path into a dense, bushy area, glad when I see a large rock.

We go around and I scan the area, deciding that we will rest here for now. "Nasrin," I call out to her, but I don't get a response.

I turn to look at her and see that she has fallen asleep, holding onto the *cryo chamber*. "Nasrin, I found a resting place," I jostle her gently and her eyes blink open.

She looks around us in confusion and rubs her eyes. "We've reached Ree? Where is she? I have questions and some demands."

She shuts her eyes again, face resting on top of the chamber, and I laugh softly at her.

"No, we have not, but soon," I say as I help her down and begin to carry the rest of the things from the cart.

I place her in a corner with the *cryo chamber* and watch her curl up to it and go back to sleep. I am reminded once more how beautiful she is when she isn't upset with me.

No, she is beautiful then, too, though not as alluring as when I am giving her pleasure. I long to do it again, but since she hasn't brought it up, I assume she must not want to think about it again.

It makes my hearts hurt.

I leave Roshan and Darya free to graze while I hide the cart behind a thick strand of bushes.

As I move back to the rock, I feel eyes on my back.

When I turn around, I don't see anything or hear anything. Maybe it's the exhaustion and the constant sense of danger.

There's no one to trade off duties with and I miss Samke again with another sharp pang. I hope he survived.

Still, I can't shake the feeling of being watched and I decide to make myself feel better by going around to take a look. My search doesn't prove fruitful, so I lay down next to Nasrin, sharing my warmth with her. She lets out a long sigh in her sleep and moves closer to me.

I lay next to her, thinking, with one hand tight on the hilt of my knife. Should the need arise, I will be ready.

36

Kuret

I don't sleep long before coming out of a dream of a green monster attacking, my hearts beating with my panic as I wake up. I listen closely, but can't detect anything and the argila go back to calmly napping after giving me a long look.

It must be safe, and I take long breaths, trying to calm down, but sleep feels pointless now. I decide to get up and patrol.

Moving as quietly as possible, I shift, but Nasrin stirs. She startles awake, eyes wide instantly, likely also remembering the attack that led to my own nightmare.

"There is no danger," I assure her, clicking to help calm her.

She pulls me close and I rub my arm up and down her back until she stops shaking. "I am going to patrol, then clean up."

She clears her throat, with sleep heavy in her voice as she speaks. "It's cold for a stream bath, but I'd like that too."

"Wait here for now, I'll be back," I tell her as I shift to standing.

It doesn't take me long to check our surroundings. Everything is peaceful., The argila hum softly while they cuddle up together. For a moment, they stir, then settle back into their dozing.

I take the time to remove my armor, propping it next to the green-haired female's chamber.

"Come, Nasrin."

I hold a hand out to her, pleased when she takes it, and lead her to the stream. When we get to the water, it strikes me just how used to bathing in it I have become, remembering the sand scrubbings I used to give myself in the past. We always had plenty of water, but not enough to waste on daily bathing.

But Nasrin's hands on my back pull me from my thoughts. Her fingers trail along my muscles, reaching around to the tie at my waist as she moves in front of me.

May I?" she asks, her breath coming even faster now.

I'm thankful I left my armor with the argila, my member already swelling in anticipation. "Yes," I grit out.

Then I moan as her nimble fingers undo the knot, brushing lightly against my already engorged flesh, hissing as the material runs down it and pools at my feet. Her hands are around me next as her black suit fades, revealing her lovely brown skin.

She moves closer to me, still holding me tight and placing my length between her breasts, her wide, black eyes staring up at me. I groan, and then move a hand to each of them, lifting their fullness and then pushing them together so their soft warmth surrounds me.

She moans as she lets go of me, instead reaching around me to hold on to the flexing muscles of my rear as I push myself between the glorious pressure of her globes. When I feel that pressure building in my spine, I slow down, not wanting it to be over, especially not before I make her cry out her bliss.

In one swift movement, I lift her, moving both of us into the deeper pocket of water, the shock of the cool water enough to help keep me under control. I quickly wash myself, using some of the grit from the stream bed to scrub off my sweat, then take my time washing her.

Her moans start up again as I massage her scalp, which become louder as I knead her hips, breasts, and the inner parts of her thighs, then I lift us just as swiftly out of the water as I took us into it, eager to have my head between them.

I lay her gently on the long grass, but she repositions herself right away. "No, it's my turn this time."

I'm not sure what she means, but I let her push me down, although I'm not quite sure I could resist her.

When her tongue strokes its way up the length of me, all other thoughts drop away. When the wet heat of her mouth covers me and tugs me as she moans, I lose control of my limbs. She can do anything she wants to me, I'd welcome it.

She somehow situates herself so her large breasts are around me again. Only this time her mouth is sucking on my tip, pulling my already weeping seed from me and opening her mouth to let it flow between her breasts.

Soon after, she repositions herself so she can better rub herself along me. All the while, the weight of her breasts hitting my tightened testicles by the end of each stroke.

I want her to go on like this forever, but I can't hold out much longer.

"That feels so good, Kuret," she moans and I almost lose control.

Before I do, I grab on to her waist. Pushing her up so her wet heat is lined up to take me, I pull her down onto me as my hips thrust upward. She throws her head back, crying out, her long white hair leaving wet trails along my thighs as I pump up into her.

"You take me so well," I hiss out, my eyes following the bouncing movements of her nipples.

My fingers dig into her soft waist as my eyes dip down to where our bodies meet, my dark skin disappearing into her lighter brown flesh. Two more thrusts into her and the sight of it is too much for me. I'm fighting to keep control, slowing us down when she cries out and her muscles contract around me.

It tips me over the edge and I let out an undulating war cry as I release inside of her.

When I come back to myself she is laying on my chest, her body still wrapped around me and we are both panting.

She lets out a laugh. "I read about that *online*. You really can learn anything on the *internet*."

I am not sure what she's talking about,. It's been quite a journey for both of us and soon she goes limp on top of me, her breathing letting me know she's sleeping.

I listen carefully to the sounds of the *forest*, but can't detect any dangers, thankfully. Too exhausted to stay awake, I wrap my arms around Nasrin and drift off to sleep.

37

Rin

When I wake up, it's still dark. The light from Kuret's chest is comforting, as is the warmth of his body, but the back part of my body is cold.

I turn my head away from him, waiting for my eyes to adjust to the darkness so I can see the sky clearly, but a faint glow lingers.

I blink, trying to clear my vision. His markings have never been bright enough to affect my sight—at least, not until now. Especially since my night vision has improved so much since my eyes turned fully black. When I move my hands up to rub my eyes, I notice the same green glow I get when I am near Kuret.

A surge of awareness goes through me. I've changed again.

With a poke to Kuret's rippled side I finish waking him. He grunts, stirring to life faster. "What is it?" he grouses at me.

"What's on my face, Kuret?"

His eyes fly open, his upper body partly rising before he freezes. Then one of his deadly looking smiles spread across his face. "Nasrin, my Nasrin. They look beautiful."

"So I really do have your marks?"

He nods as he wipes a hand across the top of his other one. "On your cheeks, yes, though the color is not quite the same. It's fascinating."

"How do you ignore the light from them so you can see?"

His grin drops a bit. "They have been on me since birth, Nasrin. I don't know."

I sigh, letting it out in one big breath, dropping the topic. There are worse changes in my body. This one might prove useful. Maybe?

We get up, making our way back to the argila, who are still peacefully laying in the same spot. We're still tired enough to quickly fall asleep again, wrapped up in each other's arms.

The sun is just starting to rise. When I open my eyes once more and I feel more rested than I have in a long time, definitely since I've come to this alien planet. I sit up and look around me.

Has it been hazy before this and I just hadn't noticed?

The sky is green and purple with a blazing sun, but it doesn't feel hot against my skin. In a different place, and in a different mood, I might have called it beautiful. Now, it's just blinding.

Oh, right. I remember now. I got new eyes, which see better in the dark, more colors during the day, but are light sensitive. More pain is the last thing I need. This place has too many discomforts as it is.

The events from last night play in my head, making me suck in a gasp and turn around. "*Alhamdulillah*, you're still here," I whisper in relief to the other female when I glance at her green hair and quiet sleeping form.

It wouldn't be surprising if someone managed to take her while we were asleep after our little trip to the stream last night.

Especially given how we have lain more in the open than we usually dare to up until now, we have set up camp not too far from where we found the other woman, with a large rock being pretty much our only protection from the elements and any potential predators but I know Kuret was watching and that let me sleep soundly.

I continue to stare at her still body, jealousy and pity mixing together in the pit of my stomach to make an annoying new feeling. I don't know whether to be happy for her that she has not yet started to experience the insanity that is this place or to be sad about the confusion that will overtake her every single waking hour, so I settle on looking away.

I can only do my best to ease her into the whole situation and make sure no one takes advantage of her the way Tehlmar tried to take advantage of me.

We owe her that, at the very least.

I stretch my hands over my head and let out a long yawn, then walk toward the cart. As I get closer to the cart, I spot the rest of my crew—and finally, Kuret.

He is shirtless and looking down at his stomach, arm and shoulder muscles rippling in a way that makes my heart leap. I'm aroused, but it occurs to me that it isn't the overwhelming arousal that I had before.

I see him much differently now and I don't know how I feel about it, especially since almost no time has passed since I was convinced he was a psychopath. Is that what happens when you have sex with someone before you are really sure of them? You get all mixed up inside? I hate it.

He has shown he can change, and I cannot deny my attraction. Like an aching that only he can soothe.

Is it real, though?

They did something to me, and I'm not sure that my body can tell the difference between somebody I like and somebody I'm stuck with.

For now, I push the thought aside. I'd rather continue to bask in my ignorance than start digging into what should not be. For now, I'll just wait and see if this longing fades.

Turning away and on to different things, I clear my throat to get his attention and I hear Roshan and Darya racing toward me, their collective low braying tickling my ears. I laugh as they jostle me and I try not to fall over from the sheer size of both of them, my hands going to scratch at their fur.

I try to look past them and see what Kuret is doing, but they keep blocking my view. So I continue to pet them until they calm down. Spending time with these two is something extremely therapeutic; they help me let go.

Time to stop overthinking things with Kuret. My body can keep saying all it likes, it's my mind that chooses, and I just need to get to know him better, that's all.

"You look brighter," a voice calls from behind me and I jump then relax on seeing my tall, glow-in-the-dark companion behind me. "I take it you slept well."

There is a marked lightness to his tone. I can tell he is still proud of himself for having found the other woman yesterday. And that he should be.

I smile at him. "I feel much better, yes."

I don't realize that he is moving the chamber until he drops it in the cart.

I glance over to see the argila nibbling on him and it helps loosen some of the fear and pity. I can't do anything about it, so I let it go.

He's looking at me with a softness in his features, his mouth opening and closing like he's searching for the right words.

He finally settles on something. "I'm sorry, Nasrin. I wish I knew how to stop these changes; I can't imagine how terrible it must feel to not know what might come next."

I swallow hard. "Thank you, Kuret."

Oddly enough, his simple statement makes me feel a lot better. Then it hits me why. Ever since I was forced to live with my brother's family, all I've heard is that I should just accept everything. What happened was my own fault.

No sympathy.

I hadn't realized just how starved I was for it, and it's strange getting it from someone I thought, at first, had room only for violence. I've been hasty in my own judgments, and I should know better. It makes that aching longing to trust him rise up again, right along with the anxiety, but this time I don't stamp it back down right away.

He is a completely different species. We aren't even on Earth. Maybe it's time to let go of all those things I learned in the past to keep me safe. They might not work here, for one thing.

See, it's logical. I snort out a breath. There's no sense in lying to myself. I will be seeking the same sense of security I felt as a child with my parents for those few short years before I knew what violence was for the rest of my life. I will never stop longing for it.

Maybe it's time to stop pushing everyone away and find out if he is worthy of my trust. I gulp, my heart pounding in fear, but also in anticipation. In hope. I open my mouth to tell him about it, but then close it with a sharp crack.

That's one step too far right now, and that's alright. I'll just have to work on opening my heart up, even if it is just a tiny crack for now, and either build that confidence... or he'll destroy me. Either way, at least I won't be giving in to fear. I've done enough of that for a lifetime.

I feel lighter when I move toward him. As I walk, I realize that my ankle pain has disappeared completely, as well as the pain in the other parts of my body.

He also seems to be moving well. "Is your leg feeling a lot better? My injuries are healed."

His lips lift at the edges. "Yes. It is mostly healed, which should have taken many weeks. It wasn't just our imagination."

I start being thankful to the genali, a habit ingrained since childhood. My hand goes up to push my hair behind my ear and I remember that it is stark white.

All the appreciation goes out of me; I doubt giving us this ability was a kindness.

"Your pain is gone?" he asks. "You look less rigid and I am glad."

I smile up at Kuret. "Yes, it is."

He starts to smile back but stops himself, probably remembering my reaction the last time he did. Guilt surges. I haven't been fair to him.

"I like your smile, Kuret," I assure him.

When it blooms, his sharp teeth showing in a wide grin, far wider than a human could ever produce, my heart confirms my words. It no longer looks scary and I love the way it shifts the patterns on his cheeks and how they surge with his joy.

"I am glad. We should get going now. I scouted the area earlier and I think I found a way to get to Ree."

He seems excited about his discovery, and it makes me feel even more enthusiastic about the day. Maybe things won't be so bad. It makes me cautiously optimistic, like things are finally starting to go our way.

Meeting up with the woman named Ree has been Kuret's plan all along, and the fact that we are moving forward makes me feel a spark of purpose.

Even if I don't feel like I've contributed much so far. I need to change that. My mind carefully ignores stabbing into that green hunter. It isn't a contribution as much as a crime. Maybe? I don't know. This place is confusing my sense of morality.

I glance at the gun I left in the cart instead of keeping with me last night. The urge to fight my discomfort about it and the memories it stirs up from another life, became dominant and that was stupid. Sure, I slept with the knife nearby, but realistically, I won't be able to use it much.

Not unless Kuret holds everything still while I stab it, and that doesn't seem practical.

Today I attach the cart to Darya, hoping to give Roshan a rest. He doesn't want to follow behind and positions himself in front of her.

I climb into the cart and make sure the gun is in easy reach, ignoring the pounding of my heart at the thought of touching it, even though I held it in my hands yesterday. The mind is so fickle.

Before we set out, Kuret hands me some remains of some creature he roasted. "How long have you been awake?"

"I woke up when the sun came up as well, not all that long before you."

If he did all that, then he's just trying to make me feel better.

The sudden thought that he might have seen me sleeping in an embarrassing position sends a blush creeping up my face, but I wrestle it away quietly.

I'm still trying to figure out a topic of conversation that won't make my cheeks flame when the path gets more rutted.

Soon after, we get to a ridgeline that is almost too slim for an argila to walk along. I use one hand to hold on to the edge of the cart for safety, and another to hold the chamber. But Kuret suggests that it might be better to put it between us. "Our bodies will act as a shield so it does not fall out."

I agree but the path is still too uneven to make any changes without falling off.

Kuret tries to make sure that Roshan and Darya go through smoothly all the while holding onto the chamber, until a sinkhole suddenly forms behind us.

I hear Kuret mutter something under his breath as the chamber starts to slide down the back of the weathered wooden cart. I reach both of my hands out to grab at it and catch it just before it falls off the back.

"Nasrin, are you alright?" he asks me, and I grunt out an answer.

The strain is hell on my back. My arms burn as I struggle to keep the chamber in some semblance of stability and somehow I succeed.

With a low bellow, Darya pulls us up and I get the chamber moved back into place.

A moment later, it occurs to me that I shouldn't have been strong enough, but I don't have time to figure out the reason.

Poor Darya is struggling to pull the cart through the rapidly crumbling ridgeline, and it's clear she's not having an easy time. I want to reach forward and tell her it will be okay, but I am still trying to get both me and the chamber steady.

This delicate balancing act is taking far more energy than I would have thought, but somehow I continue to manage it.

"Pull yourself up. Take my hand," Kuret calls down, his voice a bit louder than the argila's braying but still strong enough to reach me. He stretches out a three-fingered hand and I grab onto it, letting him pull me up.

At the same time, Darya pulls hard, with Roshan urging her on, manages to get the cart out of the rut it was stuck in.

I am still pulling the chamber forward when the back of the cart falls into another hole that wasn't there before, and the chamber slips out of my grasp. "No!" I exclaim, clawing at the empty air in a desperate attempt to catch it.

I watch as the chamber falls into the sinkhole like a heavy stone in a stream. The cart follows close behind, getting caught on a jagged outcropping along the inside wall.

Kuret leans down, trying to grab it and find enough leverage to lift it out, but it's no use. Without hesitation, he decides to climb in himself to retrieve it. I express my objections, but he waves away my concerns and lowers himself down into it.

After our impossible attempts at getting the cart unstuck, we both freeze when we hear a wet, honking sound.

Jumping to my feet, my eyes meet Kuret's and he has the same panic in his eyes.

He looks ahead as he hops off the cart, his body going tense, and eyes wide with realization. "They are close. I will go and try to hold them off."

He doesn't let me speak before screaming a battle cry and running ahead with one hand on the hilt of his blade and a large stick that I hadn't seen him pick up in the other.

"Never again!" he bellows out as he charges.

And with that, he's gone.

All the commotion is too much for the argila, who start bleating and trying to move away from the rut where Darya's stuck. Roshan bites desperately at the straps holding Darya.

I hop on the back of the cart and climb forward until I reach the point where the harness is, then try to undo the knots, but my hands are shaking too badly.

I hear the honking getting closer, and I look up furtively.

Kuret's hair is a swinging blur in the distance, and I watch him punch an arm right through one of the genali.

I wonder where the rest of them are, but then a bullet hits far too close to us, clearing my mind of any questions. I give up on the knots, grabbing my knife and slashing at the straps connecting Darya.

"Run! Go protect Darya!"

The argila race off before I am even done with my sentence. Understanding my message, Roshan heads straight for the female, while another projectile whistles close by and buries itself in the ground by my foot.

I let out a yelp and scurry away.

He brays and pushes his nose against the female argila to get her to move faster before running off behind her.

I exhale, grab the gun, and jump down from the cart, crawling forward on my stomach in hopes to stay hidden. I'm beside the cart and in the path of the crack in the ridgeline. And I look inside it, gasping in relief when I see the green-haired woman's chamber not too far from me.

Then I watch in horror as the shale shifts again, nothing about it looking natural. With nothing to hold her chamber from falling down the ridgeline, the chamber tips, crashing against rocks and flipping before disappearing from view.

I crawl forward on my forearms and try to take a better look, my heart sinking when I see part of her body hanging out of the container.

It means that it is broken, and she's officially in enough danger I can't just leave her there while we fight.

My mind starts to race at all the complications of her being out of the chamber, but a bullet buzzes past my head, and brings me back to the fact that a battle is happening around me. I hear Kuret cry out, but it's not one of pain, so I focus my energies on the green-haired woman.

Another bullet buzzes past and nearly hits me, but I roll out of the way and get on my feet. I try to find a tree to hide behind, but all of them are too far away. So I grip the braceaaer's weapon and hold it out in front of me. Fear fills my heart as I hold it up and shoot into the void. Hopefully, I don't mistakenly hit Kuret.

A honking laugh and another shot follow, but thankfully I am able to hear the direction it is coming from and start moving. I'm not fast enough as a searing pain shoots up my side while I roll away and my back hits against the side of the cart.

The wind is knocked out of me, but I hold in the cough that threatens to come out and lay still. The pain is extreme, and I hear a wheeze escape my lips. I hope nothing is too severely damaged; the pain is nearly blinding. From the corner of my eye, I can see a genali hunter starting to make his way toward the crack in the ridge, so I push myself onto my stomach and start dragging myself toward the green-haired woman.

There is a shot and two wet screeches followed by a familiar grunting and the genali moves to a different location. Kuret must have taken one of their guns and figured out how to use it.

While the genali are distracted, I shift quietly, biting my bottom lip to suppress the pain, trying to get my body into the trench that the shale made as it slid down. I hope to use it as cover as I make my way down to the broken chamber.

There are more screams and the genali runs to hide beside the cart and I push myself deeper inside the trench.

My hands shake as I raise the gun, everything in me screaming that what I'm about to do is wrong, but I ignore it. The slime raises its own gun, probably in Kuret's direction, and I stop thinking about it and pull the trigger three times.

Two of them hit, and the genali lets out a scream that pierces right down to my soul before sinking down into a puddle.

Tears blur my eyes, but I hiss at myself. "Stop it."

My need to protect the woman far outweighs questions of morality. Kuret is doing what he can, but it's up to me to save her.

I'm pushing myself up to look for other targets when the ground suddenly gives way beneath me. A scream escapes as I fall, the breath knocked out of me when I hit the hard ground. Shale tumbles down, covering me for a moment before I roll away from it.

I keep rolling until rocks start hitting me, then force my eyes open, choking on dust as I try to clear my lungs. When the air clears, I can see that I am in a long passage. From the tug of gravity, I can tell it descends. The walls of the tunnel have odd striations, like the stone has been cut with something. I must have fallen deep enough into it that it's solid instead of shifting shale.

My throat starts to tighten from the small space, but I force myself to stay calm—this isn't the time to panic.

Then I notice a light down the long tunnel and catch a glimpse of green hair. I don't know how, but she's down here with me. I hear a few screams coming from behind me and work to get breath back in my lungs so I can get to the trapped woman.

38

Rin

I hate small spaces.

They pull me right back to being a little kid, with only fragments of the memory left in my mind. But I still remember the fear in my *māmān's* eyes as she pushed me inside our two-foot pantry, where my *bābā* locked us in to keep us safe.

There were always threats of violence, but we lived in a relatively safe area. So we had gotten complacent, and the crisis took us by surprise.

As I finally pull a breath in, and cough it back out, I'm hearing *māmān's* whispered prayers and the sounds of violence. I can't move into a fetal position and cry right now like I did then.

A honking laugh in close proximity to where I am brings my mind snapping back to the situation. A genali is leering down at me, and my arm is raising the gun without any thought.

A moment later, there's a hole under his left eye and he's falling. I roll to the side, eyes screwing shut as I wait for him to fall on me.

I hear a wet thud and open them again.

A few inches from me lies a genali corpse—a gray and pink, mushy mess that turns my stomach. Seeing this, brings my deep-seated rage bubbling from within, and I spit at the corpse in defiance.

I retch and look away. Should I try to climb back out, or go down the underground passage to get to the woman? I can't decide. My mind goes to Kuret and I wonder how he is doing or whether he needs any help. But the emerald color of the woman's hair reminds me of Tehlmar's limp head in Kuret's hand and I realize that I am worrying in vain.

He can take care of himself, especially if he has a gun now.

Kuret can handle the *haroomzade* while I do my best to save this woman. The cracks in the rocks are tearing away at me and I hold in a curse when one sharp piece of shale slices at my face. It is a kind treatment in comparison to what the rest of my body is going through.

There is enough space between the opening of the crack and me, but just when I start to think that I am safe, black, beady eyes peer through the crack and meet mine.

Immediately, I grab my gun and fire a shot to its face, watching life leave its eyes before it can make any sounds.

My hands tremble. I just took multiple lives. I know it was in self-defense, but the more I do it, the less I'm able to keep ignoring my actions.

The sight of it makes me nauseous, but I swallow it down. While I continue to move myself down the shale that is lining the bottom of the passage, and thankful that the suit is made of a material that can withstand this.

How has this not already caved in? The thought makes me hurry, heedless of the cuts added as images of both of us being buried alive spur me on.

I lose sight of the chamber as I slide, clutching to the gun in a way that gains me more injuries. Soon after, I'm next to it, but she isn't in it.

I panic, then see a blood trail leading up out of the hole and scramble out to warn her of the fight.

My eyes ache from the sudden light, but it doesn't take long for them to adjust. When they do, my heart skip a beat at the sight of multiple genali racing toward us.

Reaching the green-haired woman, I see blood streaming down the side of her face. Her half-lidded eyes looking around, probably wondering where she is.

The woman is staring, seeming confused. "Get down!" I yell out at her.

She is still frozen when I grab her and yank her away.

I'm terrified, but I can't let them hurt her. "Stay behind me," I yell out, then start shooting.

Half of my shots miss, but some of them fall. I'm convinced we are about to die when I hear the woman finally speak. "Cover me."

I glance over and see that, somehow, she has somehow found a rifle. Without hesitation, she turns back to shoot, not caring about killing them or trying to kill the thrilling sensation I feel of blood splattering everywhere.

Soon after, she's yelling at me that we need to leave, and she's right. We need to get away from this. Fast.

We keep firing, ducking down now since they are firing back, screeching out as we each take wounds.

There are too many of them and I look around wildly for somewhere to hide. Then I see a cave opening at the bottom of the slope and to our right. I yell for the woman to follow me, as I scramble forward, my body screaming out at me in protest.

Bullets hit the shale around us that feel like shards digging into my sides. So, we pick up speed, the honking, wet sounds behind us spurring us on.

When I get close, I realize it's just an outcrop, not a cave, but it's the best protection we have.

There are only a few of them left now, but I doubt there are many bullets left in our weapons.

"What now?" the green-haired woman asks, panic clear in her voice.

I can still hear shots in the distance, so Kuret must still be alive. I want to run toward him, but I can't lead the woman back into more danger.

"It's time to run," I tell her.

"Oh, you think?" she says, her voice incredulous.

I don't know how we manage it, but we evade them, running into a valley until my throat feels like it's on fire from the heavy breaths. We finally duck into a thicket to catch our breath.

I ask her if she's alright. The English comes out of my mouth in an odd manner. Annoyed, I grumble in Farsi, even though I should be completely used to all of this by now.

We bicker back and forth about it for a moment, and then I'm complaining in another language altogether. One I don't recognize. Finally, I force myself to stop.

I let out a huff. No, it was the right thing to do, and finding out more about her is easy enough. "What's your name?"

"Olivia," she groans out, poking at where a bullet grazed her.

From a quick look, I can tell she was luckier than I was, though her head wound looks nasty.

I'm trying not to think about burning pain above my hip and the damage I must've done by running with a bullet wound there. Pressing my hand to it, perhaps to trigger my mysterious healing power to stop the bleeding, I cannot do much right now.

We're huddled together, I don't even have to look at her to know she has too many questions, most of which I cannot answer.

"What's going on?"

I let out a sigh I didn't realize I was holding when she asks me that, relieved she didn't start with questions about why she was in that chamber or why her hair is green.

Things I don't know.

I answer her question a little too gladly. "Those *khar* want to take us hostage again."

She shoots me a look that lets me know that says she isn't fully satisfied with my answer, so I wait for follow-up questions but get none.

"What language was that, the one you cursed in?"

"Farsi."

For a second, I want to launch into a mini-lecture on who I am and what language I speak, random thoughts charging through my panicked mind, but I stop myself just in time.

She hugs her body closer to herself, shivering slightly even though the sun is blazing down on us. "I understood it. I understood that you called them donkeys."

There is an excitement in her voice that I cannot place. It confuses me because when I was rescued, the only thing that went through my mind was utter panic.

If I could, I would have screamed for hours on end, but she is excited that she can understand my language. As if she has gone through far worse than this and just wants to focus on something innocent. I immediately feel more protective, while my respect grows for this new woman.

But also a bit of wariness over how... odd she seems.

"I am Nasrin." I introduce myself with a forced smile and she shoots me one back.

Her smile is wide and genuine. I feel a bit guilty for my caution toward the woman, but I push it off and try to focus on the conversation I'm supposed to be part of.

"Nasrin is such a pretty name," she says, pushing her gem-colored hair behind her ears.

Her hair is long and shiny, not at all reflecting what she has been through.

"You can call me Liv, if you would prefer that."

Her smile is so infectious that I can't help warming up to her, even as I wonder how unhinged she must be to look so unaffected by our frantic escape.

I grin. "If we are also giving nicknames, then you can call me Rin."

Her eyes light up and she opens her mouth to say something, but the ground starts to quake below us.

I get on my knees to crawl forward, and she follows me. But then I hear two more loud screams of death echoing through the valley. None of them sounds like Kuret, so I relax a bit. I sit back down and she follows, wincing as she does the same.

To avoid disclosing more of our location, I tap her hand and point to the sleeve of my jumpsuit, then point to the thin black band around her waist. I mouth *imagine* to her, watching as her face shifts from confusion to understanding.

Olivia shuts her eyes tightly and her face scrunches up as she replicates my jumpsuit, down to the high neck and foot coverings.

While she does, I thank *Allah* for the opportunity to be with another human. Being around Kuret and the argila has made me feel good, but still a little alone and alien, which is what I am to them as well even if there is a silent kinship between us, one that I appreciate.

Once she's clothed, I get back on my knees and crawl toward a ledge in front of me, a little farther from the commotion. If we get on it, we can wait until the fight is over before figuring out how we'll get back up. And we can figure out how to reach out to Kuret, once he's done dealing with all the threats.

I climb onto it and stretch my hand down to pull her up.

"This makes me think of *Titanic* and how Jack could have just freaking gotten on the door with Rose," she says and I look at her in confusion. "You haven't seen *Titanic*? Oh my God, have you been living under a rock?"

Her ease with laughter makes me start to chuckle as I realize that she uses humor to cope. It must be much better than overanalyzing everything like I do. "I have not seen it but once I can, I will," I assure her and she nods her head. I feel the continual growth of our silent kinship. I hope the feeling is mutual.

We sit there in silence, the noise from above sending fear deeper into my heart, and I am torn—part of me wants to stay here with Olivia, but the other part is screaming to rush back and help Kuret.

Olivia picks up a dark gray rock and starts to fiddle with it, her face an impenetrable mask with only a small smile attached.

A part of me wants to ask her to talk to me and tell me how she's feeling about waking up on a new planet, but I decide against it.

This is not the time or place for something like that. Anything could happen, and either of us could be dead in minutes. I wouldn't want her fear or sadness to be the last thing she speaks of, or the last thing I hear. Besides, we will have all the time to properly get to know each other once we have gotten to safety. If we don't, then the time spent together will be enough.

I don't realize that I am staring at her until I hear her softly call my name and place a hand on my knee. "Sorry, I got lost in my thoughts," I say.

She smiles stiffly and goes back to fiddling with her rock. "I understand. I don't mean to pull you from it."

I shake my head. "No, don't be sorry. I finally have an actual human being to talk to and I should take advantage of that."

Her face morphs into one of concern. "Am I the first human you have come across?" I nod my head and she lets out a short sound. "So you haven't seen Ree?"

The name strikes a chord in my brain as I recall all the times Kuret has mentioned her. It must be the same person that we are supposed to go to. My eyes widen as I realize that this must not be Olivia's first time out of the chamber. Probably she has information that can help us get to Ree faster.

I open my mouth to ask all the questions in my head, but I hear a concerning crack from underneath us. We scramble to move, but it's too late. The ground splits opens like a gaping maw.

My hands reach out to grab both of hers as a human-sized sinkhole opens beneath us. The only thing keeping her with me is my desperate, slipping grip.

"Rin!" she yells, her eyes wide with fear.

I push myself back against a bush and pull against her. "Can you get your feet on anything?" I ask her as I struggle to support her weight, still not sure how I can even manage it.

I've never been strong, and there is a searing pain in my side yelling at me to let go, but I just tighten my grip.

She looks down and then back up at me. "I can't see anything. It's all dark."

I attempt to adjust myself, but I start sliding down with Liv as more of the bushes give way, as if they have been cut from underneath. Our hands are forced apart and I swallow down the scream as I search for something to hold on to.

A sharp squeal comes from underneath me, followed by a thud. I look into the dark cavern that has formed in the ground and see some rapid movement, surprised I can even make anything out. But whatever is there disappears before I can catch a glimpse.

I take a deep breath to motivate myself to jump into the hole, but the ground shifts and it starts to fill it, soon far too small for me to fit into. Before the big pieces completely fall in, I see a hint of green and other glowing colors. It's moving and I can see the outline of something large.

"Hey, you there! I know you can hear me. Help her up!" I scream at whatever it is that is down there with her but I don't get a response.

Ya Allah, what if it is a predator that thinks it has found its next meal? I can't let her die.

"Olivia! Olivia, are you there? Please say something!" I yell into the darkness, my heart somewhere between my toes and directly pounding over my brain.

A muffled cough comes from the hole and I reach forward to start digging but soon realize it is futile. I try to call for her again. "Olivia, if you're there, please let me know."

Another cough follows. "Nasrin, I'm okay. There's someone else here," she informs me and relief pours over me like cold water.

I adjust myself so that my eye and mouth are directly above the hole. "Please give my friend back. Please," I beg.

A gruff voice starts speaking, and it takes my brain a second to realize that it is not English. "This one... belongs to you?"

I'm not sure if I should say yes, hoping it'll give her back, but I don't get a chance to decide.

"Zha is part of my hoard now. Go away."

Zha? What?

Vitriol fills my mouth but before I can speak, Liv does. "Fuck no, I'm no one's but my own," she spits at the creature.

I'm proud of her, but still terrified. The hissing sound of its voice gets too low for me to understand, but I know it's saying things to her

"Rin, I'll be okay," she shouts out to me and it sounds too much like a goodbye.

"Olivia! Where are you? I'll get to you," I say as a fresh energy overtakes me.

My fingers dig hopelessly at the dirt and roots, my fingers bleeding soon after.

When she speaks again, her voice sounds much farther. "I'll be okay, I promise. I'll find you once I can."

I shake my head as my eyes burn with the familiar sting of loss. "No, no, Olivia, please. I'll dig my way down to get you out. I'll find a way. Just hold on."

"Get to safety," she tells me, her voice barely audible. "I'll..." I can't make anything else out after that.

My heart's in my throat as I keep digging, grabbing a broken off branch to do it, then another when that one breaks.

Tears run down my face when I concede.

I know that I am speaking into a void, but I continue to call out to her, hoping that, by some miracle, she will reach out her hand and try to grab onto mine.

"Olivia, please. Please bring her back, please."

Another gunshot reminds me that I'm in as much danger as she is and so I stop talking. I'm about to move away when the ground

I was digging so rigorously at and getting nowhere suddenly gives way.

39

Kuret

Killing off the genali is even more fulfilling than I thought it would be, though my hearts are tight with my grief to not have Samke here with me, both of our undulating cries building on the other.

I stop counting how many there are after six and continue to kill whatever crosses my line of sight. Each one must be thinking that they will be the one to kill me. It has to be the only reason why they continue to throw themselves at me.

If they were one of the green hunters, they might have a chance. Or if they were better at using their *guns*. So far, all they've managed to do is give me small wounds.

As I slaughter my way through them, the screams, grunts, and putrid blood melt together to a background din.

I am familiar with the battlefield, at home here in this chaotic space; I soon find my rhythm and I have space in my head to properly appreciate how good all this feels.

Not only am I exacting revenge in a small measure for all the horrible actions carried out by the genali, I am also restoring my honor and protecting Nasrin.

Panic strikes me when the cart comes into view during a momentary lull as the remaining genali circle me and I do not see the argila or Nasrin anywhere.

The sound of *guns* firing starts up down the slope and I attack with renewed ferocity, tossing down the *gun* I found when it stops firing, throwing a sharp piece of shale at the last genali standing, distracting it just long enough to run forward and take it down with a crushing blow from above.

I take a moment to gather as many weapons as I can, mind screaming at me that I don't have the time, but I don't know what dangers we will face. I shove them into the pack at my waist as I run.

My hands are dripping with blood as I race to the cart. I tell myself that they are most likely hiding behind some of the giant trees that line the now-broken ridge, but they don't answer when I call out to them.

I quicken my steps as I start to make my way along the ridgeline, not wanting to run for fear of the ground starting to open up again and I am only a few steps away from the cart when I hear a thumping in the ground below me. My nerves are strung thin, trying to stay alert for any possible stray hunters trying to sneak up on me while simultaneously looking out for Nasrin and the others.

Standing still, I look around me to see if I can find the woman I am supposed to protect, but I hear the thumping sound again, followed by muffled screams in a language I do not understand. I unsheathe my knife in readiness, just in case there is any need.

I am wary at first, convinced that it is a ploy by these honorless hunters to deceive us after their defeat. So, I decide not to follow the source of the sound. First, I need to know where Nasrin is but I do not want to call out to her and alert them. I must stay stealthy.

However, when I reach the point where the cart was stuck, I hear the same voice again, except this time it has turned into continuous wailing, and I realize it is a trapped genali.

I leave it to its fate, then look around for signs of where Nasrin could have gone before spotting multiple genali puddles below. I move toward them cautiously until I see a trail of red blood.

My hearts stop simultaneously. What could be happening? I grip my knife nearly tight enough to break and move closer.

I snatch one of the *guns* from the puddles, then I break out into a run, gasping at what I realize are two trails of blood splatter. The green-haired woman must be with Nasrin and both are injured.

Judging by the greater amount of blood, they paused at an outcropping, then ran again. I follow, finding an injured genali and finishing it off with my blade.

I know I should be cautious, but I'm panicking at the amount of blood and break into a sprint, sliding down shale into a small valley. Up ahead, in the direction of their trail, I see two genali circling.

Did they find them? My chest squeezes and I almost charge right toward them, then remember the *gun* in my grip. It still feels awkward. Nothing like a bow, but I've gotten better at using it in the past few frantic minutes.

I raise it, still not quite sure how to best aim it and squeeze off multiple shots, the grip awkward in my hands.

One of them falls, but the other dodges to the side, moving behind a bush. I keep firing, but keep my shots high, not sure if Nasrin might be there too, just hoping to keep the genali pinned down as I sprint.

It works, and before I know it, I'm looming over the slime, bludgeoning it with the wooden part of the *gun* until it stops moving.

Whipping around, I search for the women, but don't find them. Their trail clearly leads here, ending in a place where it looks like something leveled the bushes.

My hearts are pounding so hard I barely hear the sound, whipping back toward it and forcing my breathing back under control.

It comes again, this time making me realize it's underground.

It sounds like Nasrin and both of my hearts constrict.

I drop to my knees and listen for the direction of her voice, relieved when it seems to be more to the left. I dig my hands into the crumbled-up rocks and dirt, throwing them out behind me furiously until I see a gap of space. Her cries are much louder, making me realize that anything could have happened to her in the time I was away.

What was I thinking?

As if to fuel myself into more fear, all the things that could have happened to her in my absence start to go through my head. Scene after scene of all the possible ways she could be getting hurt keep going through my head like deadly projectiles. Just when I started to feel like my honor could be restored...

All I can do is hope I can get to her in time.

What if the green-haired woman in the chamber has been killed? Worse still, what if Nasrin has been crushed under a large rock or hurt by a dangerous, underground-dwelling animal? What will I say to Ree if I am unable to save either woman?

How will I live if Nasrin dies?

The thought of losing Nasrin leaves a bitter taste on my tongue and a clump of uncertainty sitting in my stomach.

I love watching her and listening to her speak and can't imagine losing her.

No, I will not let it happen and keep tearing at rocks and dirt.

I decide when I dig enough to see an opening that I will dive through and get her out. I lie down flat and reach my arm down as far as it goes to dislodge a particularly large rock that had been getting in the way. A little more effort and I have exposed a large enough section of the ground. I'm starting to get somewhere and my chest fills with joy.

I can hear her clearly now, the poor female shrieking her voice hoarse for a reason I have not yet figured out. She's yelling something out over and over in a language I don't know.

Her anguished cries are punching a hole in both of my hearts, and I stand up and push a foot into the gap, yelling out her name.

She doesn't seem to hear me.

I need to get there faster. I won't be able to forgive myself if anything happens to her or the emerald-haired woman.

Loose rocks fall through to make the gap even bigger, big enough for me to squeeze through and slide down to reach her.

Sand gets in my eyes and sharp rock fragments try to tear at my skin as I struggle to reach her, her voice getting louder the more I move through. The tight fit is terrible and the weird stone the ground is made of is scratching deep gouges all over my body, but I persist.

I want to anchor my legs, but the space is too small and I can only use one hand to push rocks away while the other stays pinned to my side.

Suddenly, I fall through, hitting my shoulder painfully. I feel around with my hands to find somewhere to stand on. There is a little hollowed-out space in the ground. It is tight so I can only barely stay crouched but it is better than the hole I just crawled through.

"Nasrin!"

The air here is thin, so I carefully continue to move back and forth, wiggling myself until I drop down. All the while trying not to expend too much energy.

A cloud of dust follows me, getting into my eyes and mouth, but I wave my hands in the air to disperse it.

Through the fog, I spot Nasrin's bright hair and her black-clothed hand stretched out in front of her. When I get closer, I notice that she is stuck under a pile of dark gray rocks. "Nasrin!" I call out as I move toward her as quickly as the tumultuous, rocky ground will let me.

"Kuret! I'm so glad you aren't hurt."

When I reach her, I notice that there is a gap in the ground, but I ignore it and get down on my knees to pull the rocks off her. She is not screaming anymore, but her face is shiny with wetness.

There's terror etched on her face.

"Are you hurt?" I ask her as I am moving the stones from her body, but her eyes are stuck to the crack in the ground below us. I look back again but it is mostly filled with stone. "Nasrin, you have to tell me if you are hurt," I say again, and she finally looks up at me.

Her eyes are overflowing with water and her lips are quivering. She starts to speak in a language I don't know and I shake my head. "I don't understand."

There is a frantic look in her eyes as she stumbles over her unfamiliar words, but I try to stay calm for the two of us.

She winces painfully, clears her throat and sniffles. "Olivia is gone, Kuret. I lost her in the-the—" She begins another round of raucous sobbing.

I attempt to pull her to her feet, but she pulls herself away from me and toward the sinkhole. "She went in through there and I couldn't save her in time. It took her."

She is now pointing down toward the darkened hole but I still don't quite understand.

She is still speaking, but I cannot make out her words anymore as she babbles. I pull her away from it and to a safe enough corner so that I can calm her down. "I cannot understand you, Nasrin. Slow down and tell me again."

I am trying and failing to keep her on task, but she is terrified.

She shakes her head up and down and then begins to draw in deep breaths. She wipes her face again and I replace her hands with mine, both of them shaking as I hold her precious, delicate features.

This time, I don't stop myself or wonder if something is wrong between us because I became her... whatever the word is. Not a donor. I pull her close and holding her face cupped in one hand and press my lips onto her wet cheek.

Then I get myself back under control.

We need to leave, but she is resisting me, trying to move toward the hole to go deeper into the ground.

I can only hope that we don't run into more hunters with her like this.

When she has calmed down, she speaks clearer. "The other girl, Olivia. She was taken by something under there." She points down.

I am still confused. "Who is Olivia, who took her?" The question leaves my mouth, then the answer enters my head—it was the sleeping woman in the *cryo chamber*. The emerald-haired woman. "Did you see who did this?"

She shakes her head. "Not really, just some glimpses of light, but they said she was theirs. Like she was property. We need to save her."

I stand up and pull her up. "We will find her, but we can't stay here. It's too unstable."

She lets out a long breath, then moves her head to show agreement, the decision clearly causing her pain.

With a grunt and the pain of my injuries surging, I push her out of the hole. Then I scramble out of it, my movement causing the ground to shift and fill it part of the way back in.

We scramble away as the bushes start sinking, me holding her tight to me.

We're both shaking and I want to hold her close and move my hands all over her to check for wounds, but we need to find a better cover.

We head into the thick *forest* nearby.

We don't make it too far into the *trees* before we hear the argila braying loudly and making their way toward us. Roshan bolts right at Nasrin first and she digs her hands into his furry head and buries her face in his short neck.

Darya comes to me and I pet her distractedly, my eyes pinned on Nasrin, whose shoulders start to quake. The argila leaves my side and goes to Roshan and Nasrin, looking inquisitively at them.

While they are wrapped up in the embrace, I look at them with concern.

How is it that keeping this one woman safe is so much harder than taking care of an entire cloister? I've never been so terrified that something might happen to someone. Even my pain over Samke doesn't compare.

I never thought it was possible to have the same sort of bond as with Samke, let alone something deeper. Though the urge to help her work through her emotions is the same as if any brother was struggling before me. Is it possible to have a bond with a female?

Watching her break down like this in front of the animals, vulnerable and helpless in the face of something she couldn't have prevented, is painfully constricting my heart.

I can't let this happen again, but how can I stop it?

She is vulnerable; I have to come to terms with the fact that I might not be able to protect her from everything, even while promising that I'll die trying.

40

Rin

People underestimate the power of a good cry and an even better hug, and I realize now how much I needed both. From landing on this planet, I have found the same thing to be true here as on Earth: that one never knows where their situation will take them.

This planet has forced me to change in so many ways and I haven't quite come to terms with it.

After my cry, Kuret leads the argila and me to a stream hidden away behind a small gathering of trees and I wash the dust off myself, checking my wounds, pleased that most of them have closed, then checking Kuret.

There's no longer any questioning between us, or that weird awkwardness after we had sex; we simply let our hands roam, both needing the reassurance. It isn't sexual, both of us too emotional over losing Olivia, but it is deeply soothing.

The water and his touch seem to wash away a lot of the worry that's been weighing on me, and for the first time since climbing into that sinkhole, I don't feel so terrible.

We drink and begin walking, with the argila trailing behind us.

The silence between Kuret and me is loud, both of us weighed down by heavy thoughts.

My mind keeps wondering how Olivia is and if she's even alive. The thing that took her, though colorful, did not sound friendly. Just remembering it sends chills down my spine and it all feels worse now, because I had started to really like spending time with her.

After that battle, going with Olivia to meet up with Ree and stay in whatever "cloister" Kuret has been going on about this whole time doesn't sound all that bad. Although, I'm starting to wonder if that's what Ree really has planned after all now that I've met Olivia, or if it's just a matter of cultural misunderstanding.

There's certainly been plenty of that since I woke up here... five thousand years ago. My bones ache with how tired I am, but we keep walking.

Did I really lose Olivia to that bright-colored monster forever? No. I can't accept that.

On Earth, it seems like the more colorful an animal looks, the deadlier it can be.

I do my best to clear my mind of those thoughts and turn to Kuret. "How are we going to find Olivia? Because it seems to me that we are back on the same track to find Ree again."

He has had a strange look in his eyes the past few minutes and is acting shifty. I don't know why, but I will definitely find out.

He doesn't face me when he speaks. "That is because we are. I can't risk having your life in danger while trying to rescue someone else."

His voice is stoic—more than I have ever heard and I know he is serious.

"So we are leaving Olivia to the hands of fate and whatever intent that dangerous creature has for her?"

Kuret stops in his tracks and I wait for him to look me in the eye and say yes. To convince me he is as heartless as the guy I thought he was when I saw him rip Tehlmar to shreds in the blink of an eye. "Nasrin, you have seen for yourself how unpredictable this place is. I need you to be safe in the cloister, so I won't worry about killing two women at the same time."

A cloister really is starting to sound amazing.

I almost laugh at how quickly I changed my mind about the cloister as soon as Olivia said Ree's name, but instead I just argue. "You are so quick to think about putting me in some kind of confinement, Kuret. And I don't think I enjoy you making decisions for me." I cross my arms and strike a defiant pose.

"I am not making decisions for you, and it is not confinement at all. It is a cloister. For your own safety," he argues. "If you are right and the thing you saw take Oliva is a person—"

"I am right. It spoke and said she was his," I argue back.

I have had enough of people thinking they can just order me around. That has been my whole life. No more.

He opens his mouth, but I interrupt him by holding a hand up to his face.

He looks away from me and I take it as a sign of disbelief. He thinks Olivia is dead and I am crazy for hearing a monster speak.

Ya Allah. How am I still facing misogyny a million light years away from Earth?

I pin my lips together and turn around, walking away from him.

I hear him click his tongue and begin walking after me, the argila following behind us. "Why do you have such a problem with being in a cloister with others like you?"

I almost tell him my earlier realization that I changed my mind, but it's more expedient to just let it stand. Then I glance back and I can see his face is screwed up into a mask of frustration, his veins straining against his neck. As if my answer matters more than I could ever know.

I stop in my tracks because his question is a valid one. Why do I, a woman, have a problem with being confined? I don't know if I actually have an answer for him or if I am just pushing back for the sake of it, but something about all of this still just doesn't sit right with me. I'm vacillating between wanting safety at any cost and remembering the horror of growing up where every possible choice for women is curtailed.

Sure, I want to make it somewhere safe and be done with all this for good, but not in another prison.

He stops behind me and I turn around to face him. "I don't have a problem with being confined. I have a problem being thrown into confinement by a man."

He opens his mouth to speak, but I wiggle my finger in his face.

"I am not finished, Kuret. If you know what it is like to be a woman in my world, you would understand exactly why I don't want to be in a cloister."

I am panting, my hand is shaking, and my heart is racing. Part of my mind is telling me that it's not the same, but the other part is overtaken by the fear. By memory.

Kuret looks at me with a firmness in his eyes, like he is going to argue, but then his face falls. "Tell me what it is like, then."

I can sense the sincerity in his words, so I try to calm down a little and prepare to tell the story. I let out a breath I didn't even realize I had been holding and swallow thickly. "Alright, I'll tell you."

I sigh again before I begin to speak.

His steely eyes hold mine with a familiar intensity as the story begins to flow freely from my lips.

"A few of my friends and classmates got kidnapped on their way back from protesting a ban against education. I should have been with them, but I wasn't available that day. It was a peaceful protest. They held their placards and boards and they called out to the government, begging to be allowed to learn and teach. Before the day ended, they were captured."

His brow is lower now and he looks confused, but he doesn't interrupt me.

"They were taken and held captive for over two months. When they returned, they were shadows of their former selves. People who were once extremely happy women were now skeletons with torn mouths and multiple injuries. They were confined, all because they wanted to learn. I wasn't allowed to see them for weeks because their families were told to watch over them. As if they moved from one jail cell to another."

"What is a jail cell?"

My eyebrows shoot up, but I remind myself that we come from different worlds. In his, it sounds like they just kill criminals.

"It's a cage. They are supposed to feed you, but for these women, they put glass in their food. They were beaten and some of them raped."

"And the males were not punished?"

"No, Kuret. The males were the ones punishing them."

"For what? No, it doesn't matter. Nothing would explain that."

"I wasn't allowed to see them after that. They were locked inside their homes. That is what a cloister is to me."

"No, that is confinement."

I shrug and wrap my hands around my body. "Confinement, cloister, they're all the same."

He just doesn't seem to get it.

"That is not what a cloister is like," Kuret says quietly. When he has my attention, he speaks again. "Cloisters are made by women and respected by men. On my planet, it is a great honor to guard and protect a cloister." Kuret makes the clicking sound again. "No. I can assure you that it will not be the same with Ree. I will make sure of it even," he promises.

Looking into his wide eyes, I see that he means every word that he says.

"I guarded a cloister. It was my life before I was taken, and I can help Ree make sure it is a fair place to live."

I let out a long groan and place both of my hands on my face. "I don't think you are getting this, Kuret. Why do women even need to live so closed off from men?"

He looks confused by my question. "To protect them."

I shoot him a look. "Whatever those hunters can do to me, they can do to you and women can also protect."

He does not seem to understand what I am saying, and I roll my eyes.

"My point is, why do we have to be in separate places to be safe? We are on a new planet. Why does there have to be segregation?"

Kuret looks completely dumbfounded by my talking. "Because it is safer for women," he maintains and I groan even longer.

"I don't see why you would disagree after what you said those males did to your friends."

I open my mouth to disagree, then close it. He has a point. But then I shake my head. "There have been males in my life who have not been like that. Ones I miss very much."

He doesn't respond. I sit with my thoughts, not sure how to explain this properly to him. Our conversation is getting circuitous and I am trying to make a serious point here.

The argila bray playfully behind us and I turn to look at them.

An idea sparks in my head. "Look at Roshan and Darya. They are male and female who spend time together and they are fine."

He turns to look at them and I see his face softening.

"Males and females do not have to live apart. They can be free together, everyone contributing to the life and what it entails."

He is still quiet, but his brow furrows in what I assume is confusion at the last part of my sentence. I suppose it was pretty vague.

"Do you understand? Instead of separation, there can be collaboration—people working together to build a better life because they're people, not because they're male or female. Females can bond with females. Males with males. Females with males. Or whatever they may consider themselves. All of those relationships can be healthy, and on my world, they all exist."

Kuret runs his tongue over his dark bottom lip and I look away, concentrating hard on the rocks in my path.

The arousal is always there, but sometimes it surges at the simplest things, and now is not the time to be jumping on him.

"We don't have to be apart. I trust you, Kuret."

My eyes open wide as I say it, especially when I realize it's true. Somewhere along the way, he gained something that no man has had since my *bābā* died. My mouth opens, then closes, then opens again, but there are no words.

41

Kuret

After Nasrin tells me the story of her friends who were taken away and kept for months, I can't help but wonder why she is still speaking about putting males and females together. Since the situation seems to have happened because of that very mixture.

Females are fragile and even if I had no way of knowing, spending all this time around Nasrin has surely proven that to me. They are a special commodity that males are always trying to hurt and exploit, and I can't stand by and let it happen.

When she speaks about collaboration between males and females to build a better life, I fight the urge to laugh—not because it is funny, but because I know that it will never happen.

Still, I do not want to drag the argument out any longer.

Ree seems to be confident in her ability to protect the females and I know that she will make sure all them are happy and thriving in the cloister she is building.

I know this because my chest tells me to trust her and it has failed me only a handful of times. "When we get to Ree, you can tell her all of this. For now, let us focus on getting you there so that I can return and look for the other woman."

Nasrin's face goes from wide-eyed to having an even deeper frown on her face than before and I ruminate on my words, hoping that I have not said something to offend her.

"No," she responds.

I tilt my head to the side in confusion. "No? What do you mean, no?"

When I look at her determined frown, I know what she is about to say before it leaves her lips.

"No, we are not going to Ree and her plans for a cloister, not before we find Olivia and make sure she is safe."

I let out a labored sigh. "Nasrin, I do not want to risk your life anymore. Just back there with the genali—" I point behind us and Roshan runs up and licks my finger, undermining how serious

I look, but I pat his head. "Back there, I was terrified because I couldn't protect you. I was unsure of your safety and nearly had my hearts drop out of my chest when I did not find you after ki—I mean, fighting them."

A mischievous look replaces the frown on her face for a brief moment before dropping away. "You can say you killed them, Kuret. I won't run away." She lets out a huff of air. "I did too. Lots of them, and I'm sorry I was so hard on you before. They deserve it. Wait. You have multiple hearts?"

The question takes me by surprise. "Is that not normal?"

Nasrin plasters a hand over my mouth, but her bright eyes give away that she is holding in a laugh. Something about her body language tells me that she is desperate to find something to distract herself.

"No, people have one. On my planet anyway."

Having only one heart cannot be a healthy way to live. I wonder how she does it.

We turn at the same time to look for the argila and find them grazing behind us. It's a stark reminder of just how different a being can be from another.

"I want to find Olivia because I am the one who let her get taken away. This place is dangerous, and anything can happen to either of us at any time. Hiding from that when a friend is in danger makes me just as cowardly and honorless as the male who took her."

Her words reverberate through my head, and I understand what she means. If Samke were here and he was taken by a hunter or a strange creature, I would scour the ends of this *forest* to find him. And then start looking all over again.

Just like I would for her.

Denying her that would make me just as honorless, and I cannot have that.

I draw my lips into a straight line. "I understand. We will go back for her but you will stay by me at all times."

Her eyeballs roll back into her head for a moment again. I wonder if she has an injury I didn't find when I moved may hands all over her body.

"Where else would I be?" she asks, back to looking at me with her amused stare.

I turn my bag to the front and open it. "This is serious, Nasrin."

I pull out one of the many guns I seized from the now-dead genali and shove one in her direction. "I noticed you must have lost the other one when the cart had the accident, so hold on tightly to this."

She peers inside the bag and her eyes widen. "You have a lot of guns in there. Well done."

My spine straightens at the unexpected praise. "In a place like this, you can never have too many weapons."

I'm surprised she agreed so easily this time. I had been expecting a long lecture from her or at least an adamant refusal but neither is offered.

She nods her head and shuts her eyes tightly for a moment. "I never thought I would talk about weapons and death like this. Like it's normal."

"I wish it wasn't normal, but they brought us here. The only other option is to let them kill us."

"You're right. It's a new world, and sometimes that means being different people." She looks me in the eye, her face softening. "I can see that you are trying to meet me halfway, Kuret. I can do the same."

I let out a relieved breath, pleased she has noticed.

I still don't feel right with her having only one weapon, so I reach down into my boot and pull out my sheathed dagger. "Keep this a little handier, in case that one is knocked away from you before you have a chance to use it."

I can remember a time not long ago, when she would never have agreed to carry any weapon or accepted my offering. But I know she knows better now.

She shakes her head up and down again, placing it in a pocket that forms in her odd clothing. It blends seamlessly and I grunt in satisfaction.

"Let us go back the way we came to look for the female."

There is a spark in her eyes when I agree; I much prefer it when they shine with pleasure. Still, it feels good that we are are once again more or less in harmony.

Nasrin clears her throat. "She has a name, and it is Olivia. We talked a bit before she was taken," she says as we begin to walk. "Roshan, Darya, let's go," she calls to the animals. They stand to their full height, shaking their legs out and sticking to her side.

I can see how her mood has greatly improved now that I have agreed to do what she wants, and it fills me with joy that joins the terror.

It's an odd mix.

She flashes one of her beautiful smiles again, and I realize there isn't much she could ask that I wouldn't give to her.

Then I think about the other females.

I cannot help but think about how dangerous it is that the female—Olivia—has come out of her chamber. It means that whatever took her, if it has not killed her off yet, has a chance of becoming her donor.

Then I remind myself that it is a non-issue. Changing your entire world view is hard and it hurts my head.

I look at Nasrin and watch her play with the argila, remembering just how devastated she was at the changes that had been made to her body.

One can only imagine how Olivia will react, but I am sure Nasrin will help her through it. She cares deeply for her already, so I can rest assured that the female will not be as scared as she was when she realizes what is happening to her.

If we get there in time to take her away from the creature.

We head back up the way we had come, my mind occupied with the mission we are heading into. I'm so focused that I almost miss it when our old cart comes into view, still stuck in that sinkhole. A pang of regret hits me—this cart has been part of the reason we even made it this far, but I push it out of mind and keep moving.

I dart to it, pulling out our supplies as we both look for dangers or lurking genali, then we move away.

It seems like we are even farther from our goal than before and the list of what must be done sits heavy on my shoulders.

It's frustrating but we must keep moving. It's not like we have any choice with all the things that seem to be against us.

Nasrin gently nudges me back into focus and points out a little cavern a small way off the path we are currently on. We decide it would be a good place to rest before it gets too late and predators start to follow our trail.

We begin heading into the cavern, preparing to rest up for the night and maybe hunt around for some game to eat, when I see this one is hiding a secret in its depths.

The cavern is shaped like a reverse cornucopia, getting bigger as I go in until it opens up on the other side into a small-looking valley surrounded on both sides by near identical cliff faces. It is beautiful.

I scout ahead to make sure it's safe before I lead Nasrin and the argila through and see no apparent threats. Any one of the caves might lead us to finding Olivia.

42

Rin

After Kuret finds us a shallow cave to settle into for the night, well away from the bigger one we used to enter the valley, he runs off to scout it. When he returns, he mentions that we need to build a barricade in the larger one.

"I didn't go far into the other caves, but from the smell and darkness, I think the way we entered is the only one with quick access to the valley. If we barricade it, we can explore the other caves without fear of genali coming in."

"You're right. Although I have to admit, I don't know how we're going to do it."

He shoots me a look, his brow bones lowered and furrowed. "I can do it easily. You just rest for now."

I frown and he catches it, shooting me a toothy smile before adding more. "You have more injuries than I do. Let me take care of it and you can help later."

A smile tugs at my own lips and I grumble an agreement, "Sure."

I know I forget sometimes, but he really does have my best interests at heart when he gets bossy. He was willing to leave Olivia behind just to get me to safety, even though rescuing women seems to be the thing keeping him sane.

I still get chills at how ready he was to just walk away, but on a deeper level, I must admit, it did make me feel pretty special.

"I'll stay here with Roshan and Darya. Make sure to tell me if you need any help."

Kuret drops his bag onto my thigh and strips his shirt off, leaving me breathless. I have to turn away to cough. "Are you alright?" He places a three-fingered hand on my shoulders and I shake it off, still coughing and nodding my head.

He looks at me funny but places his shirt on the ground and walks away.

I watch his retreating back and my eyes cannot help but betray me; they're glued to every movement his body makes. While his back is turned to me, I can indulge myself in a good long look at him.

It's not like he doesn't take his liberties—I see him watching me all the time. Once he's back, we are hopefully going to touch each other again, and this time not to check for injuries.

When I was much younger, I used to watch these cheesy soap operas with *māmān* and the scenes she liked the most were the ones where the male lead was doing some physical labor without a shirt.

I never quite understood the appeal.

Watching Kuret haul those tall, heavy logs from forest to the cave makes me feel like *māmān* watching her shows and giggling, just without the giggling part. Only a moan wants to rise up and the only thing protecting my pride is that I've somehow managed to contain it.

In between ogling him, I take some time to gather large handfuls of the long grass and pilling them as high as I can on the cave floor.

I settle down on the carpet of grass and the argila fold their creepy legs and sit on either side of me. I place a hand on each of the heads and scratch.

Spending time with the argila always seems to have a way of calming me down and sitting here running my hands through their silky fur makes me feel more hopeful.

When he has carried enough logs, he starts to make holes in the ground and pierce the sticks through the ground. He repeats these actions over and again multiple times until there's a respectable barrier mounted at the mouth of the cave. Then, he pulls out one of the odd genali knives and starts to sharpen some other slimmer sticks into the semblance of a stake, pointing them sharp side out through it for extra security.

After making sure the barricade is secure, Kuret attends to both of the argila, setting down grass he gathers from the valley and securing them to a stake he had driven into the ground earlier before sauntering off deeper into the valley. The flash of the memory of him straining to move that last log makes me squirm.

I feel ashamed when I realize I should have been doing more instead of just gathering a bed and gawking. Olivia deserves better than this, but it also feels like I'm at the end of my energy.

43

Kuret

I'm outside of another one of the caves, hopeful that I am right about genali not being able to come in now, but knowing there's no way for me to be completely sure.

I can still hear Nasrin and the argila. Her breathing has been elevated since I started working and I'm hoping it doesn't mean she is more injured than I realized.

She would have told me, I remind myself.

I'll need to scout this one thoroughly, and I suppose many others.

My mind instantly goes back to the emerald-haired female, Olivia, and I hope that Nasrin is not thinking too much about her being missing. While I might not be completely in agreement with her plan to find the captured female, I will do my best.

If not because of Ree, then because I know it is what Nasrin wants and I want to make her happy.

If I had my way, we would already be heading to Ree and I could return to hunt for the other woman, but Nasrin has made it clear that she will not allow that to happen, which is why I'm stuck here.

Thinking about the other woman, something occurs to me finally. I had been dismissive of what Nasrin said about the kidnapper she had seen, partly because it sounded implausible and partly because I simply didn't want her to be right, but looking back at it, I can make some assumptions.

The monster must be a cave dweller and it probably is the reason those sinkholes kept appearing at random. It must have been after her even before the genali attacked.

Did it know they were there and decided it couldn't wait any longer?

My hands clench. We could have used help, not another creature intent on taking females. What is wrong with these terrible people?

From the description Nasrin provided, it won't be an easy fight. I must prepare myself for what is ahead.

The only thing that doesn't make sense to me is its bright skin color. Creatures that mainly live in caves usually have dark, or muted coloring, likely due to the lack of light, a mystery I'll explore later.

I make sure I am prepared before I move back toward Nasrin where she is sitting by the animals. We need to start making progress, and I can't leave her here unprotected. Once I'm convinced I can keep them safe, then maybe I can go looking on my own.

A few strides later, I hear it, ears twitching in alarm. Thunder and a lot of it. Rain is scarce on my world, but when it comes, it is dangerous. I turn my body in the direction of it and see the dark clouds, eyes widening in alarm when I recognize just how violent it looks. The sorts of storms that flood a desert and level all but the best-made buildings.

I change my walk into a run.

44

Rin

I decide to walk to meet him, my body aching with exhaustion, but guilt driving me. A moment later, I see him. I see him running toward me, his energy seemingly endless.

"We should go look for Olivia again," I call out as he approaches.

He points behind me. "We can't. There is a storm coming."

I start to reply, but he veers away without waiting for my response, heading back toward the argila. So much for searching for Olivia. He slows down, but his pace, is still too fast for me to talk or argue. I feel hopeful that we will find some clues about Olivia's whereabouts soon, though not if we don't start right away. Not that I'm sure how, but I avoid the thought that finding her is a lifeline amid everything being so uncertain.

Especially when it comes to the growing tension between Kuret and me.

As we approach the cave, I hear a low bellow that is undoubtedly a sound of pain from an argila, and I break into an even faster run somehow, dodging rocks amid the long grass, not even sure how I see them, worried whether they are okay.

My mind races, spinning through all the possible scenarios, every way things could have gone wrong. The worst case? The genali hunters circling back and harming Roshan and Darya. But anything—literally anything—could be happening.

A fleeting thought enters my mind. This must be how Kuret felt each time he came running to my rescue.

I sprint into the shallow cave and freeze. Darya is crouched, her legs folded under her, eyes squeezed shut as another long, agonized bellow escapes her. Roshan stands beside her, licking her face with gentle care. He is mopping her face with his tongue when his eyes meet mine, but he doesn't leave her side, bleating quietly at her in encouragement.

I immediately understand. The realization hits just before her next heaving cry.

A moment later a small wet creature is wriggling under Darya when Kuret comes in behind me. "Are they under attack? We need to—"

I don't let him finish as I pull him into a hug. "No, Darya just had a baby argila!" I exclaim, my voice breaking with joy.

Darya is lying down and licking her newborn while Roshan brays happily as he runs up to us.

I release Kuret for a moment and reach out to scratch Roshan's head. "Well done, my darling. You handled everything so well without us," I tell him and even though I know that he can't understand me, his bright yellow eyes are filled with appreciation when he looks at me.

All this time, I assumed she was just naturally that much bigger than Roshan, but she was pregnant. She's been running around at the end of her pregnancy.

I feel a moment of shame that I hooked her to a cart, but then realize they all look settled now. She doesn't look like she's extremely distressed. She looks proud.

Roshan leaves to join his new little family, just as proud as any father, though it seemed like they had just met, despite being clearly happy to see the other.

I turn back to Kuret again, just in time for him to sweep me up into his arms, a large grin spread across his face.

For someone who once seemed unfamiliar with the concept of pets, he's gotten attached quickly. Maybe I made an assumption. I'll have to ask him later.

He joins in my joy and walks over to see the new baby and pet the parents, murmuring something I can't hear. When he makes his way back to me, I cannot help but jump on him, hugging him close as the new-baby giddiness pumps through me.

There's a howling outside and with this new development, I decide that Kuret's right about staying here for now. "Let's get them settled in better," I urge him, and he moves to help me.

We change the grasses surrounding them, taking the time to wash up again at the stream again afterward, though the wind is whipping through the valley now.

The rain begins to fall as we run back, laughing as we each clutch armfuls of grass against our chests. We lay it out thickly to form our own surprisingly comfortable sleeping area in another section of the relatively shallow cave and then lay down, Kuret pulling me against his chest and stroking his hands down my side.

"Is it really possible for your people to stop pregnancy?" he asks me after the argila all fall asleep.

"Yes. On Earth, it's called birth control, and there are several forms of it. Not many people get access to it, though. Not where I live."

He doesn't seem to hear the last part of my sentence. "The women on my home planet would benefit greatly from something like that. They would not have to live in fear. It would change everything for them."

I try to imagine what life on Earth would be without any form of birth control, but the thought feels too distant, too impossible to grasp.

There is a dreamy look in his eyes when I tilt my head back to look at him, and I cannot help the smile that dances on the edge of my lips. He reaches his hands down and grabs both my hands in his.

"I enjoy learning from you, Nasrin," he says softly as he brings up a pair of our hands to rub at the side of my face.

I start to look away, but he stops me, his smile growing to match mine. "I am being serious."

There is an intensity in his gaze that I can't deny. It makes me shift my body so I can plant a kiss on his lips.

I think I might have convinced him of something, but I don't want to scare him away.

"I know, Kuret. We are friends and friends enjoy learning from each other."

He opens his mouth to speak, but I go first.

"And as friends, you should call me Rin instead of Nasrin."

He mulls over my name, the sweet whistling sound he makes now shorter. I don't know which I like better. "I never thought I would be friends with a female. Can your friends still call you Nasrin? Because I enjoy how it sounds when I say it."

My face splits into a smile. "I really like how you say my name."

He chuckles. "I can say it all day, if you'll let me."

45

Kuret

"It is still strange to me that you do not give your lives to have children," I tell her.

Her eyebrows furrow but I catch the faintest hint of a smile tugging at the corners of her lips. She looks away and then back at me, an amused glint in her eyes.

"Well, some women might argue that it is a type of death, though that's mostly when you speak to those with very young ones and not a lot of support from others. The children grow up eventually and then we have our freedom, though we miss them. Most of them go on to have their own *careers* and *families*, leaving their mothers to do whatever they wish."

"You know your children?"

My voice comes out lower than I expect, and I clear my throat. I mean, it's logical based on what she's said, but it still feels so foreign.

This is unheard of amongst my people. I have no memory of my mother, and I know she never knew hers. They were dead. I try not to let my shock show on my face, but I know I am failing horribly.

Nasrin absently twirls a blade of grass, twisting it around her fingers and staring at it like it is the most interesting thing on earth. "Of course. We get to raise them until they are independent enough to socialize with the rest of the world.

She looks like she wants to say more but decides against it.

I am unsteady from all the information and have nothing but more questions for her. "You're saying your children never kill you?"

She cocks her head to the side. "Sometimes they do, when there are complications, but it happens very rarely."

It's still hard to comprehend, even though I believe her.

While relief washes over me knowing I'll never lose Nasrin to the dangers of childbirth, I can't help but marvel at how different things are here. Before I was taken, I had thought my world was all that there was, my way of life being the most honorable, but I am evidently wrong.

Females can live through childbirth. Then raise their children.

Everything I assumed comes crashing down, but in the most pleasant way possible. If our females could live...

How can I get this home to them?

I don't realize that I am lost in my thoughts until Nasrin places a hand on my shoulder and softly squeezes.

"Kuret, are you alright?"

I struggle to find the words to explain what's happening so she naturally has no idea how different this all is to me. I look at her with an urgency that seems to shock her. "I have more questions but I have asked so many already..." The wind howling through the valley is the only sound around us for a second as I struggle to find the words to convey my discomfort.

Nasrin shakes her head and pulls her hand away from me. "You can ask whatever questions you have, Kuret. I have many things to ask you as well."

I turn and see there is a small smile playing on her lips and I relax. She has never been one to lie, and I am relieved that I can speak freely to her and not be spat on. "After having these children, do you keep all of them with you?"

She nods her head. "Newborns are tender and cannot live without their mothers, so yes."

My eyes widen. "Even the male children are kept with their mothers?"

Nasrin looks at me with wide eyes as well, surprised by my question. "Yes, we keep all of them. Why would we not keep the male children? They could die without their mother."

"Females do not keep their male children among my people," I mutter. "Not past weening."

Her eyes increase in size. I know that she is just as surprised as I am at the differences in our cultures.

Her hands are in front of her and she is fiddling with her small fingers.

I put my hand out in front of me and try to mimic her, though it isn't really possible because she has more fingers. She catches me and lets out a soft, chuffing sound that pleases me.

"You know, I was holding onto the hope that we had more in common, but I think this conversation has made me realize just how different we are."

I chuckle. "I knew we were different the moment I put my eyes on you."

She has no idea how true those words are, but I will do my best
to explain it to her.

"Your people are much less panicked than mine, and tender,
and it explains much of the difficulty we experienced when we
met."

This makes her laugh again, a sweet, trilling sound that is
muffled when she places her hand over her mouth. "I'm not so
sure about that. And I am not as tender as I seem and far, far
more panicked. It's always been my way of coping, and even more
important here. Everything was too different for me, and I needed
to feel some stability."

I smile at her. "I understand what you mean."

She picks up a few more long grasses and weaves them
together. "Can you describe a cloister to me? Not the kind that
Ree is building but the type you know of." She looks at me and I
smile softly at her in agreement.

I clear my throat before speaking. "On my planet, almost every
woman dies in childbirth. It's why they wait until the end of their
lives to have children. The cloister is where most of the females
live and the males protect them and the community."

Nasrin is still fiddling with her leaves when she asks her first
question. "There are males in the cloister protecting it?"

"In the outer parts of it, yes. I was a cloister guardian. We do not
live there. We just make sure that it is always safe for the women.
We protect them from predators that may try to harm them from
the outside and from males who may try to ruin their lives."

She nods her head. "Why do they only keep the females?"

Reaching out, I take the woven leaves and begin to separate
them with careful fingers. "One of the reasons the women are
so afraid of being around males is because of how fertile they
are. After a woman has been with her donor, she always ends up
pregnant with three young—two males and one female. After their
birth, they are left to be taken care of by the cloister, but the males
are taken away once they are weaned."

"But if all the pregnant women die, how do they feed them?"

I hadn't thought of that before. "I don't know."

She grabs the blades of grass and throws them behind her, then
picks up two more from the pile. "So the girls are raised in the
cloister and the boys are taken where?"

She hands one of the new blades to me and tears hers in half
to start tying it into knots again.

"They are excluded and raised by other males to become
protectors as well. If they are battle-hardened enough when they
grow older, they also get to be donors."

My hand reaches up to the tip of my left ear. The one I could pierce now, if I wanted.

I can see her discomfort plainly on her face, but I understand that, from what she has said of her people, all this must seem odd.

Nasrin bites on her bottom lip as she empties her hands and wipes them against her front. "It sounds like such a circuitous life," she says.

I mimic her and nod in agreement. "It might be, but I have never questioned it before. It creates an easy justice system. If a man lies with a woman before she is of age and she gets pregnant, he has to stand up for it and claim to be her donor. She is also questioned, and if she says it was not consensual, he is sentenced to death."

"What about the children?"

"I don't know," I say. "I never tried to find out. We knew what our role was, and we did it earnestly. Everything else was a distraction."

Her puzzled expression shifts into one of compassion. She looks at me the way she looks at her pet argila and I'm not sure how I feel about it. Except that there's hope in my chest and I like how it feels.

46

Rin

It all makes sense to me now.

All of our endless quarrels about cloisters, donors, and even the meaning of life, seem to have settled through a few uninterrupted conversations. Conversations not cut short by hunters trying to kill us. "I am really glad you asked me the questions," I say to him. He turns to me with a grin, one that no longer unsettles me. His grin, once terrifying, now feels reassuring. I take it as a good thing that he smiles more often, though if we meet other humans, I may have to explain to them he is not trying to bite their heads off.

"I am as well," he agrees.

I sigh deeply, letting the weight of my thoughts settle before I speak. "The general idea of a cloister is good, but I don't have a pleasant history with being confined. It has never been for my benefit or the benefit of the women I knew."

The words feel inadequate, a mere shadow of the truth I want to convey. I can't properly express the despair of being trapped my entire life, the suffocating fear of oppression. But I hope he sees the meaning behind my words and reluctance.

Kuret makes the clicking sound. "You mentioned it to me—how your friends were taken and hurt."

The moment the words leave his mouth, a cold sinking sensation coils in my stomach. All the levity I had been feeling over the course of our revelatory conversation is instantly dispelled. He has been so open with me, sharing his truths without hesitation. Perhaps it's time for me to do the same.

I swallow thickly as the memories flood my mind again—memories that I have been trying to suppress since the moment it happened. "I didn't tell you everything. It was not just my friends who were hurt that day. I kept protesting after that."

I draw in another breath, forcing myself to steady my trembling voice. "We went out that day with our boards, walking the streets and yelling what we wanted and when we wanted it; it was even covered on the news and we thought we were breaking through. On the third day of the protests, we were told that someone who could influence our decision wanted to see us."

Kuret inhales sharply, his voice grim. "They deceived you."

I nod my head and laugh bitterly. "You are right. It was an ambush. They beat us mercilessly. I nearly died. Only a few of us managed to escape."

The words feel like stones leaving my mouth, heavy and unrelenting. The memory is as fresh in my mind as if it had happened yesterday. The cruelty involved was unfathomable.

"I still wake up screaming about it sometimes."

He sighs sadly and places a hand on my arm. I pull it lower so that we're holding hands and he stares at our intertwined hands with an interested warmth, albeit with some confusion.

"Did you convince them to give you what you wanted?"

His naivety is endearing, and it nearly makes me crack a smile.

"Not at all. We were perceived as terrorists, accused of threatening the peace of our land. Every single one of us who participated was punished. Some people were publicly flogged but *bābā* was able to make sure I was not. Instead, I got banned from doing my job—or any other job for that matter—and my family was told to keep me under control. That meant I didn't leave the house."

The same fury that consumed me on that day burns in my chest now as I think of the other women who stood beside me. "All we wanted was the freedom to be taught and to keep the girls in schools. But even that was too much for them. They wanted to make examples of us."

I swallow hard, the memory of those oppressive days forcing its way to the surface. "I went back later. To protest, I mean. After my *bābā* died and I felt like there wasn't much to live for anyway. He was the only one stopping me from being married off and shut away for good. So I snuck out, and they threatened me again. Nothing changed, and I think it's the reason my brother and his wife betrayed me."

I push the painful memories aside, unwilling to dwell on them any longer. "Can the women on your planet have more than one round of three children in their lifetime? Has it ever happened?"

The question is a bit random, even to me, but anything to steer the conversation away from my own past. Honestly, I would have asked about the color of the clouds on his planet if it would shift the mood.

He seems just as glad as me about the topic change. "They have children near the end of their lives. Very few survive, and the process is so dangerous they don't want to risk it again. As far as I know, we've never discovered if it's possible."

It's a disturbing topic, but it feels good how easy conversing with him is now. I've spent more time with him than Roshan today, I realize.

It feels good, though.

I wonder what society would have been like on Earth if the situation were the same. I imagine the mass panic and forced puritanical ideals that would follow and realize the entire planet would likely be just like the place where I grew up.

"Human women can have multiple children in their lifetime. As many as this," I raise both of my hands and display all ten fingers in his face. "Even more, but it's rare."

He looks at me, confusion flickering in his eyes. Then, slowly, I see something shift in his expression—a glimmer of understanding. Though calling it understanding might be generous.. He's shocked and I think I've delivered enough of those for one day. It's light outside now, but the wind is blowing so hard that we might as well sleep.

I turn my back to him again, pushing myself back up against his chest, a contented sigh coming out as he splays his hand out on my stomach and pulls me close.

I really want to go search for Olivia, but judging by the howling sounds outside the cave, it isn't safe. Considering we are in some sort of odd mountain-surrounded valley, I assume that must mean it's really bad out there.

47

Kuret

The howling wind wakes me a few times, but I simply fall back asleep each time, my body demanding the rest I've been withholding and my mind no longer overriding it because of how safe we are now. No one will be moving around in that storm.

It's daytime now, though it's hard to tell with how thick the clouds are. If it's this violent in such a protected valley, I can only imagine how destructive it must be elsewhere. I hope Ree, Thivoll, and the rest of the women are all safe.

For now, I allow myself the luxury of rest, my mind drifting in and out of sleep until my body feels sated. Rin wakes up soon after, stretching her body out and making the most endearing little squeaking sounds. Her arms get tangled up in her long hair and she grumbles about it.

"I should have cut it a long time ago," she says with a yawn. "I keep tripping over it, getting it caught on things, now it's trying to choke me."

"I could braid it for you," I say without thinking, then pull in a sharp breath.

She sits up, eyes wide. "What do you hear?"

"Nothing. Sorry, on my honor. There is no threat."

She flops back down with a huff. "Then what?"

"Braiding is something only a brother does for another," he explains, his tone carrying the weight of tradition. "And mostly only with their close bonds. Never for a female and as far as I know, they don't usually braid their hair."

"I see," she says, tilting her head slightly. "Well, you don't need to do—"

"No," I say, cutting her off. "I want to."

She smiles at me. "Alright. But, no offense, I'm not sure how your fingers manage it."

I look down at my hands. Sure, my fingers are thicker than hers, but they are just as nimble. When I look back up she has a wicked look in her eye and I use the hands she just offended to grab her.

She's starts laughing as soon as I touch her sides and it's so rewarding I just keep touching her until she tells me in heaving breaths to stop.

"I can't breathe, Kuret."

I don't tell her that I've found the perfect way to end an argument. I'll let her find out later.

Instead, I gently shift our positions, settling her in front of me, before starting to work on her hair. I instantly know what she means about my fingers being able to braid her hair. It is much thinner than mine, soft and slick, but I keep at it until I figure out the different ways it needs to be held.

After finishing the braids in the back, I have her move so I can access the ones on her side, this time pausing to undo some of my own braids so I can access a few of the ornaments.

Her eyes widen when I show her how I have woven in the little sculpture. "It's beautiful. Are you sure?"

"Yes. Samke, my bond brother made it to mimic an avioid from my world."

I unbraid another. "This is a rock I found with a natural hole in it. They are rare and are considered good luck."

She holds the object in her palm, inspecting it with curiosity. "There is a smooth section here. Is that from you rubbing it so much?"

I gently take it from her, turning it over between my fingers before weaving it into the newest braid I've crafted in her hair. "Yes, it has helped me work through many problems and fears. I have had it since I was very young."

"I can't take something so special," she protests.

"You aren't taking it. I'm giving it and it will give me great pleasure to keep touching it. Preferably while buried inside of you."

She lets out a low moan and starts squirming.

"Turn around to the other side and stay still so I can finish," I say with a playful tone, my fingers deftly tying off the braid with the ends of her hair.

She huffs out a breath and clacks her blunt teeth at me. "You're the one being the tease, Kuret."

I smile, amused, and pull another braid out of my own hair. "This wood bead I won in a race from one of the most annoying of the qendi."

"Are the qendi the name of your people?" she asks, her voice gentle.

"Yes."

She hums out a breath and I focus on finishing up the last few, not yet sure which braid I should pull out to share another of my treasures. We will need to start gathering more. She has a lot more room and we have memories to start building together with them.

The idea sends a surge of pleasure through me. I look forward to every braid, each one tying us closer together.

That thought might have left me appalled before, or at the very least made me question my sanity to be pursuing a relationship with Nasrin. Especially one with any resemblance of what I might have shared with a pairing I made among the males of my kind.

This is a new world, and she isn't qendi. From all that she has said, humans can build those bonds no matter their gender and with anyone they like. It pulls back a memory of a much younger version of me and I search my braids until I find it.

Yes, that is a perfect symbol.

"This ornament," I tell her, showing her the woven metal, "I made for myself, when I was first testing out different roles among my brothers. It is ugly, but I've always liked the reminder of a time in my life when options seemed limitless."

She holds it in her hands, spinning the hoop through her hair so she can see all side of it, as I finish tying the end of the braid. "I think it's wonderful. You could have chosen that path."

I let out a bark of laughter. "If you had seen what my teacher made, you would not say such a thing."

She smiles back at me, and I take a moment to admire the braids I have made. "You are beautiful, Nasrin."

Her marks flare and she startles, still not used to them. After a moment we both start laughing, then I see her face change, a hunger in her eyes I have started to recognize.

48

Rin

Electricity ripples across my stomach and down to my core, making me swallow thickly when my eyes move from his eyes to his lips and back again.

"Thank you for doing this with me. I know you could have just thrown me over your shoulder and dragged me back to Ree, but you decided to help me and I appreciate it."

His marks flutter, the glowing patterns shifting with the unspoken emotion. He seems pleased, then snorts, the sudden breath of air making his braids clack together. "I don't know, Nasrin. We haven't talked about it, but haven't you noticed how much stronger you are now?"

"I thought I had imagined it."

"Try to lift me."

Now it's my turn to snort. "Are you insane? I'd break my back."

"Just try it."

I roll my eyes, deciding to humor him so we can move past this conversation. I stand up, take a step forward, crouch down so I can grab him right above his knees, and after a moment of thinking about how it will just make him fall over if I do that, I chide myself for even thinking it's possible and lift.

To my surprise, I manage to lift him off the ground. The shock is evident on my face, but he's already preparing to lean over my shoulder as I easily move him upward. "What?"

"Stand up all the way now," he orders and I follow his directions, my jaw drops open in disbelief.

Then I start giggling. "I'm the one that can carry you thrown over my shoulder."

I can't stop laughing and have to tip him back onto his legs before I drop him. A growl from him and his hands all over my body is all it takes to stop me, though.

"That was beyond attractive, Nasrin," he purrs into my ear. "I need inside of you. Right now."

Then he's spinning me around as my suit recedes and pressing my front into the side of the cave wall, thankfully free of mushrooms and dry from the light that must hit it during the evening. As soon as he pushes a thick finger inside of me, I stop thinking about it.

"Already wet," he hisses out, then makes a deep click of satisfaction before I hear a rustling sound. A moment later, he's lifting me higher, pressing into me, filling me up.

After making sure I've adjusted to him, he starts stroking into me, the new angle opening my eyes to all the possibilities we haven't even explored yet. Each thrust is far more intense like this. I'm already whimpering out my pleasure by the fourth stroke.

I place my hands on the wall so I can push myself back against him, increasing the pleasure as he slaps into me.

"Harder," I urge him.

He surrenders, no longer holding back, as our bodies collide, a slapping sound echoing out of the cave. Over and over, as I crest higher and his breathing becomes more erratic. I'm not prepared when the pleasure hits and I have to quickly clamp down on the scream that starts to rise.

Once he hears it, he increases his pace, pounding into a spot inside of me that takes my breath away, harder and harder until I come again, this time losing track of what's happening around me for a long moment and coming back to awareness as he spins me, then pushes back in as he uses the cave wall to keep me upright and uses his large hands on each thigh to spread me as wide as he can, pushing my knees up toward my chest.

Then he pounds into me, his mouth open and showing all of his teeth and it's so intense it's right on the edge of pain. But I stare into his bright green eyes and take it, urging him on with my gaze until he comes with a roar.

Both of us are panting when he pulls me back from the cave wall, his hands checking my skin to make sure he didn't hurt me. He's twitching inside of me as he rubs his hands all down my back, and cups me to him, grinding into me to keep chasing the pleasure.

After a moment, he moves us back to our bed of grass and I look around our little cave. It is spartan but serviceable. Soon after I'm falling asleep again on it.

✳✳✳

I wake to the feel of his hands in my hair again. His hands reach around my neck and he pushes all my hair to the back and starts to run his hand through the braids gently, his fingers massaging my scalp.

My eyes flutter shut and I lean against him, gasping softly when a deep rumbling in his chest sends vibrations across my entire body.

"Your hair," he starts speaking, his chin rubbing against the sensitive tips of my ears. "It's changed."

My first instinct is to panic and pull my hair to my face and see what he is talking about, but he beats me to both actions.

He pushes my hair forward so that the braids are spilling over my shoulders and I see that the stark white has been pleasantly interrupted by stripes of black. "It looks so beautiful. I only wish you could be imprinted on me the way I am on you."

I turn to hide my blush.

There is a wistfulness in his voice that lets me know it is something he truly has been thinking about.

I turn around, wrapping my hands around his neck.

He is so much taller than me that my feet are nearly off the ground, but his hands go to cup my rear and he lifts me up.

I feel tingling in my cheeks just as the bioluminescent patterns on his start moving and I lower my face to his.

His mouth meets mine halfway and sparks travel through my body and straight between my legs.

When I roll my hips against his hands, he moans softly into my mouth and lowers me so we are pressed against each other. I feel his hardness against me and smile into the kiss.

He pulls away and looks at me tenderly, his mouth with a slight smile of its own.

I can feel myself melting into him, both of our essences mixing and becoming one singular being. Hearing myself think that almost makes me recoil, but it feels real to me, almost magical.

Each time we touch each other we discover more about each other's bodies. I thought it would be tricky, but when I am with him, our bodies just know what to do. It's something primal about our connection that I have been having a hard time understanding, but I have decided to not care and instead just lose myself inside of whatever this is.

I kiss him again, a little more fiercely this time. By the time he lets me down from his arms, my black suit has nearly receded from my body and the corner of the cave we are in is illuminated beautifully with green light.

I hadn't even consciously done it, but my body seems to have taken control from my brain and I'm not opposed to that in the least.

He is still fully clothed and staring at me with a glazed look, like he has seen something different.

I clasp my hands over my chest self-consciously and the light from them makes me look down in shock. "*Ya Allah*," I gasp as I look at my hands and notice that they are glowing a beautiful shade of green, a little lighter than Kuret's because of the silver sheen all over me. "Is it everywhere?" I ask him, unable to contain the giddiness in my voice.

Kuret's voice breaks when he replies to me. "It is."

I can't tell if it's from seeing me naked or from the glow on my skin, but a wave of self-consciousness hits me like a train. My body must look so alien to him, so different from what he's used to. This is an individual that isn't even used to the females on his own planet even talking with him, and here I am before him, some sort of genetic amalgamation.

A storm of what-ifs floods my mind and I start panicking; what if I have unintentionally rushed things? What if he doesn't like what he sees? What if, what if... The what-ifs run through my head like wild animals across a field, but I push them out of my mind and move my hands from my body.

Whatever it is he sees, it's me now. And I won't hide from that.

If he didn't want to be here, he wouldn't be.

I decide I don't want to listen to the voices of self-doubt in my head anymore.

A fortnight ago, I would have screamed bloody murder and tried to separate my skin from my body but being here and having Kuret stare at my naked body with all the adoration in the world makes me realize that maybe I don't need to change the entire world at one time.

I can begin focusing on the world around me, gradually working my way up to the place I want to be.

He's become the center of it, but not in a way that confines me. He's a partner, and a protector.

I've been resisting all of this for so long, even though my body has been ahead of me, trying to get my brain and heart to catch up. Well, it finally has, and I find my usual boldness again to let him know about it.

"I love you, Kuret. I know you don't have marriage in your culture, but you have a bond brother. Surely we can be our own version of that."

His marks flair, and my new ones flair in return. "Yes, Nasrin. You are my bond... female. And I am your bond male. Forever."

He moves toward me now, pulling me tight against him, making me feel cherished. I squeeze him back, for once happy with my newfound strength.

We can protect each other, and the argila. We'll find Olivia, then we will help find the others.

Together.

I reach a hand up and rub it against the side of his face, watching his eyes flutter close as he leans into it lovingly, then opens his eyes again, his stare intense. "You are the most beautiful thing I will ever lay my eyes on, Nasrin."

The pleasant shock of his words makes me pull my hands away, but he holds them in place and his eyes open.

"And you get more beautiful each day."

He pulls me to him and seals his declarations with a soft kiss that I deepen as I start to tug on his shirt. In record time, he unfastens it from his body and starts to undo his trousers when we are interrupted by a soft braying sound that is unmistakably the baby argila.

I gasp and cover my chest with my hands and imagine my jumpsuit covering me up while Kuret distracts him by making clicking sounds and lifting him into his arms.

"Well, hello there, little one," I say with a smile after I am fully clothed, my face hot from the shame of being interrupted. I almost feel like a parent who got interrupted by their child and the thought of it makes me grin wider.

I scratch at his head and he nips playfully at my hand, making Kuret gasp dramatically and place him back on the ground.

He crouches as if to scold the baby, but the furry ball races out before he can get a word in, standing at the mouth of the cave to give us a naughty bleat before making his way out.

Kuret stands with his hands beside him, a cross of amusement and annoyance on his face. "That one is going to be trouble, don't you think?"

I nod my head. "He is, and I think I have the perfect name for him."

Kuret looks at me with a wide, toothy grin. "What is it?"

"Azar," I say, feeling very intelligent. "It means *fire*."

He moves back to me and his lips come down on mine once more before turning back to watch the baby's antics. "Azar is the perfect name for him."

He walks to the mouth of the cave, and stares out of it, looking picturesque in the faded light of the sun before he speaks again.

"We should head out to continue our search for Olivia." He turns to look at me with a mischievous smile. "We can pick up where we left off when we return."

I tuck my hair behind my ears and nod, silently thanking him for grounding me and refocusing me on our mission.

Rising to my feet, I brush the dust off.

"We'll find her soon," he promises, extending his hand for me to take.

I pull one of his braids. "We better, or we're going to grow old together in this cave."

"Well, I like part of that plan, but how about we find somewhere better than a cave long before our bones give out from lying on a pile of grass?"

I snort out a breath. "I like your thinking, Kuret."

He smiles, but then turns more serious. "The wind isn't violent now. I think we can look for her."

"I agree. Where first?"

49

Kuret

We spend days looking, but don't find anything. We're both weary, but Nasrin keeps pushing herself beyond her limits. Her species is more fragile than my own, and so it has been a careful dance to get her to rest without her getting upset with me.

When she does, it doesn't cause the same anxiety it did before. I know it's a reflection of her own fear, not because of something I have done wrong. We are doing the best we can.

I open my mouth to tell her that maybe we should rest a few more hours, but a loud thumping sound makes me whirl around. I hear unsettled bleating from the argila and it lets me know it's an intruder.

When I turn back to Nasrin she already has weapons in her hands, eyes trained to the outside of the cave. I scoop up my pack, checking it for weapons, then move out onto the wet ground, my bare feet making squishing sounds as the rock transitions to grass.

I turn to motion for Nasrin to stay in the cave, but she ignores me, hands clenched on her *gun* and her face looking grim, but determined. I briefly consider arguing, but another loud thump urges me into faster movement.

It's coming from the entrance to the valley. The one I thankfully spent time fortifying. After another loud whack, I break into a run. Whatever it is, we'll need to kill it before it causes too much damage that will take time away from looking for Olivia.

As we get close, Nasrin reaches out a hand to grab me, pulling me by the braids so I move my ear close to her mouth, her panting breaths tickling against me.

"I can understand them. They're arguing. One of them is giving the other a hard time about how they shouldn't be using their tail to knock."

As she speaks, I can hear a language that sounds like rocks grinding together and I wonder at her ability to make sense of it. "Should you try to speak before we shoot?"

She considers it for a long moment, but then after a hiss of pain, starts making the same odd sounds. A few moments later, she's back to speaking my language.

"If you can be trusted," she yells out, "then speak in Kuret's language and tell us about the other humans you have found. What are they named?"

My marks flair when a female starts speaking on the other side. "My name's Kira. I'm here with Drasuk. Ree and Eli are the other humans I've met."

Both of us instantly relax, though I can still see some apprehension on her face. I've never known anyone as slow to trust as she is, though from the stories she has told, I can understand why.

"Is that enough of a pass code?" asks the voice on the other side, snark clear in their voice. "Or should I do a dance over here before you agree not to shoot us."

"How do you know we have guns?" Nasrin asks her.

"Drasuk can smell them. May we come in?"

We both look at each other. I wipe a hand across the back of another and Nasrin emulates me, while also nodding her head.

"Yes, I'll just..." I trail off when my carefully constructed defenses are disassembled in mere moments by small human hands, a blue tail, and lots of claws.

The shock of pink hair pulls my notice first, then the hulking blue form with thick skin beside her, then my gaze flits back to the woman and the manticorid traits she has, including a long, dancing blue tail with a venomous manticorid tip. It helps settle me even further to see signs that she has been around Thivoll.

The woman points a thumb at the large blue creature. "Like I said, that's Drasuk. He can't understand us, so I don't suggest making any sudden moves in my direction. He's hopelessly smitten with me and all that."

The large grin on her face afterward lets me know she's trying to be funny, but the steel in her eyes and just how deadly he looks lets me know the threat is real.

A glance over at Nasrin lets me know that she's staring in awe at the blue creature, mouth hanging open. Kira notices too.

"Doesn't he look like such a cute big dragon-dino dummy? He grows on you, though. What do I call you two?"

Nasrin shakes her head, blinking rapidly. "Uh. Sorry. I'm Nasrin, this is Kuret. He met Ree a while back."

Kira moves her odd, swirling eyes back in my direction. "Ah, you must be one of her foot soldiers she's always tying herself up in knots about. Clearly at least *you* aren't someone she sent to their death. We just need to find that bird-man so she stops droning on about it."

I'm not really sure what she means, but decide it isn't worth asking. "Where is Ree? And Thivoll?"

"Let's get this nice stockade you built back in working order," Kira says, "find someplace more comfortable and we can catch up."

As soon as Kira moves the first log back in place, Drasuk takes over the task, tail working simultaneously with hands so the job is complete in a fraction of the time it took me. It's humbling, but I'm more excited about the possibility of having such a clearly able companion to help me protect the cloister.

It's been exhausting and there is this ever-present nagging reminder that one male is never enough. With Thivoll, Drasuk, and I, we should be able to at least get enough rest.

Nasrin beckons them back to the cave and Kira starts speaking again. "Have you checked all possible entrances?"

I'm taken aback for a moment, thinking at first that maybe Drasuk prompted the question, but he is scanning our environment, clearly not aware of the conversation. It's a guard's question. Not a female's line of thinking.

I shake myself out of my shock. "Partly. There are caves, but none of them seem to lead out, at least not quickly. There is still a threat, and we should be wary."

She nods, eyes scanning the environment. "What about the stream? Is that a point of entry?"

This time I know for certain it is her own question, and from her confidence and intensity, it's based on experience. "It comes from underground and returns underground. Are you a-" I stutter over my words for a moment. "A guardian?"

She glances back at me. "Why do you sound surprised?" She looks over Nasrin. "Why does he sound surprised?"

Nasrin snorts. "In his culture, females are in a cloister. I don't think a single one of them fight."

"What the fornication? Ugh," Kira says, disgust clear in her tone. "Another language that doesn't know how to curse."

She turns back to me. "I guard the feces out of things, Kuret. Yes, I am a guardian. A *marine*."

"He isn't a *misogynist*, Kira," Nasrin says. "I thought so at first, but it's just a cultural thing and he's learning."

Apparently, being whatever that is would be a bad thing and Nasrin's right. I am learning. I mean, it's not like I didn't trust her when she said males and females could integrate, it just hasn't made sense, at least not until this moment.

The pink female with all those scales, spikes, and claws, is clearly a very capable protector. Then I feel even more stupid. Nasrin has been protecting herself too. But it's so different from what I know. Our females live in fear inside their walls. We protect them... but maybe the fear that locks them in there would lessen if they also protected themselves?

Yet again, my world shifts, this time even further lowering the burden of panic and anxiety. It isn't all on me. I mean, it's my sworn duty, but now I understand what Nasrin means about how roles can blur.

I realize I haven't been keeping up with the conversation when Kira lets out an explosive curse.

"No way is Ree making a cloister. Fornicate that. Although, we do have a safe base now that we found Eli, so there is a bit of basic overlap. Except instead of walls its monsters in the water. She landed on an island protected by Wroahk. He's a *kraken*."

"A what?" I ask.

"Stupid translators," Kira huffs. "He lives in the water. A *shark*. *Octopus*. Uh. A *fish*. How can I not find a word that translates?"

Nasrin snorts. "His language doesn't have a word for *ocean*. I think he's from a desert world."

"Gross," quips Kira. "You never get the sand out of your butt crack."

Nasrin groans. "As if that comment isn't gross?"

There is a defensive tone to Nasrin's words, and I don't really understand what I'm missing. Was there an insult in there I didn't get? It seems like she doesn't like Kira for some reason, but I'm not sure why.

"Hey, lighten up, Nasrin," Kira snarks back.

Nasrin whips around, anger clear in her features, and this time I know for certain that it's not tied to what is going on right now, but something already established before they met. Are their people enemies on her planet?

"Lighten up? That's all you *Americans* care about, isn't it? That *American* snark of yours is a privilege. And a trap. You use it like a weapon, as if it means you are making progress in the world, but you aren't.""*Whoa, whoa*, there partner," Kira says, her own tone taking on a sharp edge.I don't understand her words, but Nasrin must, because she is even angrier now. "I will not! You ignore the suffering around you. Ignore the rampant loss of *human* rights and that precious 'freedom' you say you represent and champion... but only for yourselves. All lies, while you support any *regime* you need to get the resources you need to feed your endless desire for *materialism*. You were a *marine*, you say? Then those battles you fought were not about justice. They were about greed. And the women of my country needed you." She all but yells that last point, her voice raw with emotions. "Maybe then I would have learned how to 'lighten up,' instead of fearing for my life because I wanted to teach."

Drasuk pushes himself between the two females, his rock grinding voice loud now as he speaks.

Nasrin looks like she regrets her outburst afterward, but she doesn't reply."Chill, *Lizard* Brain," Kira orders him. "She's just telling me some hard truths and we'll do better together if we just face them."

Kira takes a long, deep breath, grabs one of her forehead spikes and then speaks again, her voice calm and measured. Nothing like the snark from before. "You are right, Nasrin. Many of the battles I fought were driven by greed, but many of them were essential and were just. But not all... and after I was discharged, it was one of the many things that just about wrecked me. I almost drank myself to death. I won't forget the faces of the people in all those countries I served in. The gutted, loss of hope looks in their eyes. Of course, I wish I did more. I mean... I don't know how I could have, but I wish I could go back and change something. But I can't. What we can do is make something different where we are. I mean, we might be stuck here, and I know we can make a better world if we are. I have to believe in that, or I will lose my fornicating mind."

I can see the anger seep out of Nasrin with each word Kira says. Then she takes her own deep breath. "I'm sorry," she says in a small voice. One wracked with pain. "I know you couldn't have changed it, anymore than all the things I tried changed it. I just get so angry sometimes when I watch *American TV*."

Kira throws back her head and laughs. "Oh, Nasrin. I get angry when I watch that too. How about we see it as a silver lining that it's all those light years away?"

My muscles relax when I see Nasrin smile. "I can easily agree to that," she says, finally fully breaking the tension between them. "And I really am sorry. I know *Americans* aren't all entitled and there isn't much you could have done... but when you grow up like I did... well, you get desperate."

Kira turns serious again. "While I know it's not the same, I do know what it's like to face discrimination and to be put in impossible situations. We'll have to work hard to avoid it here."

"Well, with all the glowing, scales, fur, and feathers... and who knows what else, should help put it all into perspective," Nasrin replies. "I have some of my own ideas on what we could do if we are stuck here."

"I'd love to hear them," Kira tells her with a soft smile, one that I never would have thought to see on someone who seems to fully embrace a sharp sense of humor.

With that, the two of them walk off, close together now and acting like they weren't just about to come to blows. Drasuk and I can't speak a word of each other's language, but we still manage to communicate how baffled we are by it all. I don't think understanding their words helped me make sense of it, either. Not beyond there being cultural differences they needed to hiss at each other about so they could be friendly.

Females will never stop being strange, no matter the species.

50

Rin

I expected the argila to be terrified or Drasuk, but instead Roshan scampers right up to him for pets. Judging by the lack of reaction, Drasuk must recognize the species and he simply complies and Roshan is bleating contentedly within moments.

That brings over the rest of his little family and the last part of my anger ebbs away as I watch Kira coo at little Azar, telling him that he's the cutest giant spider thingy she's ever seen.

I hope Kira's right about us being able to make a new world. Innocents like Azar need protecting. I realize with a start that the most important thing to talk about slipped my mind after my little tirade. I hadn't known just how much resentment had been bubbling, but Kira was right. I feel better now that we faced it head on.

Of course, it will take more than just one conversation, but clearly she wants to make a world where those hard conversations can be had, just like I do.

"We found another woman. Olivia. Green hair. Then something stole her from us. We are in this valley because it took her into one of the surrounding caves. It's a cave dweller and got her from us by causing sinkholes."

"Fornicate," Kira curses. "A hunter?"

I shake my head. "I don't think so. It spoke and claimed ownership. It could have killed me, but it didn't. It didn't look like the genali, braceaaer, or whatever Tehlmar was."

"Tehlmar?"

Kuret growls. "A waste of breath male that tried to force Nasrin. Tall, green hair, even longer ears than mine, spikes instead of feet."

"Great. We haven't seen one of those yet, but I'll get them added to the kill list."

I should feel bad about the spike of satisfaction that causes, but I don't have the energy for it. We're on their kill list, after all.

Kira switches to Drasuk's language then speaks again. "Can you smell another human besides us?"

He takes in a long breath. "Very faintly, now that you mention it. But it's coming from multiple directions."

"Great," she says, her tone weary.

"We should go back for reinforcements," Kira says, looking disappointed as she stands upright instead of giving Azar more belly pats.

"It isn't safe to move Darya yet, I think," I tell her. "And I'd like to keep looking while you are gone."

Kira nods. "That makes sense. If we find Olivia quickly, worse case Drasuk can carry Darya back to the island. There isn't a lot of grass there, but once we get past the monsters in the water, the argila will be the safest they can be on this cursed planet. I'd love to learn more about both of you, but I think we should go back right away."

After that, they are gone within a few minutes, and I'm surprised just how sad it makes me. I was prepared to dislike her, especially with her brash, snarky tones, but the speed that she left and how focused she was on doing the right thing by Olivia completely won me over.

I know she'll be back as fast as she can.

My lips turn up at just how certain I feel. Is this what happens when you finally let yourself trust someone? First Kuret, and now I'm finding more allies? In an American, no less?

Then I think back to Oliva. She had an odd accent, but there was a little bit of American there, I realize. And Australian, maybe?

Kira's right. Now is our time to let go of our preconceptions and the cultural baggage of our past. I need to let them tell me what kind of people they are by their actions, not by the country they were born in. We probably won't ever see Earth again, and it's busy tearing itself apart over those things.

What would my *bābā* say if I revived those same fights light years away by holding on to my own preconceptions?

"I won't," I promise him in a whisper. "I'll make you proud."

We need to find Olivia and get her back to the island.

A surge of guilt tries to rise for the time we lost to the storm, to endless wrong turns, and talking with Kira and Drasuk, but I push it to the side. We needed the rest, and now we'll have help soon. Still, we shouldn't linger.

Azar's playful braying pulls me out of my heavy thoughts, and it brings a smile to my face.

"Keep it down over there," I call out playfully.

Kuret and the argila turn to look, all of them staring at me like I'm a central figure in their lives. Like they trust me, and it feels good to return that trust. As if it has mended something that was broken.

This time with Kuret and the argila have been the most calm I have experienced since coming to this planet. I look at them and feel my face widening into a smile. It's like having my own small family with an even smaller family within it.

As Darya's baby awkwardly runs toward me, I bend and open my arms up for him. The little animal has really warmed up to me and I love it like I love its parents. It is also growing at an alarming rate, already a few inches taller.

Luckily, there will be plenty of grass to feed Darya as she nurses him and they all seem content.

Kuret walks toward me with his sharp grin as I struggle to lift the rapidly growing baby argila. "*Ya Allah*, he is getting so big."

I can still lift him just fine, of course, thanks to whatever new strength I gained, but it's awkward with all of his wiggling limbs. I set him down so he can go back to scampering.

Still, I'm relieved when I don't have to prod Kuret into searching and before long we have taken care of our basic needs and are back in a cave.

We begin to make our way through the labyrinthine corridors of the inner part of the cavern in silence. We wouldn't want to alert any predators deep in the cavern or Olivia's captor to our approach.

I stay behind Kuret as we carefully feel our way forward in the dark, his marks providing enough light to move, but not enough to do it quickly or with confidence.

"This would be faster if we separated," I blurt out.

"No, that would be—"

"Never mind, I know that was a bad idea. I'm just anxious to find her, and ridiculously low on sleep, and it's making me say stupid things."

He snorts out a breath and whispers back. "I have said many stupid things since we met."

I chuckle. "You really have, Kuret. But you have also said a lot of smart things too, and I do appreciate all you have done for me. And for Olivia. You didn't have to."

All he does is grunt, but there is a pleased lilt to it and it makes me smile.

"It's not just about the danger of separating, lovely Nasrin. I want you near me."

It sends a thrill through me and a wider smile on my face.

Then Kuret stops suddenly and I run into him with a small oof.

"There are tracks here," he says in a hissing whisper. "It looks like whatever it is, it's big, heavy, and has multiple legs."

My brow furrows and some of the flashing images from when Olivia was taken rises up into my mind. It happened so fast, and their body was so strange that I hadn't really made sense of it at the time, but when he says multiple legs it jars something loose.

"That sounds right, Kuret," I hiss back.

I'm all but dancing behind him as we continue on, the cave becoming brighter and brighter as we go. Then we round a corner and my heart sinks. It's another cave in and it looks just as unnatural as the ones from before.

"I recognize this pattern," he says pointing out scored marks on the wall that disappear behind the pile of rubble. "They must be in this cave system, but we won't get to them through this one."

Disappointment wells up, but then I think of just how vast this world is and the fact that we've found any sort of clue is promising.

He turns to me, and I can see the excitement in his eyes and it fills me with even more hope. He isn't fighting me on this anymore, instead, just as driven as I am to find her.

The surrounding cave, previously too dark to see much at all, even with my improved night vision, glows in a beautifully hazy blue and the color reflects a lovely hue in the depths of his green eyes.

When we turn back around and head back out, I don't feel as defeated as I expect. I just have to keep hoping that she is alright and doing my best to find her. Soon, we'll have help, even.

And I know Kuret won't leave me to do it alone. When we are almost out of the cave, I reach a hand forward to grasp the back of his armor. He slows, then turns to me.

I open my mouth to reassure him we will find her, but only a screech comes out as the ground drops out from underneath us. It's a blur of movement after that. I expect a hard impact with the ground, but instead something reaches around my waist.

After a moment of thinking it is Kuret, I realize the color is wrong. A quick glance down confirms it is red, and the shape of the limb is all wrong. I scream again, eyes darting around for Kuret's green, finding it instantly, but then it's gone again when I'm snatched closer to the chest of the monster holding me.

Then there's a grinding that joins the roar of Kuret calling for me, interrupted by the sound of falling rocks. His voice is muffled now, but he's still screaming out my name.

The monster shifts, letting me get a glimpse behind us, but it's only a fall of stones. "Kuret! Are you hurt?!"

"No!" he yells back, but the relief doesn't have time to sink in before the creature whips me in the opposite direction and starts running.

"Take me back!" I yell at it, then my mind catches up and I know who it is.

It's the one who took Olivia and my mind must remember the language because I feel the pain in my throat. "Stop!" I yell out in its language. "We just want to keep Olivia safe. Take me back to Kuret."

It looks down at me, pink eyes glowing, tusks snapping, and my breath stops. Does it plan to kill me?

"Zha is mine, but you will provide zha company. If Kuret follows, I will kill zha."

"You can't kill Olivia!"

"I never said I would kill Olivia."

"What? You just said..."

I think back over what they said and realize that zha might be a pronoun. To test it out, I try to say him and her, but they both come out of my mouth as zha. Odd, but I don't have time to figure it out. I need to get away. I try to squirm, but their arms just tighten.

"Zha?" I ask it. "I am company for zha?"

"Yes, zha. Not me. I don't want company."

I let out a long breath. So, it probably isn't going to kill me, but also not likely to listen to anything I say. Great.

51

Preview of Emerald

Kroaicho

I return to the enclave with my arms full—an array of gleaming rocks, stalactites, and other shiny treasures gathered meticulously from the deeper cave systems. Each piece is carefully chosen; each represents a piece of a hoard I am building back after losing so much in this foreign place.

I cradle them close to my chest, feeling their solid weight, and imagine how they will gleam under the pale glow of the bioluminescent mushrooms scattered throughout the cave. They are humble beginnings, yes, but even a small hoard can eventually grow into something vast and worthy.

As I near the enclave, a sudden absence registers—a cold, creeping emptiness that sends a jolt through my core. The human. I sense it immediately. I lower the rocks gently, my body twitching to full alert. The atmosphere is wrong and unbalanced.

I scan the darkened cave, my eyes narrowing into slits as I process the space. No Olivia. No muttered insults or sarcastic quips echoing in the damp air.

Just silence.

My nostrils flare, drawing in the cool, musty cave air, searching for zha's scent. Thankfully, it hasn't faded yet. Zha is nearby, but moving away—fast. I grind my teeth and clack together my tusks, my jaw tightening with irritation.

Zha is always trying to escape. Always complicating things. Why does zha make everything so difficult?

I drop to all six limbs and break into a dead sprint, my claws clicking against the damp stone as I dart through the narrow passages. The echo of my own breath reverberates against the walls, but I ignore it, focusing on the scent trail winding its way through the cave network. Zha is heading deeper into the caverns, toward more treacherous terrain. I push myself harder, muscles burning as I weave through the maze-like tunnels.

Stupid, impulsive human.

The scent grows stronger, and soon, I reach a familiar section of the cave. My momentum slows as I near a portion with a glassy, slippery rock floor, a naturally dangerous area even for creatures as agile as myself. I approach cautiously, claws gripping the wet stone.

The dim light from the bioluminescent fungi reveals zha's prone form a few feet away from a massive chasm, zha's body is limp and dangerously close to the edge. My irritation spikes, followed by a tight, uncomfortable feeling I can't quite identify.

"Foolish, foolish human..." I mutter under my breath as I approach zha's still form.

Zha's eyes are closed, breathing steady—unconscious. I stand over zha, my shadows stretching across the glossy rock. I should leave zha here, and let zha learn the consequences of zha's reckless actions. But my body moves before my thoughts can catch up. I reach down and scoop Olivia up, tucking zha against my chest.

Zha is so light, fragile even.

Almost immediately, zha shifts closer, seeking warmth. Zha's small body presses against mine, head nestling against my skin. My bioluminescence flickers, shifting into a deep purple, a reaction I quickly tamp down.

I glance down at zha, feeling my lips pushing against my tusks to reflect my annoyance. Zha needs a companion to tell zha not to wander. I think back to the one that was with Olivia and my body slumps.

Two humans? It is the only way to get peace, I realize.

"This is why a hoard never includes pets," I grumble, my voice a low rumble in the silence. "Never."

About the Authors

This pen name represents a collaboration with the goal of creating stories just like we prefer: spicy slow burn, strong character arcs, and all about the... shall we say delectably different.

Ky is our public face...

the one of us who posts on social media, who decided it was *smart* to get a PhD in History (and so now regales you with the book related historical mythology in our newsletter), who tends to have all the wild ideas, the writing voice we follow, and who keeps all of it moving (sheesh, that's a lot... thanks, Ky!)

On a typical day you can find Ky hanging out with her own Mr. Delectably Different, loving on her fur babies, or convincing her two kids that she really is funnier than they'll admit.

She's a musician, sculptor, graphic designer, and lover of weirdness. Most of the time, she's either working her 9 to 5, writing, or running out in the wild.

Legends Start Somewhere

Want to read more stories in the Alien Hunting Grounds Universe?

Join our newsletter for a free prequel short story! You can access it at kylabreene.com

Myth Awakened: Vimala and Jentoll

Vimala

I was once a courtesan for kings... until a rival sent an attacker in the middle of the night. One moment. One coward with a blade. I lost everything.

My beauty no longer sustains me, but I refuse to simply fade away. And yet it is hard to maintain hope after so much loss. Will this otherworldly avatar of Vishnu be my salvation?

Jentoll

I've given more than enough to my people. To my failing empire. I gave an eye. My tail. Pieces of my sanity... far too much precious time. And now it's crumbling to dust. Falling to a far different sort of rallying cry. One for peace.

Let the next generation bear that task. This is my chance to flee. To find a new home.

Two wounded hearts, both seeking refuge.
Will they find it in each other?

Join our newsletter to find out: kylabreene.com